MODERN LOVE
and other stories

M. DARUSHA WEHM

Modern Love and other stories
by M. Darusha Wehm

published by *in potentia* press 2018

ISBN 978-0-9917831-7-5

"A Wish and a Hope and a Dream" first appeared in *Cast of Wonders*. September 2017

"Reflections on a Life Story" first appeared in *Nature* 540, 476. 15 December 2016

"War Profiteering" first appeared in *Mothership Zeta*. July 2016

"Showing the Colours" first appeared in *Procyon Science Fiction Anthology 2016*, Jeanne Thronton, ed. (Procyon Press) 2016

an interactive version of "Alexander Systems" first appeared in *sub-Q magazine*. May 2016

"The Edge of the Abyss" first appeared in *Contact Light,* Megan Chee, ed. (Silence in the Library Publishing) 2015

"Home Sick" first appeared in *Use Only As Directed*, Edwina Harvey and Simon Petrie, eds. (Peggy Bright Books) 2014

"People Pleaser" first appeared in *Baby Teeth*, Dan Rabarts and Lee Murray, eds. (Paper Road Press) 2013

"The Care and Feeding of Mammalian Bipeds, v. 2.1" first appeared in *Escape Pod*. November 2012

"Modern Love" first appeared in *Andromeda Spaceways Inflight Magazine*. May 2012

"I Open My Eyes" first appeared in *Luna Station Quarterly*. March 2012

"Homecoming" first appeared in *Luna Station Quarterly*. December 2011

"The Interview" first appeared in *Podioracket Presents Glimpses*, Brian Rathbone, ed. 2011

Novels

Beautiful Red
Children of Arkadia

Andersson Dexter novels:
Self Made
Act of Will
The Beauty of Our Weapons
Pixels and Flesh

Short Fiction

Modern Love and other stories

Mainstream Fiction by Darusha Wehm

The Home for Wayward Parrots (forthcoming)

Devi Jones' Locker:
Packet Trade
Sea Change
Storm Cloud
Floating Point

A Wish and a Hope and a Dream————————7

Bodies At Rest, Bodies In Motion————————17

Alexander Systems————————27

Career Opportunities————————47

Lucidity————————49

Reflections on a Life Story————————57

Showing the Colours————————61

The Foreigner————————71

Love On The Wings Of A Zephyr————————77

Chekhov's Phaser————————81

The Edge of the Abyss————————95

Major Tom and the Lucky Lady————————111

Modern Love————————125

Home Sick————————133

People Pleaser————————145

Illumination————————147

Fame————————161

Homecoming————————179

I Open My Eyes————————181

War Profiteering————————185

The Ninth————————189

Perfect Understanding————————193

The Care and Feeding of Mammalian Bipeds, v. 2.1——197

The Interview————————————————211

Fire. Escape.————————————————219

About the Author————————————————245

YOU HAVE ALWAYS been a princess.

When you are six years old, your hat is a cardboard cone covered in glitter glue with a cellophane veil. Your dress began life as a pillowcase in the free box at the Goodwill. Your best friend Ines has a store-bought costume, her gown soft and sky blue like Princess Karima's. You aren't envious, though. You love your pillowcase dress and hat that makes you almost as tall as your mother.

Ines twirls around and around until she nearly falls over, clutching you to stay upright. "Ooh, I'll never get used to riding a magic carpet."

You giggle and say, "That's why I ride in a carriage pulled by eight golden ponies."

"Can I come to the ball with you, then?" Ines sinks to the ground, her skirt billowing around her like a cloud.

"Aren't they adorable?" Ines's father says, his eyes crinkling.

"Yeah," your mother says, "off in their own little world."

"Come on," Mr. Solano says, "that's one of the great things about being a kid. All that imagination, all those dreams." He looks at you then his eyes dart back to your mother. "They can be anything they want at this age. Might as well let them enjoy it."

"You're right," your mother says, handing him an old ice cream bucket. "Thanks for taking them. I can really use the rest."

"It's no trouble," he says, then kneels down to where you and Ines are sitting, playing with the material of her dress. "Come on, my two little princesses, let's go get some candy."

You get up and your mother adjusts the sash on your dress. "Only two pieces on the way home," she says. "You want it to last until Christmas, okay?"

You nod, excited about the prospect of even two pieces of candy. It's been forever since you've had candy.

Your family has been eating spaghetti with ketchup for days. You love spaghetti and ketchup, not realizing that it's just what's left at the end of the Food Bank hamper. You also don't know that your mother lost her job, which is why she is there when you get home from school and has had time to make your costume. You know your father is working double shifts, though. That's why he isn't there to see you in your pretty dress. Your mom goes to take a photo and you and Ines stand together, grinning at each other while she fumbles with her old phone.

"Come on," Ines says, grabbing your hand. "We need to hurry if we're going to get to the ball on time."

✳

WHEN YOU ARE nine, both your parents are working. You get the official Princess app for your birthday and every day after school you and Ines lie on the Lady Dawn Pink™ comforter she's had on her bed since you were little, looking at the latest photoshoots and reading about the princesses.

"Did you see that Cheyenne just got back from a trip to New Zealand," you say, paging through the latest updates. "They wouldn't let her bring Wolf into the country with her. Isn't that awful? It's not as if he's some ordinary dog. He's, like, partially part of her."

"It's like last year," Ines says, "when that one country wouldn't let Princess Karima travel on her flying carpet within their border."

"I know, how dumb. What's airspace security anyway?" you say, rolling your eyes. You both go back to the pictures.

"I can't decide if Karima or Cheyenne is my favourite," Ines says a few minutes later.

"Rhona," you say, your fingers tracing the flowing curls of her beautiful red hair.

"Rhona?! But you she doesn't even look like you. She's so... pale."

You don't look like any of them, with your skinny legs and bitten fingernails. You shrug.

"She's beautiful."

"They're all beautiful," Ines says, her forehead wrinkling. "When I'm ten, mom says I can get my hair cut like Karima's." She holds up the ends of her long, black hair, effecting a makeshift bob. "She said no to the eyeliner, though." Ines lets her hair fall back down. "How about you?"

You don't know what to do with makeup. Your mother wears little, but one afternoon when both your parents were at work you spent a hour in the bathroom with her eyeshadow, blush and lipstick. The best you could do was make yourself look like a clown. You can tell that Ines would never look like a clown. But she's pretty to begin with, everyone says so. You are clever. Or strong. Never pretty.

"My hair's okay the way it is," you say, running your fingers though the short cut. "I'd look dumb with long hair."

Ines shrugs and the two of you look at pictures of her with with different haircuts until it's time for you to go home.

At night, when you can't sleep, you imagine you are Rhona, with a gown of green velvet, a mind sharp enough to trick a wizard, a face pretty enough to bewitch an entire kingdom and a long trail of flaming red hair.

✳

WHEN YOU ARE twelve, Ines gets weird. All she wants to talk about is romance. You think it's because of Princess Mei Ling's wedding last month.

"Don't you think Cheyenne's prince is better-looking than Mei Ling's prince?" Ines asks. You don't know what to say. You don't care about the princes.

"I mean, I know he's older," she says, not waiting for you to

9

answer, "but I think he looks distinguished. That silver hair at his temples makes him look, I dunno, classy, like one of those actors in a black and white movie." She flicks through the images on her phone. She bought the Princes app with her first babysitting money and now you sit apart in her room, each looking at your own pictures on your own phones.

"Do you ever dream about your wedding? I think about it all the time. Mei Ling's was so beautiful," Ines says, not seeming to notice that you haven't said a word, "I want gold leaf on my wedding cake. And a dress like hers, but with blue accents, not pink. And what did you think about her prince's uniform? Guys look great in uniforms." She stops talking and looks over at you. "Want to watch the video again on the big screen?"

The Solanos have a big tv in their living room, and you often go over to watch movies. You nod, even though you think the wedding was kind of boring. But all the Princesses were there and Rhona looked incredible in her formal gown. You watch it all again for the millionth time, impatiently sitting through the wedding part to get to the ball. When Mei Ling enters the main salon on a flying horse, you gasp with delight as if you'd never seen it before. When Rhona dances with her prince, time stops.

That night, you dream that instead of Rhona's prince, it is you she dances with, your arm around her waist, her head on your shoulder. You twirl around the ballroom, your feet not quite touching the floor, her hair flying behind you both in a trail of auburn curls.

✳

WHEN YOU ARE seventeen, you work part-time in a bakery. Your alarm goes off at 5:30 in the morning, Rhona's voice singing her theme song sweetly in your ear. It almost makes waking in the dark bearable. You spend two hours each morning decorating the elaborate fairy cakes that each cost more than you'll be paid that week, then you go to school and try to stay awake in class.

Ines texts you in history:

```
new p movie opens 2moro lets go!
```

You've been saving all your bakery money and summer job wages in a college fund. You know now that your parents can barely keep up with their debts and won't be able to help, and you don't have the grades for a scholarship. Your father has steady work in construction, but it was never enough when your mother couldn't find work. Your mother went to college and she's always told you that an education is the most important thing. "Wishing for something won't make it so," she says. "You have to put yourself out to get anywhere in this world."

She says that it was her degree which got her the job she has now, assistant to a junior manager at a big firm downtown. "Who would you hire?" she asks you, "someone just out of high school or someone who's been to college? You can't just expect to get a good job without it anymore." Sometimes you feel like you want to scream whenever you hear the word *college*.

But you know your mother is right. Your parents seem to work all the time — you can't remember the last time the three of you did something together that wasn't a hasty meal or a half hour in front of the second-hand, tiny tv. Between school and the bakery, it feels like you work all the time, too.

You text Ines back.

k

You get to the theater two hours early and still barely get in. The audience is mostly teens and college age women, a few boyfriends and just a smattering of guys there of their own accord. But there are hardly any little kids — this isn't one of those origin story films. It's a grown-up story about post-princess life, featuring

Bianca — the first of the princesses, a stately matron now — and Lianne, who became a princess when you were a kid. The story begins as Lianne arrives at Bianca's castle in her carriage, glorious and shining with her footmen bustling about. She enters the Great Hall to find a table groaning under a feast of delights.

Ines elbows you and whispers, "Those are the fairy cakes *you* make." It's true, the bakery where you work specializes in replica royal sweets. Being around such beautiful things is the main appeal of the job. You nod and shush her.

Over the next ninety minutes, you are transported to a magic world that you can barely believe exists in the same universe as your own life. Glorious silken gowns transformed from ordinary box-store dresses. Flying chariots whisking the princesses to fabulous balls or feasts laden with luscious food no one eats. Lives of glamour and leisure. For a moment, you wonder if it is even real.

Then comes the moment you've all been waiting for. Everyone has been talking about the rumour that a new princess would be revealed in the film. Your breath catches in your throat when you see her for the first time. You know it's her: she is too radiant, too perfect to be working in some grimy urban store. Bianca and Lianne have gotten lost on their way back to Lianne's château, and walk into a small Korean grocery in some nameless city, looking for directions. The girl behind the counter must be about your age, but her days of worrying about grades and college are over. The princesses recognize her true nature immediately and take her away with them. No one objects. It is as if it were ordained in the stars.

They say that the movie story is based on her real life, that she really was discovered in some store just like that last year. Seo-yeon, an urban princess, elevated from the streets to a castle in the clouds. Your eyes fill with tears. You can't count the number of times you've wished for that moment. To have what you've known all your life finally be reflected in someone else's eyes. That you, too, are more than you appear to be.

If Seo-yeon could be plucked like a flower from her life of toil, surely it could happen to anyone? Even to you?

✳

WHEN YOU ARE twenty-two, you pull a crumpled bill from your pocket. It's enough for a draft beer at the campus bar and you've earned one. You are thirty thousand dollars in debt, you can't remember the last time you slept more than five hours in a night, but tomorrow you will walk onstage with hundreds of other people and walk off with a degree.

The bartender slides the beer toward you and takes your money, her dark eyes lingering on you for a moment. You're not in the mood to talk, so you take your beer to a quiet table near the back. You sip and look around. There aren't as many people in the place as there would be on a Friday night, but at three in the afternoon on the day before graduation it's crowded enough. You recognize the students' uniform of thrift store coats, broken book bags and five-year-old phones.

You notice a guy from your post-structural economics class a couple of tables over; he gives you the eye-contact-and-nod then goes back to his animated conversation. He's wearing a pale yellow t-shirt with a faded image of Princess Bonita printed on it. You know he's wearing it ironically, but you had that exact shirt when you were a kid.

You remember working with whatshisname — Charlie, Carl, something like that — on a class project. You made this infographic that showed how many people out of a hundred ever got out of the economic class where they were born. It was a good chart. You got an A minus.

Your phone buzzes and you flip it over. Ines. You haven't seen her since Christmas, when you were both home and her engagement news overshadowed the holiday. She found her prince.

going home after grad lets get 2gether

ill be back this wkend
coffee?

yah
wanna ask u about cakes!!!

You wonder how she and Mikhail can afford a fairy cake for their wedding. They are both going to be paying off their student loans as long as you are, and neither has a job lined up after graduation. Your mother told you that they think they will have to live with Ines's parents after they get married.

"It's no coincidence," Carl or Charlie's slurred voice interrupts your thoughts from across the bar. "We're living in a new feudalism, ruled by unrealistic hopes to join an unattainable elite. Statistically, the rags to riches dream isn't real, but we think if we just work hard enough, it'll happen for us. We all think we're kings in peasant's clothes, but we're just children playing make-believe. It's time we decided to live in the real world." Other voices rise to join his in belligerent agreement and you recognize arguments you've heard yourself make on other afternoons like this one.

Maybe Ines has it right — buy an expensive cake, have a fairytale wedding day. What's another few thousand dollars? At least then you'd have something to remember, one moment when you were someone's princess. But it's so hard to let the dream go.

You don't feel like a peasant, you never have. But you know if you keep pretending that one day you'll meet your fairy godmother, she'll wave her wand and suddenly everything will all be fine, that you'll spend your life being a servant to a fantasy.

You finish your beer, thinking of those days when all it took for a magical transformation was a rolled up piece of cardboard and a pillowcase dress. You flick your finger over your phone, Rhona's beautiful face filling the screen. Those blue eyes. That red hair. Can't you live in your imagination with her just a little longer?

After all, you've always been a princess. Haven't you?

"YOU DON'T LOOK like an Ishmael," he said, an eyebrow arching. But it *was* a costume party. She could be anything in there.

She laughed, throwing her head back and revealing the hollow of her neck. She looked very thin, he thought. "I guess not," she said, "but I've always wanted to say that when someone asked my name."

"Ishmael it is," he said. "You better call me Isaac, then." His seventies afro shortened while his moustache grew, and the loud disco suit he'd been wearing morphed into a ship's dress whites. A martini shaker appeared on the table next to him and he gave her the pistol-finger.

"Very clever," she said, shaking her head in what he imagined was admiration. He mentally made a list of all his friends who liked — or at least had an awareness of — cheesy old television. "But isn't that cheating?"

"You're the first person I've talked to tonight," he said, "no one else saw the other outfit. Besides, this one's better." He tugged the jacket down and grinned. "So, Ishmael." He sipped from the red plastic cup in his hand. "You appear to have me at a disadvantage."

"Oh?"

"You've got me figured out, but I can't tell who you are supposed to be." He took in her utterly generic jeans and pale blue t-shirt adorned with a line drawing of a sparrow.

She leaned in toward him and looked around as if fearful that the other partygoers might overhear. "I'm the Empress of the Universe."

"I see," he said. "I must say, you look almost as much like the Empress of the Universe as you look like an Ishmael."

She grinned. "I'm in disguise."

He barked out a laugh, spilling his drink in the process. He grabbed a nearby napkin and dabbed at her arm, revelling as always in the simulacrum of touch. It wasn't exactly right, he remembered that well enough. But it was so close.

He was disappointed when she took the napkin from him to finish cleaning herself up. "In disguise," he said. "Very good. You might even win with that one."

✳

I SHRUGGED AS I dabbed at myself with the napkin. I had no interest in the contest. I'd never won, not in any of the years of Halloween parties, and I'd been to them all. Even the ones where were actually together in someone's flat or house, as opposed to being simulated in this section of Emil's enhanced mind.

I looked at the ineffectual napkin and shook my head. "This isn't doing anything," I said, and caught a glimpse of something familiar in Isaac-the-bartender's eyes. I tried not to think about it too much.

I accessed the system responsible for creating this 'body' and had it clean up the stain on my t-shirt. If only real life were so simple to fix. I caught myself envying Emil — having this much control over his environment full-time. Then my stomach roiled, and a wave of self-loathing threatened to drown me. This was no game, it was more a prison than playhouse; this environment which was rendered by complex implants in Emil's brain. Implants without which he was completely incapable of communication as a result of his paralysis, a result of the accident we... No. I didn't want to think of that tonight. Not tonight.

"Nice talking to you, Issac," I said, thankful that the software controlling my voice made me sound lighthearted. I made my avatar smile and walked toward a knot of people near the music system. It would be loud, hopefully loud enough to make me forget. For a while.

18

✳

HE WATCHED HER walk away, wondering if it would be awkward if he followed her. After a moment he headed for the area of the simulation that looked like a kitchen.

"What's with that girl who isn't even dressed up?" the woman with snakes in her hair said as she poured a large gin and tonic. "I mean, who comes to the Halloween party and doesn't wear a costume?" Her friend, who looked like a cross between an fox and a vampire, didn't answer. "What's the point? Hell, even if you're out of ideas there are, like, a hundred presets to pick from. There's just no excuse."

"Blue t-shirt?" Isaac said, interrupting, and the gorgon nodded. "She *is* in costume," he said. "You should go talk to her."

"You figured out who she is?"

Isaac shook his head. "Nope. Whoever it is has gone in a whole different direction this year. Unlike some of us, *Lauren*."

"Damn it," she said, as the snakes uncoiled, making her hair look like it had doubled in size. "How could you tell?"

"You do something with your hair every year," the vampire fox said, shrugging. "It's always obvious."

"Well, at least you can tell I'm in costume," she said, and turned to walk back to the main room of the party, a sibilant hiss following her.

"Just because we change bodies, it doesn't change who we are," Foxy said, giving Isaac a toothy grin. "Right, *Emil?* And, yeah — great party." Isaac felt a paw on his arm then watched as his companion dropped to all fours and walked out of the kitchen.

He shook his head. That must have been Hui. She was the best guesser of them all; every year she'd been the first to figure out who everyone was. It was so bad that years ago they just gave up on having a prize for identifying people. Now it was all about the costumes.

Alone in the kitchen, he switched to a bird's eye view of the party. It was still early, they were all still well-behaved. Of course, their drinks were just pixels and code, but what they did in real life was up to them. And plenty of them would be taking breaks from the simulation and enjoying whatever refreshments suited. Parties were always smoother when well-lubricated, and he knew it was tough to spend a long time in a simulation. He'd taken months to get used to it, so he figured most of the rest would be popping in and out.

They were his closest friends, many of whom he'd known since before the accident. It had changed his life, confined him to this facsimile of a world, but he knew he was lucky. If it had happened only a few years earlier, this technology that allowed him to be half human, half simulation wouldn't have been available and he'd have been trapped in his unresponsive body. He knew well enough that no one could stay sane for long in that condition. As he looked at the simulation he'd created of an apartment, furniture, a whole life he could still share with the people he loved, he felt a surge of gratitude for the wires and chips in his head.

He scanned the rooms and picked out about a dozen people he was sure he could identify, but none of them were Diego. He wondered if this was the year he'd finally skip the party. He wondered if that would be good thing. Emil knew that Diego was as shattered as he'd been by the accident, only Diego's injuries couldn't be fixed with technology. Seeing Diego only once a year, in the skin of another person, it was almost worse than not seeing him at all.

Emil left the party for a moment, pulling up a simulated memory file. It was from before, but the implants worked with neural memories, rendering them into the same kind of simulation that now mediated all of Emil's experiences. Both more and less real than memories, it was like stepping back in time, into a party maybe five years previous.

It was Tyra's house, an over-large split level on the edge of town. She'd decorated like it was going out of style, though — plastic skeletons and crêpe paper bats overrunning the place. Emil found himself dressed as a matador, hand-in-hand with a hardened Klingon warrior, bat'leth at his side. He simultaneously remembered and remembered remembering the body in the rented Star Trek costume: Diego, a skinny bookworm with perfect eyelashes who stopped Emil's breath that summer. The summer before the accident. He exited the program and for a moment wished he could feel his face. He was sure there would be tears.

Hui's words echoed. Changing bodies doesn't change who we are.

✳

I HOVERED AROUND the edges of the group by the music. I could feel the memories, the despair starting to climb inside me and I fought to keep it at bay. It's hard to imagine that all it takes is one moment, a singular moment of metal and plastic colliding and a person could be locked in his head, unable to move or talk. But still alive, still awake.

It must have been horrible. No wonder every year since, he's volunteered to host the party, here in the home he's made in his mind. I looked around — it was uncanny. If you didn't pay close attention it looked like any luxury apartment. But it was too perfect, too clean. And the 'costumes'; for a group of people who never grew out of playing dress-up, the opportunity was too tempting.

"Nice t-shirt." The voice came out of a sleek chrome and black leather sofa, and I jumped. At least my real body did, but my avatar simply smiled.

"Thanks," I said. "I think you've got 'most unexpected' sewn up this year."

"Ha!" the sofa said. "Very funny. But you have 'most inscrutable' for sure. Or maybe 'most meta'? Dressed up as a person who couldn't be bothered to dress up? Kind of impressive."

I laughed, revelling in the moment of normalcy. Friends, making jokes. No one accusing anyone of anything. It was freeing.

"Would it be inappropriate to sit on you?"

"Nah, I'm game."

I perched on the sofa and tried to pick out Emil from the gryphons and rainbows and impossibly beautiful people in the room. Once, I'd have thought I'd know him anywhere. Each year I found I was wrong.

✳

HE GRABBED A bottle of champagne from the fridge and walked back out to the main space. The usual two dozen people stood around a mostly faithful representation of his living room, drinking, talking, one couple making out in the corner. Most of them had been friends since university, and even as they grew apart and changed over time, this core group still managed to get together once a year for the party. It was their own private Las Vegas: what happened on Halloween stayed on Halloween.

He scanned the room, looking for the Empress of the Universe. Hui may have been the undisputed champion, but it had been a long time since he'd been so baffled by one of his friends. If he didn't know better, he'd have thought someone sneaked in.

He saw her by his bookshelf, which displayed a selection of the book, film and music titles currently in the entertainment drive of his system. She sipped from her plastic cup and seemed to scrutinize the shelves.

"You must know Emil's taste by now," he said as he walked up next to her.

She shrugged. "People change," she said. "And there might be something good I want to borrow." She smiled and drained her cup. "You going to open that?" she asked, glancing at the bottle.

"Why not?" He wrestled with the cork for a moment before it popped out. He poured some in her glass, then swigged straight from the bottle. "Cheers."

"That's not very bartendery," she said.

He shrugged. "I've never been good at staying in character," he said. They stood by the bookshelf, drinking in silence, staring at each other as if they might be able to see through the projection that rendered their images.

"I wonder if this is what it really looks like," she said, finally.

"What?"

"This," she swept her hand to indicate the room. "Emil's... place. When it's not being used for a party."

He didn't know how to answer. Most of his old friends never talked about it, about him, about the accident. It had become one of the unwritten rules of the party — don't talk about Emil. They weren't his rules, though. This was his life now: he worked, had friends, traveled, all mediated through the software and hardware in his brain. He knew it sounded like a kind of technological heaven to some people, but it wasn't. He wasn't better than human, just different. If he could have a functioning body again, he'd trade all the immediate connectivity and virtual experiences in the blink of a microchip's cycle. But that wasn't a possibility.

This life wasn't perfect, but it was immensely preferable to the alternative. Emil wasn't embarrassed or shy about it, how could he be? But so many of his friends acted like talking about it was taboo, like mentioning it would somehow be pulling back the curtain on a stage magician, revealing that it was all just a cheap parlour trick. Even now, when they visited him in his own realm, they pretended that it was just another party, that the impossible costumes and improbable physics were just another option from the fancy dress rental.

It wasn't everyone, of course. He and Hui met regularly, and everyone in his life that he'd met after he'd changed at least put in the effort to be understanding. As much as he wished the old gang could get over whatever it was that kept them away, Emil usually didn't fight it, not anymore. He didn't want to endure that moment when they looked at him — at the simulated version of him that his implants created — and compared it to what he had once been.

There was something about her, though. The Empress of the Universe seemed to want to find a way to bridge whatever chasm there was between them, one disembodied, the other... Emil didn't know her story. Another unwritten rule — no asking, only guessing. Was it possible? He peered into her eyes, knowing they held no clues to the identity of the person who animated the body, but wishing that he might still see a glimpse. Could it be... him in there?

"If you want to see how Emil lives," he paused, thinking abut how to phrase it, "I understand he takes visitors."

Her face seemed to change subtly, something like recognition or maybe just hope written on it. Emil fought the urge to see what his program had done with her avatar, and why. But he didn't want to know, not like that. Just because he had new abilities, that didn't mean he had to use them.

"I wish ..." Her voice trailed off and he was sure he saw the shine of tears in her eyes. "It doesn't matter," she said.

He let his hand rest on her arm, marvelling at the sensation of real flesh he felt. Hers and his. He thought he'd never get used to it. "It matters. What do you wish?"

She looked at him, her eyes locked on his, then her face changed. She smiled as if the conversation had never been serious. "I wish I really were the Empress of the Universe."

"And what would you do with your great power?"

"I would make every day Halloween," she said, "and then I would really be the Empress of the Universe." She laughed and drained her glass. "Anything left in there for me, barkeep?"

"Sure," he said, and poured champagne into her red plastic cup. His hand barely trembled.

✳

NOVEMBER FIRST WAS always tough. A physical hangover could be counteracted with drugs and neurostim, but a psychic hangover was nearly undefeatable. I looked forward to the party so much, when it was over it was almost like I'd been punched in the gut. Halloween was like stepping back in time, like for one night I could be the person I used to be, before.

It had been years since I'd met any of those people in the real world, my "closest friends." I knew they talked about me, the ones who still met for the occasional drink or meal. Even the ones who'd moved somewhere far kept in touch online. Except me. I was alone. How could I face them after?

There had been an investigation and they said it wasn't my fault. That it was the conditions and the other driver crossing the line. But it was me who'd been at the wheel, me who had been responsible. And I had just walked away, while Emil lay there, broken and unmoving. His beautiful body reduced to a shell, animated by wires and painted in pixels. And I did that.

I lay in bed, watching the sun slant through the window. Something had changed, somehow. At first I couldn't even identify the feeling, it had been so long. But finally I knew what it was — I really did wish that every day were Halloween. I wanted to be out there, wanted to be *back* there, at the party. The only place where I felt like a human.

I rolled over and picked up my handheld. I'd always kept the contacts up-to-date, but never used it. When I hit the connect button I was so surprised I didn't have time to be afraid. *How long has it been since I wasn't afraid?*

"Hello?" The voice sounded hungover, too. That wasn't a surprise. It was the only thing that wasn't.

"This is the Empress of the Universe," I said. "Well, I was yesterday. Today I'm just Diego, I guess."

I waited for Emil to answer, fear, exhilaration and anticipation nearly drowning me. As the moment stretched out toward infinity, I looked out the window and saw a flock of birds take flight off the roof of the building next door, their tiny bodies moving together as if they were individual components of some complex machine. I felt something warm and real and safe returning to my body, like birds returning to their nesting grounds after a long, cold winter — there, at that moment between question and answer, between gravity and flight.

"MORNING, JEANNE," MICHAEL says, not looking up from his workspace. His hands are flying over the translucent tabletop, manipulating images, text and settings at an incomprehensible pace. He's sat next to me for four years and I still don't know what he does.

"Morning, Mike," I say, sliding into my seat. "How goes it?"

He grunts. "Same shit, different day."

I pick up the helmet from its stand and shove it on my head. It covers my face down to my nose, blocking my vision completely. I feel the smartfoam conform to the shape of my head and choke back the momentary claustrophobia. It passes. I do up the straps and settle in for the morning shift. At least the time goes by quickly.

The buzzing in my ears makes my stomach lurch. Light flashes across my eyes and I don't know if it's a real light on the eyepiece or if it's just in my head. I breathe slowly and deeply, tamping down the nausea. My hands feel around the straps and my chin and I finally fumble off the headset. Sweat pours down my face as I put the helmet back on its stand.

"You going for a smoke?" I ask Mike.

"Yeah," he says. "See you in the box." I nod, though he still has yet to look up from his workspace. The conversation is more ritual than communication.

I walk through the bull pen toward the break room, past the hundred or so people who work on this floor of the Alexander Systems building. Some are technicians like Mike, some are controllers like me and the rest are in sales. The sales people are there to make the rest of us remember that there is a lower circle of hell to which we could still descend, I guess.

The break room is crammed with people — eating lunch, talking on their gadgets, scrounging cigarettes. I try to avoid the latter type as I push my way through to the box. Smoking isn't allowed in the office, but they've built a plywood wind shelter out on the fire escape for us. It was taking people too long to get all the way down to the ground floor then back up again, and they couldn't get people to stop nipping out for a smoke. So the box appeared.

I light up, cupping my hand around the flame. It is cold and the plywood doesn't do much for insulation. I scowl at the new sales rep who's mooching around the box looking for a handout. I am spared having to talk to her by Mike's arrival.

"Hey," he grunts, lighting one of his own. I nod back at him. We don't talk much, Mike and I, but we're what passes for friends here. He takes a couple of drags, then grabs me by the elbow. I start — Mike has never touched me before as far as I can remember. "C'mere," he says and steers me to a dark corner.

My heart pounds. What is going on? I've known Mike for years and he's never once expressed any kind of interest in me like that... He leans in toward me.

"I've applied for a promotion," he says almost silently, then stares at me intently.

"A *what*?" I say, all thoughts about Mike making a pass at me vanishing from my mind. Technician was as high as anyone got here. There are no promotions.

"There's a way out, Jeanne," Mike says, the zeal of a fanatic in his voice. "I was surfing the internal HR site one night and there was this new link. Opportunities. There's maybe ten openings right now I qualify for. Can you believe it? I could get out of here." He grabs me by the shoulders and I smell the tobacco on him. "We could both get out of here," he says.

✳

THE AFTERNOON GOES by in a blur. Most afternoons do, to be fair, but this time I could tell you what I was thinking without a moment's hesitation. Promotion. It couldn't be real. Poor Mike must be delusional, or worse, the victim of some cruel practical joke. The site was fake, it had to be. Everyone knows there's nowhere for people like us to go.

When I get home I sit on the edge of my bed and flip the screen out from the wall. I poke the screen a few times then finally find the HR page and stare at it. There is nothing new, nothing that looks anything like a page with jobs. It's just the usual explanation of how people get placed where their skills are best suited and that we should like it or lump it. I even use the search function — nothing for *job opportunities, promotion, application*. Nothing.

I let my head fall into my hands. What is wrong with Mike? He doesn't love the job, none of us do, but does he hate it so much that he's created an alternate reality for himself, one where there is something to look forward to? And is that really so bad?

✳

THERE IS A bluish light all around me; I can make out shapes but I can't tell what they are. People moving, maybe machines. Maybe it's just the light. It should be soothing, but I can feel my heart pounding in my chest. I'm panicking. I try to sit up but I can't move. My arms, legs, head — I can't move any of them. I can't feel restraints... am I paralyzed? I can feel myself hyperventilating, my heart feels like it's going to explode...

A horrible noise pierces my panic. I open my eyes and silence the alarm. I sit up, sweat glistening my body. I stand, trying to shake off the memory of the nightmare and light a cigarette with trembling fingers. Even after my coffee is gone, I can still feel the coldness of that light around me, the terrible fear of paralysis.

Mike is head-down as usual when I get to the office, but he looks up when I approach the desk. "Jeanne," he says, his face splitting into a manic grin. "I have an interview."

"What are you talking about?" I hiss quietly, slipping into my seat. "There are no job postings, Mike. I checked the HR site last night. There's nothing there, man."

He shakes his head. "They aren't always there," he says and I know he's gone truly loopy. "The links only showed up for me last week and they're gone now. But I got in just in time. It's tomorrow, my interview. Wish me luck, okay?"

He really believes this. I shake my head. Does it really hurt anything, I wonder. Letting him hope? "Sure, buddy," I say, readying my helmet for the morning shift. "Knock 'em dead."

✳

MIKE GOT THE job. At least that's what he tells me as he packs up his desk. "It's great, Jeanne," he gushes. "Almost double the salary, real vacation time, responsibility." He shakes his head and puts his hand on my shoulder. I automatically recoil, but try to cover it up. I don't think he notices. "I hope you see it soon," he says and I'm sure I hear pity in his voice. "You deserve a promotion." He picks up the half empty box and hefts it in its arms. "Catch you around, Jeanne," he says and walks out of the office.

I sink back into my chair. I don't understand any of this. I look around the office at the rest of them — no one is paying any attention as Mike leaves. It's obvious he isn't coming back; where do they think he's going? I mash the helmet on my head and try not to think about it.

I've got a cigarette glowing hotly between my lips when one of the scroungers sidles up to me; a too-pretty little woman whose name I don't know. "Can I have the butt when you're done?" she asks, not looking me in the face. Her voice has that submissive sound, like she's taken a few knocks and halfway expects another one. I've probably told her to fuck off a time or two before, but now, with Mike gone...

"Here," I say, shaking a half-smoked tailor made out of my pack.

"You can have this." I pass it over to her and see her eyes dart up to mine.

"Are you sure?" she whispers, a mix of awe and fear in her voice, as if she's afraid I'll snatch it back. I nod and tuck the smoke into her hand. I strike a match and our hands glance off each other as I light the cigarette for her.

We smoke in silence for a moment, then I say, "You see Mike leaving today?" She nods, still not looking at me. "What do you think that's about?"

"I dunno," she says. "Fired, maybe." Her voice is even quieter now and I strain to hear her. Fired. That makes more sense than anything else. I hadn't thought of that. But he seemed so happy. "It's too bad," her voice comes to me as if from a long distance and I pull myself out of my thoughts and look at her. She pinches the cigarette off with enough left for another round and tucks the end carefully in her pocket. "He seemed like a nice guy," she says and turns to push her way back to the floor.

✳

I STILL CAN'T make out anything around me, just that horrible cold, blue light. I try to close my eyes, but I can't even do that. I can feel my body, just barely, but I can't seem to make it do anything. I remember not to panic, I remember that I've been here before, remember that I've been here forever.

I can hear voices, just outside... outside where? I don't know where I am, but I can tell that the voices are from some other place, another room, another world. I can't make out what they are saying. I know they are talking about me.

I wake up to the alarm and feel like being sick.

I spend the workday catching up on things that seem to have piled up over the last few days. I barely have time to get out to the box. The small woman I gave a cigarette to smiles at me shyly, but we don't talk. The afternoon disappears.

I am on the train going home and I have this feeling. It's the eeriest thing I've ever felt as I look around at the other people. They seem unreal. I seem unreal. This isn't the way my life was supposed to be. I am as sure of it as I am sure of anything.

I get home to my apartment and slip in front of the screen. I don't know what I'm expecting. I type "this is not my life" in the search box. Hit *Enter*.

Films, novels, songs, a million blog posts. Of course, I can't be alone in this feeling — who wouldn't wish that there was more to life than this? It's nothing. Just existential malaise. I turn away to reach for the cigarettes when something catches my eye. In the summary of one of the blog posts the phrase "recurring dreams" is sandwiched between complaints about delayed trains and the shops always being out of bread. Recurring dreams.

I click the link.

404.

I go back, looking for a cached image of the site, but now it's not even in the search results. I rub my eyes, incredulous. I saw it, I know I did. But there's nothing I can do to bring it back, no search that finds that post.

I spend the rest of the evening alternately trying to convince myself that I imagined the whole thing and wondering if this is like Mike's job site. It's there and it's gone.

I don't sleep at all that night.

＊

I WALK INTO the box, my mind filled with images of blue light, the sound of far away voices. I don't even see her at first. "Hey," she says, her hand reaching out for my arm. She stops short of touching me, but the gesture draws me back to reality. "I owe you one," she says and opens her hand. A beautifully home-rolled cigarette lies in her palm. "My account just reopened," she explains and lifts her hand toward me. "I can pay you back."

I look at her, the hopeful expectation on her face. I pick up the cigarette with two fingers and try to smile. I don't think it works. "Thanks," I say. "What's your name?"

"Laura," she says.

"I'm Jeanne," I say and light the cigarette. It goes down rough and I don't mind. "You're in sales, right?"

"Yeah, just started a couple of months ago," she says. "You hear anything from Mike?"

I shake my head. "He's gone."

She nods, but I think she's just agreeing to keep the conversation going. She doesn't know what's going on. I sit on the bench and smoke for a minute or two. She talks about a new coffee bar that's opened near her apartment. "They let you stay as long as you want," she says. "It's so nice just to get out once in a while, don't you think?" I look up at her.

"You ever get the feeling this isn't where you're supposed to be?" I ask.

She shrugs. "Sure. I've taken a few minutes longer on break once or twice. Who hasn't?"

"No," I say, leaning forward, my hands gripping my knees. "I mean all of this. Your whole life. Don't you ever feel... Don't you think this isn't really your life? This isn't how it was all meant to be?"

I see a look of fear cross her face. "Uh..." she says and I realize that there is no one I can talk to any more.

"Never mind," I say, forcing a laugh. "It's just been a rough morning."

"Yeah," she says, choosing to believe my excuse. "I hear that." We don't talk again until it's time to go back to work. She waves at me and smiles as we separate in the hallway. I wonder if she's even a real person.

✳

I HAD ALMOST convinced myself that I had just imagined Mike and his promotion when I finally see it.

Internal Job Opportunities <u>Click Here to Apply Online</u>

I click there.

Opportunities for Jeanne Dennis at Alexander Systems
• Team Leader, Technologist group 75 <u>Apply Now</u>
• Assistant to the Manager, Floor 8 <u>Apply Now</u>

I am numb as I click the Apply Now links. At first nothing seems to happen, but in a minute I hear the chime. There are a pair of acknowledgment messages waiting in my inbox. I stare at the boilerplate text and my mind whirls. Am I delirious? Dreaming? Mad?

I copy the text into a file on my system, half believing that the messages will have evaporated from my inbox in the morning. I light a cigarette and see that my fingers are trembling. I stare at the screen for an hour then finally go to bed.

All night long, I dream of voices and blue lights and cold. When I wake I feel like I haven't slept at all. My hands shake as it takes three tries to light my first cigarette. I spill coffee on the threadbare carpet. I sip and smoke in front of the screen, afraid of what I won't see there.

I have reason to be afraid, but not the reason I thought. The messages are still there.

✳

THEY WANT TO interview me. I get the message two days later, a cheerful note from some HR person, inviting me to an interview. It's online, they say; I can do it at home. I'll get an hour's paid leave to come home early for it.

Paid leave. If Mike had mentioned anything like that to me I'd have known he was crazy. But it's right there on the screen for all to see. An hour's paid leave.

I throw up all morning on the day of the interview. I've taken two weeks' worth of personal time rushing to the toilet — if I don't get this new job I don't know how I'll make it up. Laura catches my eye on the way to the box, waves at me. I shake my head. I can't even smoke I feel so nervous. And what would I tell her? She'd never believe me, not in a million years. I watch the clock and try to stop my stomach from leaping out of my body.

The interview itself goes by in a blur. Two faces, blandly corporate, stare out at me from the console screen. All I can think is that my apartment must look like a disaster. They smile at every answer I give — there's no way of knowing what they are thinking. Afterward, the only questions I even remember don't have anything to do with the job — "If you saw someone hit another person on the train, what would you do?" "If your desk mate started to cry, would you ask what's wrong or just keep working?" "Imagine a typical day in the life of your next door neighbour. Can you describe what it's like?"

When it's over, the smiling faces nod and the one on the left says, "Thank you for your time, Jeanne. You'll hear from us by the end of the week." They disconnect and I feel myself breathe for what feels like the first time all day. I did everything I could. I'm so tired that I crawl into bed without eating anything and close my eyes. If I dream, I don't remember it.

※

I CATCH HER eye on the way to the box. I smile, trying to contain myself. I want it to be a surprise, my good news. I want to share my happiness with her. Maybe some of it will rub off. She waits for me in the crowd of people and I push my way through. "Hi," I say, and pass her an almost full pack of high grade cigarettes. "Take one," I say and lead on to our usual bench.

I can see confusion in her eyes but she pulls out a cigarette anyway then hands me back the pack. I look at it, look at her. I don't even want the cigarette, but I extract one and light it without thinking. "Guess what?" I say, unable to keep the grin off my face any longer.

"What?" she asks, and it looks like concern on her face.

"I got a new job," I say, the words tumbling out, "a promotion. Team Leader for group 75. I start on Monday." I look at her and can see my own face reflected in her eyes. I look like a raving lunatic and I try to rein it in.

"There's this secret job listings page," I explain, "I don't know if it only shows up after you've been here a while or what. Anyway, remember Mike? Well, he saw it, applied and got a better job. That's where he went. I didn't believe it at first either, but then I saw it and now here I am." I know I'm rambling, but I can't stop. I need her to believe me. I need her to know that there is a way out.

I can tell that I'm not getting through. "That's great," she says mechanically, the way you'd talk to a slow child. "I'm really happy for you, Jeanne."

I force myself to calm down. "I understand," I say. "Mike... I didn't believe it either." I finish my cigarette and throw the butt on the ground. Someone will pick it up, salvage the remaining grains of tobacco. I reach out and lightly touch Laura's arm. She doesn't wince, at least. "I know you think I've lost it," I say. "You just got here; it will probably take awhile before you see it. But it's real, it is." I stop myself again. "Just watch the HR site. Promise me." I take her face between my palms and stare into her frightened eyes. "Promise me you'll watch the site."

"Ok," she says, her voice trembling. I let my hands drop from her face and look at my fingers. I can't remember the last time I touched someone's skin.

"I have to go," I say. I reach out toward her and she extends her own arm, tentatively at first. I press the pack of cigarettes into her hand. "Thanks," I say then turn and walk out of the box for the last time.

✳

I AM SURROUNDED by the blue light. It feels like I have been here my whole life — paralyzed, suspended, smothered by the light. I hear the voices, closer now, clearer. "She's coming around, sir."

"Careful now. This is a difficult adjustment. Everyone handles it differently."

"I have the tranq ready."

"Good."

My eyes are open. They have always been open, but for the first time I blink. It feels like a colossal effort, yet it also seems like a victory. How long has it been since I closed my eyes? Before I can finish the thought, I feel like I am falling into a pool of cold water. No, not falling, *rising*. I fight not to panic; I try to breathe but I still can't seem to make any part of my body other than my eyes do anything.

"Heart rate's up," one of the voices says.

"Not a problem yet, but keep an eye on it."

I gasp. Air! Slightly metallic tasting, but clean and pure and filling my lungs. I can move my shoulders now and I raise my head slightly. It's harder than closing my eyes but I can see machines and two people at the foot of this tub I'm lying in. "Jeanne," one of them says, the one in charge I think. "Jeanne, everything is going to be fine. No one is going to hurt you. Just relax and we'll have you out of there in no time."

I try to sit up, try to thrash my arms and legs, but they don't move. I can hear talking, but I no longer care what they are saying. I have to get out of here! My breath comes hard and ragged, then darkness encloses me again.

✳

I OPEN MY eyes, blink a couple of times. The blue light is dimmer now and I am lying on a couch. I'm wearing some kind of dress made of the softest fabric I've ever felt. It's warm, comfortable. I feel like I should be terrified but there's this calmness filling my body.

"Hello again, Jeanne." The man smiles warmly. "You've had a bit of a shock, so we've had to give you a mild sedative. It will wear off over the next few hours, but we thought it best to make you a little calmer." He leans in toward me and I don't even feel like flinching. "You'll start to remember soon. I'm sure you'll have questions once it's all come back to you." He turns and gestures away from the couch. I notice for the first time that I am in a small sitting room. There are no windows but the door is open.

"If you need someone, just call. This is best done on your own, but we will be monitoring you from out there."

"Wait," I croak. "What about the job? Where…"

He pats my arm and I feel calmness wave over me again. "Just remember." He walks out the door.

I don't know what I'm supposed to remember. I packed up my things, left the office, took the train home…

When the first one comes it is almost physically painful. Images, but more than pictures. Memories, they must be, but such terrible memories. A knife, wet with blood. I can feel its stickiness on my fingers, which are clenched around the hilt. So much anger.

A person I don't recognize is lying on the ground, screaming, with blood everywhere. I can't look away. Now I remember — her name was Sandra. They told me at the police station her name was Sandra. I told the officer that it was her own fault, that she brought it on herself.

"She nearly died," the officer shouted at me, slamming his hand on the table. One of the other officers pulled him from the room. I sat there, covered in Sandra's blood, smirking.

I feel sick. I lean over the side of the couch and retch, but nothing comes out. It feels like my stomach is trying to tear itself from my body and I can't stop heaving.

No one comes through the door.

I have no idea how long I am in the room. Eventually I stop retching, but the memories keep on coming. My arrest, the trial, Sandra sitting in the courtroom glaring at me. The prosecutor told the judge that this was the fourth time I had been stopped by the police, but the first time I had been violent. However, since it was such a brutal attack, they said they had no choice. It had to be the Alexander System.

I don't know what that means, but I remember going crazy when the sentence was pronounced. I tried to escape the courtroom, punched out one of the officers, screaming the whole while that I wouldn't let them change me, wouldn't let them destroy who I am. It took three people to finally restrain me and I remember the prick of a needle. Then it all fades out.

I sit on the edge of the couch, my head in my hands. I hear the door open and footsteps approach me, but I don't look up.

"Your sentence is complete," the voice says. "You've had your anti-social tendencies neurochemically corrected and you've completed the assigned year in the virtual retribution centre. You are free to go."

"Free…" I repeat, tears falling silently down my face. "You don't know what the word even means."

✳

THE FIRST WEEK I don't even leave the apartment they've given me. It's spacious, airy and light and I don't deserve it. I remember that everyone lives like this, I understand that my experiences at Alexander Systems were a fiction, but I can't help but feel like I've been rewarded somehow. And I have, I suppose. I've been rewarded for serving my sentence, for taking to the drugs which adjusted my brain chemistry to become a person who would never stab a neighbour over some perceived insult.

But I don't deserve a reward. For two days I don't even get out of bed. At first I think I will never get over the memories of what I did. She could easily have died — and regardless of what I said in my defence, I know that was what I was trying to do. Murder.

They tell me I have to go see a counsellor once a week. Somehow I manage to navigate between my apartment and the office. The streets are clean, the people all seem so happy and... easy. No one looks like they're late for work, no one looks like they've ever missed a meal. I feel like everyone can tell that I don't belong.

The office is blandly attractive, just like the counsellor. She tells me her name is Kristina, that she is trained to help people like me. She smiles at me and I avoid her by walking over to the large window overlooking the park. I can see couples walking, holding hands. Children chasing butterflies and each other. Machines tidying, composting, making everything orderly.

"It's pretty different here than it was inside," she says and I start at the sound of her voice.

"What do you know about it?" I say, then immediately feel bad for getting angry. "I'm sorry," I mumble, but she shakes her head.

"It's a good question," she says. "I don't really think anyone can understand unless they've been there. But I have." I stare at her, not knowing what to say. "I got six months for punching my ex-boyfriend's new partner in the stomach. She was pregnant at the time."

"My god," I say. Kristina nods.

"The baby was fine," she goes on. "My bark was worse than my bite," she smiles. "But it was just the culmination of a lot of bad behaviour. Anyway, when I got out I was completely disoriented. I remembered my life before, but it was like... I don't know, like remembering a film I'd seen or something."

"Exactly," I said. "I recognize everything, but it's like it isn't real, like it doesn't belong to me."

"That's normal for people like us," she says. "And it's something even other people feel every once in a while. I know it's hard to believe now, but you've served your sentence — you're part of society again. You deserve happiness as much as anyone else. It will get better. It just takes time."

I nod, but I don't believe it.

Months go by; I visit Kristina once a week and we talk and I guess it does help. Somehow, the horror fades. I wonder if it's an effect of the drugs, of whatever they did to me, that I can somehow remember my crimes, feel truly guilty, and yet still live. Kristina says no, it's just me getting better, but I don't know what to believe.

✳

I ONCE WOULD have said that it happened by accident, but I can't stop feeling like my life is scripted, like I'm part of a movie. Kristina tells me this is normal for people like me and I nod. She tells me that in time I will come to know this as the real world and I nod again. I knew Alexander Systems was the real world, but it wasn't. My tiny apartment. Mike. Laura. They were real, but they aren't. I don't say any of that to Kristina. What's the point?

So, when I see him in the lobby of a theatre part of me isn't even surprised. My heart pounds, though, and I rush through the door. He is with a woman I don't know and I try not to scare her but I am so happy to see him. "Mike," I say, walking up to him, breathless. "God, it's good to see you."

He does a double take when he sees me, but he smiles. "Jeanne," he says. "I'm glad to see you, too. I hoped you'd be getting out soon. How are you doing these days?"

I look around. The theatre is full of people and this woman with Mike is standing there, looking right at me. It's not safe to talk here. "Fine," I say, "great." I look at Mike, hoping he knows that I'm lying. "Say, I should let you go, but maybe we could talk sometime? Here's my contact info." I pull out my handheld and squirt the data in his direction.

"Sure," he says and my handheld chirps with a new contact. "Good to see you, Jeanne."

As I walk toward the door I hear the woman say, "Is that someone from... you know?"

"Yeah," Mike says, "she was a friend."

"Were you two...?"

"Naw," he says, "it wasn't like that inside." I leave the theatre and walk back to my apartment.

It wasn't like that inside, he's right. It never seemed strange at the time, but no one was close, not really close. There were no couples, no dates. It was just work, loneliness, more work.

✳

I DREAM OF the box. I am sitting on a bench, smoking a tailor made, when she walks up to me. Laura. Cute, pretty Laura. She's wearing a summer dress, the straps touching her shoulders so lightly they almost aren't there. The wind blows her skirt around her legs so it looks almost like she's flying. She is smiling at me and she lifts her hand to wave. It's slow, so slow, like the moment could last forever. Then she's in front of me and I can feel the warmth of her all over my body. She tilts her face up to mine and it feels like time stands still as she inches closer, closer. I know she is going to kiss me and I feel so happy I could die. Then I wake up.

✳

"DON'T YOU EVER think of the people still in there?" I ask Mike. I've finally gotten through on a voice channel when he's alone. That woman — Jill or Julie or something — is almost always there.

"Honestly?" he asks. "Not really. I mean, I did my time. I'm not even the same person anymore, not really. It was my punishment, just like it's theirs. I try not to think of it at all."

"But..." I start to argue, but he cuts me off.

"Look, Jeanne," he says, "it was hard when I first got out too. That's why we have the counsellors. But it gets better, I promise you. At first I thought about it all the time. But it's not real, Jeanne. It was built to punish us and thinking about it all the time is just a kind of punishment, too. Why spend your time dwelling on the past, when the present is so much better?"

"But, what if this isn't real either?" I say and it's the first time I've said out loud what I've believed since I left the room with the blue light. I hold my breath, waiting for his answer, but he laughs.

"Come on," he says, "who cares if it's real or not? Seriously, where would you rather be? In there, even if it is real or out here even if it's not?"

I don't answer and I can hear him sigh.

"Look, Jeanne," he says, "I've got to go. I know it's tough right now, but trust me, it really does get better. Talk to your counsellor, it really helps. Get out, have some fun. Try to remember what a normal life really is."

"Yeah," I say.

"Look," he says, "call me again once you get a bit more... acclimatized, okay? We'll get together then."

"Sure," I say and break the connection. Maybe he's right, maybe it doesn't matter what's real and what isn't. But at least I know what matters to me. I know what I have to do.

✳

"YOU CAN'T GO in there." The guy standing behind the console doesn't sound entirely certain of himself. I'm not surprised — I'm sure there isn't exactly a long line of people trying to break in to this place. He moves to block me as I keep barrelling toward the door to the room they'd trapped me in. I put my arm out to shove him away, but he's more solid than I expected. He starts to grab for me and I pull the knife from my waistband.

43

"I don't want to hurt you," I say and mean it. I have to fight the nausea that is rising just thinking about what could happen if he keeps trying to get in my way. "But I will if you try to stop me," I finish and mean that, too.

Time slows and I notice that he missed a patch on his chin when he shaved last. He's wearing an ID tag that says his name is David Baynes. He smells of fear.

I guess he can tell that I'm not lying and he backs away from me. "What do you think you're going to do?" he asks as I open the door and look at the bed of goo where my body lay while my mind was trapped in that other world. "Destroying this cell won't do anything — the Alexander System is completely decentralized. You could destroy this whole facility and it wouldn't make a difference. You can't accomplish anything here."

I turn to look at him, the knife heavy in my hand. "Yes, I can," I say. "And you're going to help me." I flick the knife at him and see him cringe. I grab his arm and pull him into the room.

✳

THE LIGHT IS that familiar cool blue but it no longer seems frightening. I feel my heart beating slowly and evenly for the first time since I can remember. "How much longer, David?" I ask. I'm cold and I can feel my body becoming heavier.

"A few minutes," he says and I idly wonder why he hasn't gone for help. I'm trapped in the bed now, I can't hurt him from here. Maybe he decided that if I want to go back that he shouldn't stop me. Besides, if they caught me and decided to punish me for breaking in and threatening the staff, I'd just end up where I want to go anyway. Maybe he figured all that out and decided to save some time. Or maybe he's still just scared.

Why he helps me doesn't really matter. All that matters is that I can feel my body lose its attachment to my mind, can see the blue light fade away into darkness. Already I can feel the beginning of a craving for a cigarette. It won't be long now.

Work, loneliness, more work. Here, I don't even have the work. But now I know. It will be different now.

I'm coming, Laura. I know it will be years until they let you out and they may never let me out, now. I know it probably isn't real. But that doesn't matter. Who cares if it isn't real if it means I'm not alone?

JO-LYNN HAD always laughed at Charlotte, her stupid sister-in-law, who believed the crap in those so-called newspapers she bought at the supermarket every week. It was no wonder that her no-good brother married Charlotte; he'd always liked them dumb and easy.

Once Charlotte moved in to the small house Jo-Lynn had been sharing with her brother Carl since their parents died, Jo-Lynn had decided it was time to move. She just didn't have an excuse to go to the city, and she wasn't about to move away then have to come crawling back when she ran out of money. She needed a plan.

She'd been out on the back porch having a cigarette when she saw the light in the sky, squinting as the saucer landed. She was plenty surprised when the aliens grabbed her and she found out that Charlotte's trashy papers weren't entirely full of garbage.

Carl hated that Jo-Lynn finished high school with honours, hated her even more for wanting to go to the city and attend the community college. "What do you want to be groping rich old ladies for," he asked, sneering, between sips of Pabst Blue Ribbon, when Jo-Lynn told him she was moving to the city to become a massage therapist. "As if some fancy college makes you better than me," he slurred, as Jo-Lynn left the room to pack.

She figured the aliens were trying to probe her that night on the table on their ship, but being one-celled organisms, they didn't know how to do it. They just poked and prodded with their pseudopodia, all night long. But by the time they finally dumped her back in the yard, Jo-Lynn had come up with a plan. Those aliens gave a damn good massage.

last night I had
the most wonderful dream

CARLY MOANED SOFTLY in her sleep, and rolled over. She dreamed and dreamed, and when she woke, she found that she still had the lingering shadow of a smile on her lips. Her body was loose with the remnants of her orgasm. She stretched, and smiled fully as her eyes slowly opened. She loved Mondays.

there was a man
so beautiful
he took the breath from my body
we were drawn to each other
as if we had magnets
in our souls

CARLY WALKED INTO the dream research lab a few minutes early, but Dave was already there. His back was turned to her, but she knew his body by heart. Dave Windeman, M.D., PhD. had been Dr. Carly Andrews' partner in research for nearly four years, but not, alas, in life. From the first day they worked together it was clear that they were the perfect pair in the lab, complementing each others' weaknesses, feeding their strengths. They were so obviously well-suited to each other, their grad students never understood why they weren't a couple off campus.

It was not a question they had never secretly asked themselves.

As she watched Dave lean against his desk and read a report, Carly felt an involuntary flush come to her face as she vividly remembered her dream from the previous night.

our mouths touched
and sparks flew from our parted lips

CARLY SIGHED SOFTLY, and walked toward her partner. Dave stood, sensing her behind him and turned. He smiled, and Carly saw the corners of his eyes crinkle. "Morning, Doctor," he said. "You slept well, I trust." He raised one eyebrow, and Carly felt herself blushing again.

"Very nicely, thank you," she said, forcing her voice to remain even. "And you look particularly well rested yourself, Doctor," she answered.

"Indeed," Dave said. "It was another impressive showing from our friends last night." He leaned back against the lab bench, and took a sip from his coffee cup. "It was the Swedish women's soccer team for me," he grinned with false machismo. "Anyone interesting for you?"

into his ear
I whispered
your name

IT WAS A Wednesday when Dave had come barging into Carly's office, his face pale and gaunt. "You look like hell," she'd said, smiling. Her smile faded fast when he didn't answer back.

"Have you ever thought that sleep problems were contagious?" he asked, his voice quivering. "Like I could have picked something up from the lab?"

"Contagious?" she answered back, incredulous. "What are you talking about?"

Her partner flopped onto the couch in Carly's office and put his head in his hands. "I took Lucidox last night," he began, and held his hand up to stop Carly's objections before they began. "I don't need the after-school special, just listen, okay?" Carly nodded curtly, her lips pursed like a scolding mother. "I've done it before a bunch of times, so I know how it should..."

"David Edgar Windeman," Carly said, cutting him off. "These drugs are for clinical research, not for, for..." She fought for the right word. "Not for amusing yourself with."

Dave sighed. "I know your opinion about this sort of thing, but I didn't come here for a lecture. Just hear me out, and then you can slap my hands, okay?" Carly snorted, but said nothing. "I know what it should be like with Lucidox. You can control everything in your dream, make anything you want to happen, happen. No surprises. Like a daydream, only more vivid. That's how it always was before. Last night, though..." His voice trailed off.

"Start at the beginning," Carly said, slipping into her researcher role and picking up her notebook and pen.

Dave told her about how his dream started out normally enough, but then other people who didn't belong in the scenario kept showing up. "It was so strange," he said. "I was completely aware that I was in a dream, and I could choose to do whatever I wanted; control my own actions, change the scenario, whatever. But there wasn't anything I could do to control the other people in my dream. It was like they were... well, like they really were were other people."

"What are you saying, Dave?" Carly asked, frowning.

"I'm saying that there were other people in my dream. People with their own ideas, their own plans, making their own decisions."

Carly pursed her lips and thought. "Sounds like a typical dream to me, Dave," she said, and when he tried to explain further, she cut him off with a lecture. "This is exactly the problem with messing around with something like Lucidox," she said. "You think that, because you're a professional, you know what you're doing, but you don't, really. And now you come in here thinking you've made some kind of breakthrough just because your drug-induced lucid dream wasn't a perfect construction of your conscious mind. You should be ashamed, Dave."

She almost convinced him that it was nothing. But over the next few weeks, their patients and research subjects began complaining of eerily similar experiences, and Carly started to believe her partner. And when she finally consented to try Lucidox herself she knew it to be true. The other people in her dreams were real.

✳

THEY SAT AT the lunchroom table, Dave's feet on the scarred plastic tabletop. "I know this seems impossible," Carly began, "but could it be some kind of telepathy?"

"You mean people sharing the same dream?" Dave asked. "I guess it's as good a theory as any." They hadn't shared their theory about other beings inhabiting dreams with their grad students and postdocs, they simply started keeping track of additional data in their tests. But they had gotten nowhere in over two weeks, so they agreed that it was time to go public.

They posted their theories on an online service for dream researchers, and shrugged off the inevitable jeers and name calling. And after dozens of attempts, no one could match any of the dreams any better than chance, there being so many typical themes among people's dreaming lives. They were becoming a joke in the community.

It was Dave who eventually stumbled on the truth, even though he thought at the time he was making a joke. "If it's not other dreamers," he said one day when they were frustrated by the lack of progress, "it must be bloody aliens."

✳

THEY READ UP on tests used by SETI, the search for extra-terrestrial intelligence, and though neither he nor Carly truly believed the alien theory, they had nothing else to try. So they called in Johanna.

She was a one in a million, Carly had once said. Johanna said that all her life, even as a child, she had known her dreams were dreams, and had always been able to control them perfectly. A natural lucid dreamer, she could be given instructions before falling asleep, and be able to remember and carry them out in her dream. So Dave, Carly and Johanna began a systematic program to try to contact the dream people.

It wasn't an instant success — Johanna began by starting a conversation with the first strange person she encountered in a dream. She related the discussion when she awoke to Dave and Carly. "It was like we were speaking two different languages, though the words he used were English. I said, 'Hello, my name is Johanna, what is your name?' and he said, 'Fruit are underwater, thank you sunset.' It went on like that for a while then I just gave up." Dave smirked and Carly frowned, and they looked for other ways to communicate.

Only when they tried mathematics did they have any success. Johanna began counting in prime numbers to the people she met in her dream. She'd had to memorize the sequence, being utterly terrible at math herself. When she awoke she was able to report the dream person's response — perfectly continuing the mathematical sequence. Carly and Dave knew they were on to something. It wasn't proof, not yet, but they were convinced. Convinced enough to try other tests with other dreamers, until they had pages and pages of similar data. Enough pages to make them realize that they had found something incredible. An entity, that was intelligent but not human, was living and acting inside people's dreams.

*

"I'M SORRY I didn't believe you at first," Carly said to Dave, one night after they'd been working late and went to a nearby pub for a quick bite before calling it a day.

"It's okay," he said, smiling and holding her gaze with his own. "I knew you'd be disappointed in me taking Lucidox for fun, but who else could I tell?"

Carly smiled. She could feel the better part of the three glasses of wine she'd had with dinner on her sense of propriety. She let her hand wander over to Dave's side of the table, and her stomach flipped pleasantly at the softness of his touch as he put his own hand ever so lightly on her arm. "So what did you want?" she asked. "What dream desire made you take Lucidox in the first place?"

She swore she felt Dave's hand on her arm stiffen but in the dim light of the pub she couldn't see his face flush. "You," he thought, as his heart jackhammered in his chest. "In all my dreams it's always only ever been you."

Aloud, he said, "Flying."

I looked into his eyes
his eyes which were
your eyes
his hand moved against me
it felt like your touch
so soft it is more a memory
than a caress

"DO YOU REMEMBER when we first started here?" Dave asked, as he filled his mug with coffee from the pot. "Could you have imagined then that we'd ever be presenting to the Royal Academy in London?"

"Of course not," Carly laughed. "We aren't even British."

The grad students and postdocs had all left for the day, but Carly and Dave were still in the lab, ostensibly to finish preparing their talk before the flight across the pond the next morning. Really, they were both too nervous to be alone, and had no other excuse to be together. They both had always been most comfortable in the lab.

✳

IT WAS THE sex dreams which had finally catapulted them into the spotlight. Even though it had taken a few weeks for it to become obvious, it was impossible to ignore that for nearly two months, in a thirty-three hour period between Sunday and Monday every single sleeping person on the planet past puberty was experiencing intense and vivid erotic dreams. The dream research community was abuzz with the revelation, and Carly and Dave's theory about the other lifeforms populating human dreams was, amazingly, among the most credible explanations.

Once they had formalized their theory, Drs. Andrews and Windeman had teamed up with several other professors at the university. Anson Sindow, the psychologist, hypothesized that the beings were trying to communicate with humanity through pleasure. Kavita Dhaliwal, the biologist, guessed that it was some kind of mating ritual within their own species that they were reenacting with sleeping humans. The physicist, Sally Jensen, suggested that it was the random result of electrochemical stimulation. Whatever it was, it was real and worldwide and completely impossible to ignore.

"So, what do you think it is?" Carly asked Dave, as he flipped through the final draft of their presentation for the millionth time. "The Sunday night special?"

"I don't really know," Dave said. "It's not exactly my field."

"Sure," Carly said, "But you've experienced it almost ten times now, and most of those times you knew it was really the other beings, not your own unconscious at work. You must have a theory."

"Well," Dave said, putting his feet up on the lunchroom table and leaning back in his chair. "I do have a thought or two." He glanced at Carly, and couldn't stop himself from remembering his most recent dream of her. He quickly looked away. "I don't think it's just a mistake, or some kind of translation error," he said. "It's too... consistent for that, you know what I mean?"

"Yeah," Cary said, laughing. "Is it the same one for you each week, too?"

Dave nodded, his heartbeat racing in his chest.

"It's so strange," she said, "having this lover that you don't even know."

"You don't know who it is?" Dave asked, his eyes catching Carly's for a moment. "You don't ever recognize anyone?"

"Oh, that," Carly said, a flush creeping up her face. "Well, who we see is just a product of our dreaming minds," she said. "Your Swedish soccer team, for example," she grinned. "But who it is, really," she said, "I wish I knew. I wonder if we'll ever know."

does it bother you
that this man I dream of
clothed in your body
is not you
are you jealous of him
my dream lover
who stole your name and your face
whom I loved last night
exquisitely

The face staring back at me from the mirror is unfamiliar yet I know it is mine. It *feels* like me, even if I still fail to recognize myself sometimes. I am told this is my actual body, that this world is the real world. The life I thought I had, the world I believed to be real — those were cleverly controlled electrical impulses sent to my brain. Not real. Not me.

Yes, I asked *why*. Of course, I asked *how*.

"There are many reasons a person might be placed in simulation," my first therapist, Kris, told me. "Rehabilitation from anti-social behaviour, military training. Interrogation." I must have looked appalled. "Oh, it isn't all like that. Some people choose it themselves, like a vacation or entertainment."

"Did I?"

Kris smiled. "If it helps you to think that, perhaps that's what you should choose to believe."

"But what was it, really?"

Kris shrugged. "Why does it matter? You're here now."

✳

It takes many sessions and another therapist before I accept that I will never know why. Two therapists later, I honestly don't care. I don't care why my body was hooked up to IVs and electrodes, why another life was created and curated, forced into my mind. I don't even care that I can never believe in reality again.

Oh, I have no doubt that my therapists are sincere, that they believe what they say, but no one will ever convince me. How could I be sure this is real when I know that the life I thought was mine was a simulation? Once you know your own eyes can deceive you, your own memory is a rewritable disk, you can never be certain. If one life can be a puppet show, any life can be. It's turtles all the way down.

✳

"How are we feeling this week, Gil?"

I'm thankful that Samia, my latest therapist, has finally agreed to say my name with the hard "g" — Jill or Gillian feels more wrong than the face in the mirror. The patronizing plural, on the other hand, I can do without.

"Fine. Better." She nods for too long, waiting for me to say more, to unburden myself. To express my feelings.

Too bad. I can wait as long as anyone.

She purses her lips, then breaks the silence. "Do you miss them?"

I don't have to ask who she means. I had a good life in my created world. Nothing spectacular, just an ordinary existence, but it was comfortable. Fulfilling in its own unremarkable way.

"Sometimes." I sigh and decide to throw her a bone. "The other day, I saw a woman who looked like her. Not exactly the same, just something familiar about the way she carried herself, the movements of her body. It was disconcerting, unnerving." I see my reflection in the window behind Samia's desk, the short blonde hair I still can't figure out how to style, smooth scrubbed skin from my failed attempts at trying out makeup.

"How did that make you feel?"

I think about the question, like I am meant to. That's the whole point of being here, to work through how I feel about this experience. To get past it.

"I feel... blank."

Samia writes something on her tablet, nodding. She nods a lot — all the therapists do. "It will take time before the experiences in the simulation no longer seem real, before you settle into your true body, your true life. It's normal to feel like this world is empty for a while. It will pass."

I nod back and arrange this face into the shape of a smile. We end the session and I leave her office, feet tracing a path back to the apartment, where I will stare into the mirror.

✳

It took months to convince me — charts and logic and explanation and unending patience. For a long time I fought them, even though I couldn't understand why they would be trying to fool me, how they could imagine I'd ever think that my life was a lie. But it was.

That was not my beautiful wife. Those were not my maddening and marvellous children. The face and body I saw in the mirror and quietly despised were never mine to hate.

✳

The therapists think they understand what it's like to know that your entire sense of who you are isn't real. They think that it is painful, disorienting, something that needs to be overcome. They don't understand anything.

I never did see a woman who reminded me of her. It was just the kind of thing I was expected to say, the kind of thing that would make Samia make a tick on her tablet and a note on my file. *Subject is experiencing feelings of emptiness.* There was no point in explaining that this wasn't what I meant at all.

I am not the person I thought I was, and that is a joy. I am not the person anyone needs me to be, not defined by my relationship to anyone else.

I am blank. A fresh canvas, the blinking cursor.

I look at the face in the mirror knowing this may be another prison, another interrogation or training program. It might even be real, like Samia claims. It doesn't matter. Here, I have no history, no expectations, no baggage. I am free and unencumbered.

Free to discover who I want to become.

WHEN I OPEN my eyes I am alone. Alone for the first time I can remember. A soldier's life is never solitary. I spend the first conscious hours of my capture hunting for food. I find the small creatures living in the dirt floor of my cell, my claws shovelling the sediment into my mouthparts at a blinding rate. I sift through it all fast, filtering out the tiny protein rich food animals. There isn't much, though, and I am still hungry when the floor is nothing but a sea of dirt balls.

The room is small, barely big enough to stretch out to my full length, but I manage to exercise my limbs a little. There seems to be no real damage. I breathe deeply, searching the air for scents, any clue as to where I am, where everyone else in this place may be. But I smell nothing clearly, only a tiny trace of one or two other people. I can't tell if the scents are from other prisoners or my captors.

I crouch on my hind limbs, counting by threes to help the time pass. We learned this technique in training and it worked well enough in the sensory deprivation exercises. I am up to 681 when the entry unbars and you enter.

I don't know what I expected. Someone bigger maybe. Someone who didn't look like me. A monster, a tyrant or a demon. But it was just you. You who could be my sibling.

I suppose the surprise shows on my body; I've never been good at controlling my colour-changing. You walk up to me and look at me, as if I were some strange, small animal you found in your territory — curious but harmless. I say nothing and the silence seems to last forever. Eventually you nod your head and the other one who's been standing near the entry — the big one — comes toward me.

The pain is severe — I've experienced worse, but not for this length of time. I don't know how long I can put up with it; I think that this is not how I thought I would die, when it stops. You wave off the guard and sit in front of me as blood pours from my wounds, looking calm, like you've done this a thousand times before. I imagine that you have.

"Tell me about the Tilth army's plans to attack Barzelay," you say, sounding bored.

"I am Andalya Lour:Odam," I croak out, "a loyal citizen of Tilth. I am the sworn enemy of Barzelay and will provide no other information." I give the answer I have been trained to provide to all questions, the only thing you will ever get from me.

"Of course you are," you say. "Just as I am the sworn enemy of Tilth. But you're only half right." You lean in toward me and I can smell food on your breath. "You will give me all the information you have, Soldier Andalya." Your voice is calm and sure and you stand, turning away from me. The guard walks toward me and I flinch. "We will learn what you know," the guard says, "if I have to claw open your head and scoop your brains out to get it."

Before I can say a word, you call the guard and leave, barring the entry again. I lean against the wall of the cell and weep.

✳

THERE IS A crack in the wall, near the corner where I relieve myself. Through it I can make out the shift from day to night. I try to count the nights, but soon I lose track. I watch the door until my eyes swim, fearing that it will unbar and becoming more afraid each moment that it doesn't. But soon the emptiness in my belly outweighs the fear in my mind and all I can think of is food.

I methodically move in a spiral around my cell, filtering the dirt over and over again for any morsel that I can find. Counting by threes is useless and I just crawl round and round looking for food. I have no idea how much time has passed when the door unbars. I am so hungry I forget to be afraid.

You throw a bundle at me and I smell food. I am intoxicated by the prospect of nourishment and tear open the cloth, thrusting my mouth parts into the mound of fresh dirt inside. I don't know if you are speaking to me or not; all I can hear is the sound of myself eating. It seems like only a heartbeat passes before the food is gone and I start to pay attention to something other than my belly.

"...sorry about that," you are saying, "but this land is not very rich in nutrients. It's not ideal for a prison, but so much is not ideal in wartime, don't you think?" You are walking around the cell, looking at the dirt balls on the floor, my waste piled in a corner. I feel my mandible contracting in shame, but I force myself not to change colour. I try not to catch your eye as I take my forelimb and clean myself the best I can.

You notice my movements and stop talking. I can feel your eyes on me and it takes all my effort not to fold myself up with my head tucked deep into the hollow my body makes. But the voice of my trainer comes back to me and I manage not to change my body position. "Never put yourself in the position of humility. Never show any of them more than basic courtesy. The enemy's regents are not your leaders — do not pay obeisance in their presence. Stay strong in yourself to stay strong for Tilth."

You do not seem to notice the effort I am making not to show my humiliation and I am pleased that I am the strong warrior I was born to be. I believe that I will endure this capture.

For the first time since I was set upon by the guerilla forces of Barzelay's army and brought here I feel calm, the fear flowing from me like water over boulders. I close my eyes briefly, then notice the walls of my cell shifting upward. The dirt of the floor feels so soft and nice on the side of my head, then the world goes dark.

✳

WHEN I OPEN my eyes, I see your face close to mine. Too close, I think, close enough that our antennae could touch. I have never been this close to another, except in combat. But I do not feel my carapace colouring brown in discomfort and I have no need to move away. Which is good, as I seem to be unable to move my body.

I can smell your scent and you radiate a desire to make me comfortable. The smell is delicious and its effect on me is immediate. My muscles relax and my body colours bluegreen in contentment. "This is much better, Andalya Lour:Odam," you say. "So much more civilized, don't you think." I excrete a scent of agreement. "I just want to help you," you say. And I find that I want to help you, too. I want to do whatever it is that you require of me.

When you begin asking me questions, I am so pleased that there is finally something I can do for you. You who have brought me food and water, kept me cool and safe here in this strange place.

I tell you everything I know.

✳

I HAVE SO little to offer, my carapace turns the colour of blood in shame. You have given me so much and I have no real information for you at all. I am only a mere soldier, this is my first mission away from Odam.

"Tell me about Odam," you say, as if we were merchants chatting over the tables of our stalls on a quiet market day.

"Odam is my hatchling group," I say. "There were twenty-one of us, my siblings and I, and once my shell was hard I trained with them for thirty cycles before we were assigned to the front."

"Trained for what?"

"We fight for Tilth against the pretenders from Barzelay. We fight to keep Tilthians free, to protect our kin and way of life."

You look at me and I see your body colour slightly orange. Sadness. Then it is gone and you are the beautiful colour of contentment again. "What does that mean, Soldier Andalya? What do you think those phrases really mean?"

"Please," I say, "call me Lour. My friends call me Lour." A flash of orange on your body again, so fast I almost do not see it.

"Never mind," you say. "Tell me more about your training. Tell me about this mission."

There is an odd voice in the back of my mind screaming at me to stop, that any information I give you is too much. I do not know why I think this and ignore it. Helping you makes you happy, makes you smell so good. It makes me feel good and I feel like it has been a very long time since I have felt this way. I do not want this feeling to end.

"We learned fighting, my siblings and I," I say. "Fighting claw to claw and with weapons. And interrogation..." Something seems wrong, my stomach clenches and I feel sick for a moment. Then it passes. "Something about withstanding interrogation."

"You're doing very well," you say, your intoxicating aroma calming me. "What about your mission?"

"We were to find the Barzelay base," I say. "There was a rumour of a Barzelay unit just across the river. We were to find it and kill all the soldiers there."

"Do you know why?" you ask. "Why that base?"

Confusion colours my body. "I do not understand," I say. "Because it was there. Because it is Barzelay. There is no other reason."

"No," you say and I am sure I smell a hint of disappointment in the air. "There is never any other reason." You lay a claw on me, softly, and I can't remember a time when anyone ever touched me with such care.

You leave the room and your scent lingers, but only for a moment. Then all I can smell is my own scent. Loneliness.

✳

I SLEEP FOR minutes or days, there is no way to mark the passing of time here. When I wake I find my limbs are still restrained but I cannot stop my body from curling into itself, the burning of red on my carapace. How could I have so quickly turned traitor? All for a sack of food, I have failed my people. I can't imagine now why I would have wanted to tell you all my secrets, tell you everything. You who are the very reason for my existence. I and all my kin live to fight you and your kind and here I have given you everything you asked for without even a struggle.

I think of my siblings, my trainers, the only other souls I've ever known outside this prison. How they would despise me for what I have done. We live to fight Barzelay, we fight so all of Tilth — the merchants and educators, the healers and priests — so they may live free of conflict and foreign rule. We fight for all of them and I have failed all of them. My whole nation, my people. I am worthless.

I long for a weapon to end my miserable life. When the burning on my carapace begins to be matched by a burning in my belly, I am thankful. Perhaps I will be allowed to starve to death and no Odam will ever know of my failure. I busy myself with the restrains on my limbs. The repetitive movement of the vines against my claw, the rough parts of my body, makes me almost forget the burning inside and out.

✳

THE DOOR UNBARS and my eyes close against the shaft of light. I smell you before I can see you and I throw myself in your direction, claws snapping wildly. I feel myself get a grip on some part of you, maybe a limb, and I squeeze with every bit of strength I have left. I smell blood and squeeze harder.

Then I feel claws, hard truncheons, electrical weapons. Pain explodes all over me and I think that I will die. My body colours green in relief.

But I do not die. New restraints are put on me and your guards stand by your side. I see a shallow cut on the second joint of your left forelimb. It does not look bad. I have failed yet again.

"Soldier Andalya," you say. "Don't be angry with yourself. No one can withstand the drug we gave you. Not you, not me, not the greatest generals in all of Tilth or Barzelay."

I spit at you, but I have eaten nothing for days. Only a puff of dust comes out.

"I suppose your training never told you of these drugs," you say, "of how there is no way to avoid telling us what you know."

"Barzie trickery," I say. "Infidel sorcery."

You laugh. "Oh, I would be pleased indeed if these were tools only possessed by Barzelay forces," you say. "But your interrogators use the same tricks on our soldiers. We are more the same than they would have us believe, Andalya Lour:Odam. Only evenly matched forces can fight forever."

"What are you talking about?" I blurt out, then remember — I am Andalya Lour:Odam, a loyal citizen of Tilth.

"How long have we been fighting this war?" you say, orange colouring your body. "Ten, twenty generations? I was born a soldier, same as you, same as all my siblings. In all your training, did anyone ever tell you what would happen when you win? What specific objective you were to achieve? How would you even know if you won?" You lean in toward me and I fight not to shrink away from your face. "Tell me, Soldier Andalya. What are you fighting for?"

I stare into your eyes, antennae pulled back for fear of touching you. "I am Andalya Lour:Odam, a loyal citizen of Tilth. I am the sworn enemy of Barzelay and will provide no other information."

I barely have time to hear the crack of claw on carapace before the world goes black again.

✳

DAYS COME AND go; there is no way to keep track. I guess that every two or three days a sack of dirt is dropped into the room. The first time I managed to ignore it for hours. Now I don't bother. If you want to drug me, you will. If you want to beat me, you will. And when it comes time to kill me, you will do that too.

Today it seems that the food is clean. I feel normal, at least undrugged. I no longer remember what I used to feel like. When I was a soldier not a prisoner.

I have no particular hatred for you, that passed a long time ago, but neither am I pleased to see you when the door unbars and you walk in. You no longer bother with the guards, though I am certain they remain nearby.

"Soldier Andalya," you say as you crouch before me. "It is almost one full moon cycle since you first came to us."

"If you say so," I say.

You look at me and colours cycle over your carapace. I've mostly given up paying attention; you've obviously had better colour control training than I have. I know the colours are all lies. But I see orange over and over again and I wonder why you would choose to show me sadness. Sadness for what? For your loyalty to the wrong side? For what you do here? For what is happening to me?

"The war is almost over for you," you say and I know exactly what you mean. "I envy you."

"Do you?" I say, almost able to laugh. "Shall we change places, then?"

"Sadly, a hero's death is not in my future," you say. "We all have our parts to play, Andalya. You will die to keep your leaders and my leaders fat and I will kill you to ensure a rich economy for my merchants and for yours."

"I will die for the honour of Tilth," I say.

You look at me, the colour of anger flashing brightly over your body, but your voice is soft when you speak. "Yes. That's what I just said."

∗

MY LIMBS ARE each tied to a separate branch and pulled apart. I cannot move any part of my body. My thorax is completely exposed and I cannot help but emit the odour of fear. I know now that I am going to die, and I know now that until this moment I never really believed that this is how it would end. Killed in action. A hero of Tilth.

You are alone in the yard, I can no longer even smell your guards. You walk toward me until you stand two limbs' lengths before me, the weapon in your claw. "I see you're not getting your subordinates for this task," I manage to say. "Good for you."

"There is no pleasure in this for me, Lour," you say, your body covered in orange.

"It is your duty," I say. "We all must serve our masters in the ways we must."

"Yes," you say, "today I will serve by killing you and you will serve by dying. Tomorrow, who knows how I will be called on to serve."

"Just get it over with," I say, closing my eyes. "I'm ready to be a hero."

I smell something — it must be you, but I have never smelled it before. It makes me think of parents, of mates. For a moment I forget myself and feel like a softshell youth. It is the most wonderful smell I've ever encountered. I open my eyes, and see your body colour yellow and blue, the colours of kinship. You lift the weapon and I can smell the electricity crackle as it charges.

Kinship, your body tells me, and I almost believe you. But I know the colours lie.

I SLIP INTO the fake-leather seat, and look at my watch. I have about an hour before the shareholders' meeting, but I have to stop by the day care first, so I want to make this snappy. I've found that the little impatient look usually stops these people from making small talk and gets them down to business. Not this guy, though. From the moment I sit down, he starts with the chit chat. I sigh softly to myself, not wanting to be rude, and look up at the mirror that lets me see a little of his face. That's when I notice that he's not from here. I can hear it in the accent, and when I look closely I can see that his eyes reflected in the mirror look a little... off. Great. Just what I need. Another bloody foreigner.

Still, I'm not prejudiced, so I give the man my particulars and he gets going. I know it's probably going to take at least twenty minutes, so I lean back, close my eyes and hope I can maybe just sleep through it.

No such luck. He's chattering away at me, about the weather and some boring local political thing, when he looks up at the mirror at the same time I glance up and our eyes meet. "You might not realize this," he says to me, "but I'm an immigrant."

"You don't say," I answer, bored and rolling my eyes, though he can't see me anymore, his focus back on his job where it belongs.

"It's true," he says, not noticing my sarcasm. "I have a home here now, but I came through the portal about a year and a half ago. You ever been through?" he asked, his eyes darting up to the mirror and catching my gaze.

I fake a smile and shake my head. "No," I say.

He laughs mirthlessly. "Well, you probably would not want to. Oh, my plane is a beautiful place. We have these amazing snow-capped mountains there that you just don't have here, and the architecture cannot be believed." He pauses a moment, and I worry that I'm going to get the tourism board lecture. Instead, he mercifully goes back to his story. "I'm sure the other planes are lovely, too. But the trip — Gott in Himmel — it's a bear. I truly thought I was going to die. It was like my flesh was being ripped off my bones. Yeugh." He shivers at the memory.

Of course, I've heard all about the terrible pain of the interdimensional transporters. They say that the scientists who accidentally created the first rift between one instance of the universe and the others only realized they had done anything remarkable at all when they heard the agonized shrieking of the poor bastard who fell in the hole. Not something that sounds much like a holiday to me. I always said I'd wait until they figured out some painless way to travel between the planes, thank you very much. Besides, I never really understood what was so great about being surrounded by a bunch of foreign freaks in the first place. It's not like you even have to travel for that.

But some people think it's the most exciting trip you can take. The Hendersons down the street took the whole family last summer, kids and all, on a tour of three different universes. That seems like child abuse to me, but it's a free country. Marsha Henderson said it was 'educational'. I'd rather just watch a documentary about it on T.V.

They've figured out that the other universes, at least the ones people can get to, are fundamentally the same. They say that we all started as one plane, then some particular thing happened here but it didn't happen there, and poof! Another branch on the universe tree. As time went by, every subtle difference going back though history led to greater and greater differences between the planes. They say that some of the atmospheres in the other planes would be deadly to people from here. The trip through the rift does something to you though, and basically turns you into whatever people are over there. Also, not something that appeals to me that much. I'd like to keep my organs exactly where there are. There are plenty of places to visit here in this plane, I say.

"That sucks," is all I say to this guy, though. I'm not sure if he even hears me.

"And once you get though the rift, the bastards at immigration are no walk in the playground, either. It took me months to get my resident's card here, even though I had all the paperwork ready before I left." His eyes catch mine in the mirror again, and I nod. I don't even know why they let otherworlders stay here. I mean, they're just taking the jobs and resources away from people who were born and bred here. It doesn't seem fair.

As if he can tell what I'm thinking, this guy says, "And trying to get a job — oh, what a pain in the elbow that was. I had a good job back home." He looks at me again in the mirror, and I make some non-committal noise. "I had high status in the community, made a good, good living, had some nice savings buried away. You know, they don't even let you in here without six months worth of cash to live off. And the trip isn't cheap either. Not that the money was a problem for me, not then. It goes pretty quick on this side, though. The exchange rate is terrible."

I can't help myself. "So, if you had it so good over there, what made you want to move here? It couldn't be for the glamourous life you have now, eh?" I tried for a joke, but it didn't seem to go over. Maybe humour doesn't translate well.

"You've never been through?" he asks again, and I shake my head. "Things are different there; I guess they are different everywhere. Here, you have your two moons. Where I come from, there's only one and you can hardly even see the blessed thing. And even though I studied about this plane before I came, I never really understood what real poverty was until I saw the people here living in their own filth, eating whatever garbage they could find. Terrible."

I thought about explaining that we have the concept of merit here, and that people can't just get a free ride on the backs of the others who work hard, but there's no point of trying to reason with these people. They just seem to think that everyone should be entitled to a good life without having to work for it. Pathetic. I squirmed a little in my seat, but he just carried on.

"And of course here, between the different anatomy and advances in medical science, doctors make barely enough to live off. Where I'm from, let me just say, such an idea would be unthinkable."

I laugh, but he doesn't seem to notice. He says, "Back home, I had money and power, but neither of those can guarantee you good health. At least not on my plane. I never planned on moving; didn't even like to travel much. But, I had a sickness that would have killed me there. I'd heard that here it was a five minute job to remove the tumour. So, in order to live, I moved."

He doesn't say anything after that, but I can feel his tools poking around in my reproductive sac. It feels like he's almost done. "Why didn't you just go back?" I ask.

He sighs, long and sad. "Things are different everywhere," he said, his voice thick with something that almost sounds like regret. "It's a one-way trip out of my plane, unfortunately. You can leave, but you can't come back."

"Why is that?" I ask, genuinely curious.

"They are afraid that the trip out changes you permanently," he says, "and the government is afraid that these changes pose a risk to everyone else. The fact that your cells change both ways in the transporter is something my people don't seem to understand," he says, bitterly. It sounds like a reasonable enough precaution to me, though. Maybe we could learn something from those other planes after all.

After a moment I ask, "So, you were a doctor back home, too?"

He snorts. He's pulling the baby out of my uterus now, and I can see my heart in its organ sac beating faster. Nothing hurts, of course, but my system must be pumping extra fluids into the reproductive sac to fill the void left by my soon to be child. I've read about how on some planes, people have their organs inside their skin. How awful that must be — how would they ever fix anything?

"No, I wasn't a doctor," he says. "I was a decorated personal carrier jet pilot. It was the best job in the world, I think. Money, prestige, you got to meet the most influential people on the planet."

"A carrier jet pilot," I ask, as he comes around the barrier with the squirming jumble of bulbous organ sacs that is my child, and places it in my hands. Under the translucent sacs that hold her organs — it's a girl, I can see her tiny uterus — I see her face squint as she starts to cry. I hope she knocks that off before I drop her off at day care. They hate whiny kids there.

"Yeah," he said, smiling ruefully, as he pulls off his gloves. "I was a taxi driver."

THE SUN WAS warm on me the day I first became aware of you, the ground was thawing and a slight breeze blew. It was the wind that brought us together. At first I didn't know what it was that touched me ever so lightly. One of those creatures that floats on the breeze like an autumn leaf? No. It was you.

The very edges of you brushed against me in the wind, your leaves touching my leaves. I'd never known you were even there. I cannot describe that feeling of only then coming to understand what it was to have been alone, in that wondrous moment of now being not alone. It was transcendent.

Then the breeze died and your touch left me. I hoped for a storm if only to have that sensation back again.

✳

THERE WERE FEWER days when the rains fell, then they stopped entirely. The air was still and I wondered if my memory of your touch was real as I became dry and thirsty. Then the rain from below began, when the heat of the day was strongest, regular as the sun and I felt a stirring in my trunk. The sun shone hard, the soil dampened and the wriggling creatures in the soil returned. And I grew. And you grew. We grew toward each other. By the time the days were long our branches were entwined, my leaves and your leaves rustling together.

The split-trunked creatures reappeared, most days when the sun was high. They were so strange and fragile, compact and frenetic. But they could not distract me from you. Even when the smallest of them would climb up me, my bark itching, newborn branches breaking, I was happy. When a cloud blocked the sun or a floating creature broke off one of my twigs, I'd feel your leaves brushing mine and it was as if the sunlight never ended, like the rain never stopped falling.

∗

THE SMALL CREATURE had been climbing me every day. I paid no attention until I noticed it was reaching the edge of me, moving toward the beginning of you. My branches were still thin there, fragile in the wind. I felt them bend, felt one, then two break and then the weight was gone. A sharp vibration in the earth at my roots, then nothing.

Our leaves rustled together and there were more and more vibrations around our trunks. Then two of the larger creatures leaning against my trunk, salty rain falling on my roots. Then silence and night and our branches entwined.

∗

OUR BROKEN BRANCHES regrew, new leaves appearing where others had fallen. The climbing creature did not return.

∗

THE SUN, STILL bright but cooling now, was high overhead when it happened. Many large creatures climbing, a coldness biting into my bark. Then a terrible vibration and searing pain — a double pain as my limbs were severed and I lost contact with you. My sap dripped to the earth like rain. My branch scarred over, I would live but what life is there without you? It was like an endless drought, like the darkest winter — would I ever touch you again?

∗

THE DAYS GROW longer now, the soil around my roots losing its solidity. Familiar vibrations near my roots, the movements of a split-trunk creature, but different. As if it, too, has broken branches. I feel its weight against me. I am leant against for a long time before it moves away on uneven limbs.

Broken branches grow. The sun and rain return. There is already a hint of moisture in the air, and I can taste the sunlight intensifying. My roots feel nutrients escaping from their icy prisons. I lost your touch once but such a joy could never be lost forever.

I can grow. I will grow. Toward you, always toward you.

I NEVER PLANNED to end up here. I've never planned anything, really. All my life has been like that: I see an opportunity and I take it. Sometimes that works out better than other times. So why should this be any different?

I'd just been by docking station three, slipping a few hundred wadded euros off the shifty captain from that rust bucket Lunacy. What a stupid name for a cargo ship. Why do ships' captains feel compelled to name their barges with some clever pun, anyway? Lunacy, indeed.

About a month before, I'd caught them dumping their trash out their airlock after their last trip off the base. They thought they were far enough off the rock that no one would see, but I just happened to be ogling a brand new BMW private shuttle through the scope when I saw them do it. If I'd followed procedure and called it into the ILSOC, the International Lunar Station Oversight Committee would have slapped that scow with a fine that made the wad I'd stuffed in my own pocket look like milk money. And the dark circles under the captain's eyes I'd seen the last few times they dropped their cargo off made me guess that he didn't have the kind of dough to cover a fine like that. The cash in my pants told me I'd guessed right.

He'd been paying me off every time they came through here to keep my trap shut so they could just open theirs and avoid the dumping fees back Earthside. It was typical for that kind of operation — an old junker repurposed for cargo transport to try and get in on the lunar cash cow. I'd been inside Lunacy a couple of times when I was making nice with a sweet young thing who'd been working on board for a while. It was amazing their shipments didn't grow legs, the security on board that boat was so bad. No one ever noticed me, though. It seemed like anyone could come and go as they pleased, and for a few nights, I was very well pleased, indeed.

I was off to my quarters to add these recently acquired bills to the little stash I had going, when my beeper went off. I jumped at the noise, and pulled the little phone from my other pocket. I could see on its display that it was a call from my boss, Laura. I was technically off duty, but I answered the call.

"Natalie?" A voice that was definitely not Laura's boomed through the tiny speaker. I thumbed the volume down a bit.

"Yes," I said, warily. "Who is this?"

"This is Jerry Cornwell speaking," the voice said. Oh, shit, I thought. Jerry Cornwell was Laura's boss. I'd never even seen the guy. "Could you pop by Ms. Baine's office please?" His voice made it clear that it was not a question.

I gulped nervously to myself. "Sure," I said aloud, turning away from the habitat section of the converted old mining station and toward the management offices for the resort. "I'll be there in a few minutes."

✳

LAURA BAINE WAS the manager of shipping and receiving for Bella Luna, where I shlepped crates for a living. Bella Luna was the new resort complex just over the horizon from the old lunar mining station, which is where us working stiffs who run the joint actually lived. The moon was becoming a great tourist destination, but while it might be a great place to visit, almost no-one wanted to live there. So, the money was extraordinarily good for manual labour, and they weren't that picky about the resumé. My co-workers were a motley crew of deadbeats, ex-cons and desperados. I fit in just fine. Laura didn't fit in at all, though. Which was why she needed me.

Laura wasn't there because she was behind the eight ball on debt or dead last on anyone's list of potential employees. She had left a perfectly good job Earthside to come up here and run S&R. I never could understand it, but she tried to explain it the first day we met by showing me her prized possession: an old prop from the original series of Star Trek.

I'd just arrived at the station, and was still feeling sick from the transport or the gravity change or something. I just wanted a slice of dry toast and a clean bed, but the new boss wanted to talk. Always wary of pissing off authority, especially in close confines, I agreed to meet her in her office that first day. The woman was almost giddy when she reached out to shake my hand.

"Natalie," she'd said, her warm hand embracing my clammy one. "You don't know how happy I am that you are finally here. It will be so nice having another woman on staff." She let my hand go, but moved a foot closer to me, even further invading my territorial zone. I had to fight not to wince. "We women need to stick together," she said, much too close to my face.

I first thought that she was coming on to me, and I didn't have enough mental fortitude to deal with that possibility right then. I took a half step back, and slapped on the best smile I could manage. "Call me Nat, Ms. Baine," I said, politely I hoped.

She smiled back. "And you must call me Laura." She walked back to her desk, and sat on its edge. "So, what brings you to Bella Luna, Nat?"

The goddamn vomit comet, I wanted to say. Instead, I told her that I had needed a job, and this was the best deal going. It wasn't exactly a lie, and if she hadn't looked at my CV herself and seen the three years at Hawthorne Women's Correctional I'd just finished doing for a botched robbery, then I wasn't about to enlighten her.

As it turned out, I could probably have said anything. She wasn't really paying attention to me. "I've been here since almost the beginning," she said, her eyes getting that misty look people pick up when they're getting all nostalgic. "As soon as I heard that the mining station reclamation project was going ahead, I knew I was going to end up here. Heck, a decade ago I even tried to find a decent job for myself at the mine. Anything to be up here." I could tell she was on a roll, and didn't think I could stand through a whole speech, so I hop-walked over to the nearest chair.

She went on as if I'd never moved. "All my life, I've loved space. Not like an astronomer, I mean, though I did learn the names of all the constellations when I was seven. But I love the concept of space, the idea of all that freedom, the vastness of it all. The possibilities." She paused, a crazy kind of gleam in her eyes. "You see that?" She pointed to a brown lump in a lucite box hanging up on the wall above her desk. I nodded. "That's the exact phaser that Walter Koenig used in season two of Star Trek." Her face flushed. Whether it was with rapture, pride or fever, I couldn't tell. But she was practically glowing. "It's no replica," she said, as if expecting me to challenge her on the authenticity of the thing. "You can take a closer look, if you like." I knew I was supposed to be impressed, so I levered myself out of the chair and maneuvered myself so my face was almost pressed against the box. "Magnificent, isn't it?" she asked.

I thought it looked like something you'd find in the toy aisle of a dollar store, but I kept that opinion to myself. "Pretty cool," I said. "So, you chose to come up here just 'cause you wanted to live on the moon, huh?"

"Well," she said, a conspiratorial look in her eye. "It's not for the fulfilling work, I can tell you that."

✳

LAURA WANTED US to be friends and I knew enough to know that getting cozy with the boss was a good way of greasing my way through this place. She liked to think that she took me under her wing, that she was offering a helping hand to a fellow gender warrior or something like that. We ate our lunch together at the staff canteen more often than not, and I made a point of agreeing to visit her in her quarters once or twice a month to watch old space shows. After a day or two on the job I knew that Laura wasn't flirting with me, she was just lonely and scared. Her juvenile visions of living off world hadn't factored in being trapped with a bunch of people who don't share your vision of a beautiful future.

"Those guys hate having a woman boss," she told me, one of those interminable nights in front of the flat screen in her quarters. I knew she was talking about my co-workers on the docks, not the crew of HMS Space Cowboys or whatever it was on the TV. I honestly hadn't noticed anything of the kind, but maybe this was the first time Laura had ever heard the kinds of things that working stiffs always said about the suit who was cracking the whip. In my experience, no one gave a damn whether the suit bottom was pants or a skirt. But I knew that this was the tenuous thread that bound her in friendship to me, and I wanted to keep her on my good side.

"Men," I said, trying to sound disgusted. "They never think a woman can keep up, am I right?"

"God, it must be terrible for you, Nat," she said. "Women always get the short end of the stick in male dominated jobs, especially physical ones. How do you keep going?"

"I keep to myself and work hard," I lied. The truth was that I got along just fine with the guys. Especially after I split Lefty Connolly's lip when he grabbed my ass the first week. After that I became a regular in the monthly poker game. But Laura knew nothing about that.

"Even so," she said, "it must be tough out there among them." She paused, but I didn't think she'd gone back to watching the hoary episode of Stargoons or Transgalactic Space Pirates or whatever it was. "I've got an idea," she said, finally, a grin spreading across her face. "I'm going to make you my assistant."

"Your what?" I said, frowning. I didn't want to end up taking a pay cut just so I could sit on my ass all day in Laura's office making coffee and answering the phone.

"Not officially, of course," Laura said. "I can't get you out of your regular jobs. But you can help me out when it gets quiet on the docks. Come in first thing tomorrow, and I'll show you around." She smiled. "This is going to be great," she said. "I'm totally snowed under with communications right now, and there's hardly anything coming in on the transports for a couple of days. And this will be fabulous for your career." I tried not to roll my eyes.

"Sound great, Laura," I said. Seeing an opportunity, I continued. "Well, I'd better be well rested if I'm going to be taking on a lot of new responsibilities." I yawned. "I should probably head back to my quarters."

"Okay," Laura said. "You sure you don't want to stay to the end?" She cocked her head toward the TV screen.

"Definitely," I said and left. It was early enough that I caught Lefty in his quarters before he'd gone to the bar. As it turned out, we never actually made it to the bar that night.

✳

I WASN'T EXACTLY well rested when I got to Laura's office the next morning, but it didn't matter. She gave me a portable computer and a corner of her desk, next to the mind-bogglingly ridiculous snow globe of the old mining station. As I shook the thing, and watched fake snow fall on the overly shiny model of what the mining station supposedly looked like once, she gave me a brief run-down on her job. I'd never really thought about what the manager of Shipping and Receiving does all day, but it wasn't a big surprise when she laid it out. You don't hump crates all day for months in a joint without having a pretty good idea where they're coming from and going to. When she was done yakking and left me alone to actually do some of the work, I took my time, and sipped my coffee, and got stuck in to the backlog of emails. Just the usual stuff — suits wanting confirmation that their gear got where it was supposed to when it was supposed to. And this was what they paid her the big bucks for?

It turned out that being her little helper was a better gig than I'd first imagined. Most of the time when deliveries were slow, the bosses got us grunts to shift furniture, paint the walls or do some other menial task they called "other related duties." I didn't mind loading cargo — it was my job, after all. But I'd never cared for being told to do some other random thing just because the boss could make me jump. Hanging out in the office with a coffee and the portable beat cleaning out the break room fridge by a good margin. So I eagerly offered to help Laura out whenever things were slow.

I didn't bother letting the guys in on my sideline job. Kissing up to the boss is a great idea; being seen to be a suck up is much less so. But usually once a week I found myself happily sipping coffee and banging away at the portable on what I now thought of as my corner of her desk. I wondered how a person got to be a manager of Shipping and Receiving. It was a pretty nice job, and I knew Laura's pay grade was a good chunk higher than mine. I was starting to think that I could easily get used to a desk job. I was even growing fond of that stupid snow globe. When Laura wasn't around, I'd stare at the thing and see if I could figure out what each part of the station was now.

The mine was totally shut down about a year before the resort opened, but the construction crews needed housing and services, so the station was converted to a kind of township for them. It later evolved to become home to those of us who work for the resort. They say that when the mine was operational, there were something like a thousand people working at the mine and nearly the same number working in the businesses that sprang up to support the miners. There were the usual suspects like the canteen, the commissary and the laundry, but there were also several bars, a movie theatre, a pizza joint and even a Thai restaurant. Most of those businesses died along with the mine, but the construction crews kept a few alive, and the resort staff population is big enough that even a few new ones sprang up.

Lefty and I liked to drink at the honky tonk by the south bay doors. It was the shortest stumble back to his room of any of the gin joints on the rock, and I knew the lay of the pool table. The first time shooting pool in lunar gravity was quite a trip, let me say, even if they do weigh the balls down. Lefty was leaving the rock for a job back Earthside, so we were kind of trying to make the most of the few nights we had. It was no great romance or anything, but we amused each other well enough, and when your entertainment options are limited, you take what you can get.

It was the day after he'd bugged out that Laura called and asked if I wanted to go for a drink. I could hear the desperation in her voice, and if I hadn't been looking for any opportunity to avoid having to feel lonely, I wouldn't have agreed so fast. But, like I said, beggars can't be choosers around here.

We met at one of the bars that catered mainly to the front staff at the resort. I think I was the only roughneck in the joint, but I knew how to clean up all right and I can keep a low profile. I wasn't worried about standing out. Laura, on the other hand, looked like she'd been hitting the bottle pretty good on her own when she came through the door. She wasn't stumbling or slurring her words, but I could tell that she'd had more than a glass of wine by the total lack of volume control in her voice.

"Nat," she bellowed as she sat down across from me. I winced. "You're here already."

"Just got here, Laura," I said, casually glancing around to see if the bar staff were getting ready to kick us out of the joint. I caught the barman's eye, and he winked at me and shrugged, so I figured we were probably still within the bounds of propriety at this place.

He came over to the table, and Laura loudly demanded, "Bourbon. Rocks. And don't be stingy with it, either."

I grinned at the bartender, who wasn't entirely unattractive, and said apologetically, "Same for me, please."

"No problem, ladies," he said smoothly, then walked back to the bar to pump the drinks.

"So, what's up?" I asked, hoping she'd talk and drink herself out fast so I could see about fixing that bartender up as Lefty's replacement.

"Oh, I don't know," she sighed. "It's just all so disillusioning, you know?" I didn't, but I smiled and nodded anyway. "I mean, is this how you thought it would be?" She waved her arm around to indicate whatever "it" was that she was talking about, and ended up belting the bartender in the gut. It looked to be a soft hit, and he didn't even drop the enclosed squeeze glasses containing our drinks, but I saw an opportunity.

"Are you okay?" I asked, jumping up out of my seat and steering him away from Laura after he hooked the drinks to the holders on the table.

"Sure," he said, smiling. I took a liking to that smile.

"My friend is just having a tough time of it these days," I said, putting on my best sympathy face. Guys dig that. "I thought that if I took her out, I might help her snap out of it." I smiled apologetically, and got another one of his thousand watt grins in return.

"I hope it works," he said, and gave my arm a squeeze before he went back to the bar. Things were looking up. But I still had Laura to deal with for the rest of the night. After that song and dance there was no way I could ditch her now, not in front of Smiley there.

I sat back at the table, and watched Laura take a long sip of what was left of her drink. "So, what were we talking about?" I asked, hoping she had forgotten.

"This place," she said, disgustedly. I looked around the bar. Seemed all right to me.

"The bar?" I asked.

"No," she said, sighing as if I were a moron. I was getting a little pissed off. The barman wasn't hot enough to put up with much more of this. "No," she said again, her voice losing its strident edge this time. "The whole place. The resort. The fucking moon."

I finally figured it out. Maybe I was a moron after all. "Space isn't everything you imagined it would be after all," I said and watched Laura nod. I thought I maybe saw tears in the corners of her eyes, but it could have just been the funky lighting of the place.

"It was all I ever wanted," she said. "The exploration, the freedom and wonder of it. 'To explore strange new worlds...'" She picked up her glass, but didn't take a drink, just watched the amber fluid float around the ice cubes in the thin plastic container. Her voice got hard. "But it's the same here as anywhere else. The same bullshit day in and day out." She took a long sip from her glass, finishing the drink, and looked straight at me. Her eyes were cold. "I thought it was going to be the adventure of a lifetime. But it's still fucking Shipping and Receiving." She laughed, but I got the feeling she didn't think anything was very funny. "It's just a different view."

Laura got pretty quiet after that and while she put back another couple of bourbons, I got the bartender's phone number. "How's your friend doing?" he asked.

"She's homesick," I said and he nodded.

"Well," he said sagely, "the moon isn't for everyone." He told me his name was Dave and that he thought I was a good friend. I looked over at Laura half sprawled on the table, and thought I saw an opportunity.

"I'd better get her home," I said, and Dave smiled and squeezed my arm again.

✳

IT WAS THE next day that my phone rang while I was counting the dough I got from squeezing the captain of Lunacy. I ducked into the ladies' room and made sure I looked presentable before I walked into Laura's office. A middle aged man sat behind her desk, his ass barely squeezing into Laura's ergonomically designed chair. He stood when I walked in the door, and extended his hand. I took it, and we shook, as I waited for the other shoe to drop.

"Please sit down, Natalie," he said, indicating the chair opposite the desk. I levered myself down, and he shoved his butt into Laura's chair. The nervousness I'd felt on my way was totally gone now, and I had an urge to laugh, but the stern look on his face made me tamp the giggles down.

"I'm afraid I have some sad news," he said, then made an effort to smile. It looked more like the effect of a mild electrical shock than any real human emotion I've ever seen. "However, there is some good news for you, I think."

"Oh," I said neutrally.

"Yes," he said, the stern look returning. "I appears that Ms. Baine has decided to leave us here at Bella Luna."

"Really?" I said, surprise in my voice.

"Yes," Cornwell said. "She tended her resignation by email last night, and her things are all gone from her quarters. We assume she took the overnight shuttle back to Earth. Something about needing to find a new challenge, she said."

"She never said anything to me about resigning," I said.

"No?" Cornwell said. "I understand you two were close."

"We were friendly," I said, warily.

"According to Ms. Baine's reports, she was showing you the ropes around here," he waved his hand over Laura's desk like a magician.

"She did let me help out when we weren't busy on the docks," I admitted.

"According to the reports, Ms. Baine thought you would make a good replacement for her when she left."

I swallowed hard. "That's very kind of her," I said carefully.

"Ms. Baine is a professional," Cornwell said. "I'm sure her judgment is sound, and that is why I would like to offer you a provisional promotion to head of Shipping and Receiving, Natalie."

My eyes grew wide. I knew what Laura made, and the raise would make a nice addition to the stash I had going. I smiled at Cornwell. "I'd be honored, sir," I said. "And, please, call me Nat."

✳

IT TURNED OUT that I was right, and becoming a suit wasn't so hard after all. I ordered a new ergonomic chair that fit me better than Laura's old one, and I've even become kind of fond of Chekhov's phaser up on the wall. Dave the bartender and I have been keeping time together, and he takes me to much better restaurants and bars than Lefty and I had ever gone to. Even with the expense of nice clothes and quality liquor, I'm still hanging on to way more cash than I'd ever seen before.

After we'd gone out a few times, Dave took me to the observation lounge on the top of the old mining station. I hadn't even known that there was one, and when we walked in the door I found that I had to close my mouth. You don't really notice the full immensity of space when you're busy on the station. But under that clear dome it's like the biggest, clearest night sky you can imagine. I have to admit that the first time I saw the Earthrise it took my breath away and I finally understood what Laura had been talking about. I can't even imagine living anywhere but the moon any more.

The only thing I miss is that old snow globe. I still find myself reaching out to pick it up and give the thing a shake every once in a while. But I know it's out there somewhere, blood and bits of hair I knew I'd never be able to get off still stuck to its edge. It's there, forever floating out in space along with everything else that found its way into Lunacy's trash room and out their airlock that night I took Laura back to her office. I was a little worried that the resignation I wrote wouldn't fool them, but I guess she taught me how to sound like a manager well enough. No one noticed me in my uniform pushing a crate over to the docks, and no one noticed me load it into Lunacy and stick it under the rest of the crap in the trash room. Sometimes it's good not to be noticed.

I'D JUST SETTLED into a comfortable pedalling pace when the radio crackled to life. I sighed. It was doubtlessly one of the local wits passing me and unable to keep the clever thought contained. "Get off the trajectory, you hippie," was a classic. "Buy a generator," was another one I heard frequently, as if it had never occurred to me to switch up my custom crank-powered personal starrunner to the stock fission-drive model you could see mouldering away at auction lots across the quadrant. Maybe this would be my personal favourite: the heart's-in-the-right-place, "Want a tow?"

I couldn't ignore the scratchy *bip-bip* of the radio's notification. I forced myself to slow down to a leisurely pace and thumbed the comms. "This is Starlite Blue, go ahead."

My shoulder muscles loosened when I heard the gruff voice come though the tinny speaker. "April, my dear, what brings you to this part of the universe?"

Usually it drove me crazy when people didn't bother with proper radio protocol, but I could forgive Admiral Grant anything. He wasn't a real Admiral, had never been in anyone's military as far as I knew, but he was the sweetest old space dog I'd ever met, and it was the only name he'd ever given me.

"Switch to channel seven-two, sir," I suggested to get us off the working channel. The Admiral could get away with anything but there was limit to how far I'd join him in radio anarchy.

"Roger," he said and after a quick thumb stroke, we were back in business. "So, what brings you all the way out to this patch of sky?" Grant asked. "I'm sure I'd have heard about it if there was your kind of work round here."

I smiled as my legs got back into an easy rhythm. Grant

sounded like a bluff old space captain who had about as much discretion as a green marine fresh off the vomit comet, but I knew better. We weren't in exactly the same racket — the Admiral traded in goods whereas I delivered information. Nothing overtly illegal in most of the jurisdictions where we operated, but not something you spoke about on the open comms, either.

"I'm not here for work," I answered. "I'm on holiday."

The laugh that came over the speaker nearly shook me off my saddle. "Who in heavens comes all the way out to this neck of the woods for a holiday? What are you looking for, an unobstructed view of dark matter?"

It's true, the Sigma system wasn't exactly a classic tourist destination. Once the Cyndex asteroid mining operations cleared out, most of the people moved on to places with more work or more fun. I wasn't looking for excitement though.

"You could say that," I answered Grant. "I think of it as the call of the sea, the lure of the open road."

"Ahh," Grant said. "You're all the way out here to get away from the traffic."

I laughed. I hadn't thought about it that way but he was right enough. There were settlements close enough here that I could resupply and rest when I needed to, but the direct trajectories were relatively free of other ships. It was, in short, a really nice route for a cycler.

"So where are you putting in?" Grant asked.

"I'll be at Cyndex colony two in-" I glanced at the nav station's projected ETA, "fourteen standard hours, give or take."

"Why don't I stop by," Grant said, "let you buy me a drink at Bao's?"

"You aren't on deadline?" I asked.

"Not this time," Grant said, "I was looking for an excuse to stop."

"It's a date," I said. "Starlite Blue clear." I thumbed off the comms and eyed the battery monitor. Another hour and I'd be topped off for the rest of the trip to Cyndex. I turned the book I was reading back on and let my legs do the work.

✳

I REMEMBERED WHEN Bao's was the most happening gin joint in the sector. Rowdy, sure. Barfights, there were a few. But mostly it was full of miners getting their R&R in every way imaginable. I saw things going on in full view of everyone in the place that I'd only ever read about in dirty books.

Now, the bar was clean, the chairs scarred but intact, and getting a table was guaranteed. They said that almost 90% of the folks on Cyndex Two left once the mining operation closed and the ones who stayed were mainly family-first types and the odd adventurer. It was the latter group who managed to keep Bao's running, along with folks like me and the Admiral who stopped by on our way someplace else.

Bao herself was running the bar when I walked in and her eyes fell on me like hungry wolves. "April May," she said, her rough voice croaking out the syllables of my name, "it has been too long. What'll it be?"

I looked past her to the beer fridge and saw nothing but the nondescript green of Steinie bottles. I grimaced. "Anything more interesting in the back?"

Bao smiled, which did nothing to make her look any less terrifying. "I've got a few Paulie's stouts; for you — two for one." I knew that meant one bottle would cost the same as two Steinies but that wasn't completely unreasonable. I nodded, wondering how much trouble it was to get around the sanctions and bring in the Paulie's.

I poured my drink into the glass Bao handed me and wondered some more. I had no illusions about the work I did. In another time or another place it would be called espionage, maybe treason. Even now it wasn't exactly the kind of thing you talked about openly when someone asked "so, what do you do?"

But the right of individuals to pursue their own interests was about the only thing that the Liberty Alliance and the Progressive Free State agreed on, so they couldn't stop the transfer of information, technology and goods between their spheres of influence. They just made it difficult, which gave people like me plenty of work.

I was thinking about the bits of info I'd stashed away from the last job I'd been on, when I heard the unmistakable voice of Admiral Grant. "Bao!" he said, his voice carrying all the way from the corridor. "How have you been, you old reprobate?"

I looked up and saw Bao grinning like a skeleton. "Much better since I last saw the back of you, Grant." She laughed and I forced myself to stop wondering about the precise nature of their relationship. He walked over to the bar, taking in the whole room at a glance. He looked much the same as the last time I'd seen him about a year previously. The same long gray hair roughly tied at the base of his head and the same tunic that looked like it might have once been part of a uniform but was so discoloured with age and wear that its origin was unrecognizable. The casual observer could easily be mistaken in thinking that the Admiral neglected his appearance, if not for his neatly trimmed and waxed moustache.

"Get me a wine, would you?" he said while slipping into the seat across from me. "April, look at you. You must be twice the size you were the last time I saw you."

I laughed. "They do wonders with muscle mass over at the Proxima spas."

Grant whistled. "You look different every time I see you. Business must be good."

I nodded and took a sip of my beer. "The day I stop changing is the day you know I've finally gotten old."

"I've never gotten into modding," he said, "but they say it can be addictive."

"I'm just keeping up with the tech," I said and he raised an eyebrow. "But, yeah, I've been at it a while."

"When did you start?" We'd never really talked about our pasts before, but he seemed interested, and it beat talking about which brand of hull paint we liked.

"Twelve."

"Sounds about right."

"Yeah, it is now. It wasn't even much of a mod, just a screen implant that kids nowadays get from Santa, but back then..." I sighed. I hadn't told this story in a long time, but something in Grant's eyes made me talkative. Or maybe it was something in the Paulie's. "The neighbours called a Child Protection company in. It was awful — they accused my parents of abuse, of turning me into a machine. At least they called a decent protection outfit. The guy they sent out took one look at me and dismissed the complaint. But the neighbours ... ugh, it was hard putting up with their disgusted looks all the time. I was so happy when they left."

"They weren't part of the Morality Rebellion were they? Those people who protested when the Alliance government came in?"

"We never called it that, but yeah. And it wasn't the government they were upset about exactly. More like the loosening of restrictions on personal choice that came with the Alliance. They just couldn't handle seeing other people doing things they didn't approve of. It was ugly for a while, but they were outnumbered. Ultimately, it was like it or leave it, so most of them left."

"They're the ones who founded the outer colonies, aren't they?"

I shrugged. "That's what they say. I've got no plans to go see for myself, that's for sure. Seems to me it worked out for everyone. They get their pristine communities with their rules and regulations and the rest of us don't have to put up with a bunch of interventionist reactionaries. Win-win." I took a sip of my beer. "Speaking of rebellions, I heard there was a border crackdown over in the Shankar system. Cargoes seized, rumours of someone getting jumpy with a laser gun."

Grant nodded, all traces of jocularity gone. "For once the rumours are true," he said. "It was a pal of mine at the receiving end."

"Bad?"

Grant nodded. "Third-degree burns with complications. Onboard medlab couldn't hack it."

"I'm so sorry," I said.

Grant didn't say anything more and I didn't know what to say to that. I'd heard the smuggler's ship was giving off a Progressive energy signature and the Alliance patrol shot at it. Not standard operating procedure, but no one in Alliance Command would lose sleep over it. Still, even though hostilities between the Progressives and the Alliance were loud and proud, casualties weren't common.

Bao arrived with a large glass of wine which she placed wordlessly next to Grant's left hand. She let her hand drop to his shoulder and I saw the slightest hint of a squeeze, then she was gone. If Grant noticed, I couldn't tell.

He took a deep draught then said, "Here's to all of us out here scraping by in the big black, caught between two monsters."

I lifted my pint glass in his direction. "To the ones who've gone before." We clicked our glasses, drank, and let the silence descend for a while.

✳

GRANT TOLD ME he was staying overnight at the station, and I'd planned to be there a few days, so we agreed to meet the next day before he left. I'd hired the use of a guest room — my cycler was my home but it was small and if I were on a vacation I might as well be able to take a bath. I'd turned off all my devices before crawling into the soft bed, all alarms and alerts forced silent. I woke after a deep sleep to the pleasant glow of the station's artificial sun. I'd picked out one of the few restaurants for breakfast and after getting dressed opened the door of my quarters to a scene of utter chaos.

Cyndex Two wasn't anywhere near as populated as it had been when the mining operation in the nearby asteroid belt was running, but there were still several thousand people living there. And every last one of them seemed to be running down the corridor outside my room.

I tried to stop a man who nearly crashed into me, but he shrugged off my arm and ignored my questions. "What's going on?" I asked again, more loudly this time, in the hopes that someone, anyone, might answer. Someone who bore the characteristic stoop of a lifelong miner stepped out of the river of people to stand beside me.

"Looks like there's finally going to be a shooting war," the ex-miner said. "Turns out the Alliance installed a military outpost just at the edge of the Nune colony. It just came online."

"An outpost?" I asked, thinking that Nune was huge, the main Progressive colony. Millions lived there.

My source nodded. "One of the new Protector class stations. A thousand fighters, they say."

"What are they thinking?" I asked, not expecting an answer.

"News feeds say it's to protect the research labs in the Altera sector." The miner looked at me. "Where you from?" Cyndex was independent, so the people living there could have held allegiance to either or neither of the two major powers. It never really seemed to matter out here.

"All over," I said, "but I'm an Alliance citizen." I got a curt nod in return, but I noticed some of the tension went out of the conversation.

"They say that research station is really important, something to do with extending the range of energy cells. I guess they have to do something to make sure it stays out of Progressive hands."

I nodded, even if I didn't really buy the theory. "This is bad," I said, "but what's with the panic? Altera's nowhere near here."

"You didn't know? The station's been locked down," the miner said. "No one in or out. Word is that it's just a matter of time before the Progressive trigger fingers get itchy and they try to remove the Altera outpost by force. They say those Protector stations can take out a lot of matter in a single strike. It's going to get ugly and it isn't going to be contained."

"Yeah," I said. "Thanks." I turned to fight my way against the flow of people to try and find Grant.

He was from Nune.

*

HE WASN'T IN the guest quarters section, but I wasn't surprised. I only looked there because it was on the way to docking. I knew he'd be on his ship.

I hit the ship's bell on the hull and waited. I didn't wait long before until I heard the squeal of someone undogging the hatch and the heavy outer airlock door opened. "You heard the news," he said, inscrutable. He stood back allowing me just enough room to get through the hatch. "Probably treason just talking to you," he said, "you might as well come in."

I smiled, but somehow our usual banter wasn't fun anymore. I guess because all those jokes about being on opposite sides were no longer just jokes. I stepped into his ship and jumped when the airlock door banged shut. I turned to face Grant and said, "If I'd known anything about this..."

He stopped me with a wave of his hand. "No one saw this coming," he said, "no one outside the inner circles anyway. I'm as clued in to the scuttlebutt as you, my dear, and I hadn't even heard a peep." He passed me as he started walking down the passage. I fell into step behind him, only a tiny part of my mind screaming at me to get off this ship as soon as possible. The rest of me knew that even if Grant was a Progressive, he was still the only friend I had in this sector. Maybe the quadrant.

"For all the freedoms we enjoy," he said as he opened a door set into the bulkhead, "freedom of information isn't exactly one of them." He turned and gestured for me to climb the ladder on the other side of the door. I did and when my head emerged through the gap in the deck I could see into a small, but comfortable sitting room-style cockpit. I made my way up the rest of the companionway and walked over to the small settee. I had an unobstructed 360° view out the flybridge. There were more ships docked here than I'd realized.

"It's no different on my side," I said when Grant appeared at the top of the companionway. "I'd be out of a job if it were." He laughed and for a moment he looked like the Grant I'd always known, but then it passed.

"Drink?" he asked.

"Definitely." He took down a bottle of something thick and dark and poured us two large measures. He handed me a glass and paused a moment before clinking his with mine.

"Cheers," he said.

"Indeed," I answered. The drink went down rough. "It's a bit early for me," I said, catching my breath.

Grant cackled. "What else are you going to do trapped on a dying, nominally independent colony world on the eve of galactic armageddon?" he said.

I laughed and took another, smaller, sip. "Drinking before noon doesn't seem like that much of a problem when you put it that way," I said. Grant settled into the armchair across from me and peered into his glass.

"It's bad for business," he said, finally. "Bad for business and bad for that holiest-of-holies, *individual liberty*. Both sides must realize that, surely."

I nodded. The Alliance was founded on the principles of an unfettered marketplace, of the right of all citizens to be free from state interference in their personal and business lives. The news feeds back home made it sound like the Progressives were practically communists, but I knew that they were libertarians as much as we were.

"They're too much alike, our two sides," I said. "Sometimes I think that's why we fight."

Grant snorted. "The only difference is we think the state is for schools and hospitals and you think it's for cops and armies, right?"

I smiled and shook my head. "It's not that simple and you know it," I said.

"No, but it's close enough."

A flash of light caught my eye and as I turned to look out the viewport I heard the explosion. "What the hell?"

"Looks like folks are getting restless," Grant said. I could see that one of the docked ships had fired on the docking clamps keeping it moored — and its crew trapped — at the station. All they'd done was damage their ship, making it harder for them to leave when the lockdown was over. Assuming total war didn't break out and we all started killing each other.

"Sometimes I wonder if a bit of regulation might not be such a bad thing," I said, "keep the idiots out of my patch of space."

Grant turned away from the viewport and walked back over to the drinks cabinet. "They still manage to sneak though," he said. "Fewer, probably, but there's no stopping idiocy." He poured another measure and held the bottle up to me. I nodded and he bought it with him to the settee. He topped off my glass and sat.

"It's a strange life for people like us," he said, staring out the viewport. "Most folks never leave the gravity well where they were born, never actually meet anyone from the other side. People like you and me, the folks out here at the edges, we see it all more clearly."

"See what?"

"The blurred lines, the shades of grey." He lifted his glass and drained half the contents. "The price of bloody freedom." He laughed — a terrible sound — and it dawned on me that he'd had a bit of a head start on the drinking. I couldn't blame him — I'd always thought that if either the Alliance or the Progressives got hot weapons anywhere near the other side, that the best we could hope for was a long, ugly war. More likely was a few minutes of madness then flames and murder and survivors who envied the dead.

"You have family on Nune?" I asked.

He nodded. "We aren't close; I left for a reason. But they don't deserve what's coming. No one does."

There wasn't anything to say; he was right. I reached out for the bottle and he passed it over.

✳

I DON'T KNOW how much later it was when I woke on the settee in Grant's ship, a few black patches in my memory. I was okay with that. I did a little deep breathing to activate my adrenaline production, then when the nausea passed got up and looked around the ship. Grant was gone.

I undogged the hatch and stepped out into the docking level. I stuck my head out the door, but the chaos was over. The hallway wasn't deserted, but at least no one was panicking any more. I made my way to the main hall in the hopes of finding Grant or news or food. Especially food. My magic muscles go through protein like a star cruiser eats fuel, and I was running on low.

I heard the sounds of people and saw that most of the station was in there, an Alliance broadcast on the screen. I looked around until I saw a food cart and followed my grumbling stomach. I ordered some noodles with double tofu and scanned the room as I waited. I hadn't seen so many people in Cyndex's hall since the mines were open. I saw Grant at a corner table with Bao, the two watching the broadcast in silence.

"Hey," the noodle guy said, bringing my attention back home. I thanked him and took my bowl over to a nearby table. I wedged myself between a couple of people staring at the news screen and began shoveling the food into my mouth. As I ate, I watched the news, too.

"... entering the twenty-seventh hour of the Seige of Nune." The pretty talking head on the Alliance feed was wearing what I thought of as Grim Expression Number Two, and they'd ginned up a flashy logo for the ticker than ran under the computer-generated face. It was a wonder what people thought of the universe if this was the only way they got information. "The military has dispatched its full arsenal to patrol the borders of the Nune Colony and all active duty personnel have been recalled to their bases. Our team embedded with the Fourteenth Spaceborne Artillery are reporting that a pre-emptive strike against the occupying Progressive force on the edge of Nune space has not been ruled out as a possibility. Military leaders are unable to share anything more at this time."

My tipped-up noodle bowl was obscuring my view, so I didn't see what happened next, but I heard a voice across from me say, "Typical Alliance bastards, just looking for an excuse to invade sovereign space."

"We're not the ones with a thousand fighters occupying territory on the edge of your largest colony," the woman on my left said, her voice quivering. I could hear similar arguments breaking out around the room.

"Come on," I said, putting my bowl down. "Things are different out here. You're both miners, right?" They each nodded. "You've got way more in common with each other than any of us do with folks on the main colonies. Who cares if you're from the Alliance and you're Progressive? It's all just an accident of birth, anyway. What's the point in letting a bunch of politicos turn us against each other?"

"No one out here with any sense has any love for the Alliance," the little guy across from me said. "Cyndex left us all high and dry when they pulled out of the mines, and it was the Alliance and their damned 'non-interference' that allowed it to happen. They let companies get away with murder. It's the only reason Cyndex incorporated in Alliance territory."

"Oh, come on," the woman said, "if it weren't for the Progressive government's repressive corporate oversight, companies like Cyndex wouldn't have to cut and run as soon as they took a little hit on their bottom line. If you're going to blame anyone for Cyndex leaving, blame the lazy bastards getting free drugs on Nune."

"That's it!" The guy across from me was quicker than he looked — he leapt across the table. He was aiming for the woman, and I leaned in toward him to try and stop whatever he was planning to do. I caught a fist on my left shoulder and before I could think it through I'd buried my right fist in his gut. He was tougher than he looked, too, and he didn't crumple. Instead, he got me pretty smartly on the chin, knocking me off the stool.

I'd never liked fighting, and I could feel the situation careening out of control. I barely heard the sound of the rest of the room breaking out into a brawl over the hammering of my heart. I scrambled under the table and got a chair in front of me like a shield. Black dots were appearing at the edges of my vision and I knew I was panicking, but my expensive new reflexes knew what to do when a half-full mug whipped past my head and crashed into a nearby table, shards flying. I curled into a ball and tried to will myself to disappear as the sounds of a riot intruded into the safe space I was pretending to make for myself. I sat there for what seemed like hours before I remembered to lower my heart rate and moderate my endocrine system, and my brain started to work properly again.

I scanned the room for Grant and saw him huddling under a table with Bao. His eyes caught mine, and I jerked my head toward the door. He nodded and I saw him say something to Bao. She shook her head and it looked like he was trying to convince her of something, but she just kept shaking her head. He looked my way and I gave him the "now or never" hand signal. He nodded again and said something to Bao. She smiled at him and shook her head again, and he looked down at the ground. I got ready to run and wondered if he was going to come with me after all, then saw him nod at me again.

I thanked providence for allowing me to at least get some noodles into me, then sprang forward from behind my chair into a momentary break in the mêlée. Out of the corner of my eye I saw Grant scrambling along the floor toward the door that I was bounding toward. We made it through at about the same time and didn't bother talking as we ran down the hallway toward docking. We didn't stop until we were aboard Starlite Blue and had dogged the hatch behind us.

✳

WITH BOTH OF US in the small cockpit there was barely enough room to turn around. "Now what?" Grant said, trying to find a patch of bulkhead to lean against comfortably.

"I don't know," I shrugged. "Find a way to get out of here, I guess."

"Then what?"

I looked at his face and wondered what we'd be losing by running. Wondered what we'd already lost. "Then either half the habitats in this sector blow each other out of the sky or they don't. Either someone comes to their senses and the Alliance and the Progressives start talking to each other or they don't. And even if it all blows over, the mess going on in there isn't going to end overnight. We're a lot safer out there in the big black than we are here where all anyone cares about is the colour of your citizenship card."

"You really think so?" he said. "Where do you think you can go? The rustic climes of the outer colonies? No one there has any use for a couple of smugglers. And you," he pointedly raked his eyes over my body. "You really want to go live in exile in some place where there's nothing for you to do but be vilified? You're really willing to give up everything that makes you who you are just to be a little safer?"

"It doesn't matter who I am if I'm dead, Grant. There isn't going to be anything left for any of us here." I breathed deeply, forced my adrenaline levels back down. "Maybe we could start our own colony, those of us who leave. Or just keep moving, I don't know. But if we stay here, we're probably going to be killed. You saw the mess back in the hall. We both know that they're going to tear that place apart. And if you go back to Nune..." I couldn't finish the thought. I don't think I'd ever been so tired in my life.

Grant shook his head. "I'm not staying on Cyndex, but I'm not running, either, April. I don't like the way this is heading any more than you, but I'm a Progressive citizen. I'm willing to fight for what I believe, for the way I want to live my life. I can't see why, of all of us, you're not doing the same."

"This isn't like standing up to some ignorant neighbour," I said. "Sure, I love my freedom, but I love my life more. I'm going to do what I have to in order to survive. And I'd have thought *you'd* understand that."

"I do understand," he said, his voice suddenly quiet. "We all have to do what we have to do. If this blows over there's going to be a lot of rebuilding to do, a lot of materials to move. And if it doesn't blow over..." He looked at me, his eyes hard and clear. "If it doesn't blow over, running won't matter."

It didn't make sense — his eagerness to fight, to maybe even die, over the conflicts of people he'd never even met. Corporate leaders, politicians, generals. But I did know there wasn't anything I could say to change his mind. "At least let me help your ship get out. I have the override to the station's docking system."

Grant smiled, but there wasn't much of the warmth I'd always known from him. "Trading data has its perks."

I nodded. "Once you're on deck, I'll spring the clamps in five."

"Thanks," he said, and put a hand on my shoulder. "Maybe I'll see you somewhere down the line, buy you a beer."

"Sure," I said. I looked out the viewport at what used to be a nice quiet patch of space at the edge of nowhere. "It's quiet out there for now, better go."

"Take care of yourself, April."

"You, too, Admiral."

He undogged the hatch and stepped on to the station. "It's Kwende," he said, then turned away. I could hear his feet pounding the metal floor as I swung the hatch closed.

I scanned my dashboard. Power levels were good, the lanes were clear, and I ignored the percussive thumps of weapons fire that made their muffled way from the station through the hull my little ship. I hit some keys on the dash and felt the docking clamps release.

"Good luck, Kwende Grant," I said to empty space as I swung my leg over the saddle and got ready to ride.

I WAS BALANCING a cup of tea in one hand, while hanging on to the side of the companionway hatch with the other. I climbed into the cockpit sideways, compensating for the roll of the boat. I was only four days out of port and still getting used to the syncopated back and forth as Lucky Lady took the waves abeam.

I got myself safely to my seat by the helm and took a sip of tea. I sighed, hooked my tether to the harness I always wore above decks, and leaned back over the rail. The sky was clear and full of stars in that complete way that only happens on a moonless night hundreds of miles from shore. I hadn't seen another vessel in days and that was just fine. Nothing to run into, nothing to worry about. Just me, my boat, the big blue below and the big black above.

I did a 360° scan of the horizon, just in case, and seeing nothing, set the timer for twenty minutes. I lay down on the soft cockpit cushions and closed my eyes. I had a rig that would steer the boat to the wind for me, and I knew that nothing should be able to make it from beyond the horizon to my position in less than twenty minutes. Even so, I had the radar set to sound an alarm if anything showed up within ten miles. I dropped off to sleep in the rocking of the waves.

The timer went off, and I drowsily opened my eyes. I sat up, and looked around. Still nothing. I smiled to myself and took a sip of tea, still warm in its thermal cup. I checked the instruments — with twelve knots of wind on the beam, we were rocketing along at six knots; pretty good for my heavy old thirty-four footer. I leaned back out to look at the stars again, and squinted. I'm no celestial nav expert, but I've spent enough time looking up to notice when there's something new. Occasionally, I'll notice a new satellite or something up there. But I'd never seen anything new that was this bright before. Or moving so fast.

✳

THE RADAR TOLD me that the thing landed about eight miles away, and I thought I could even hear the splash. I certainly saw the burning fireball falling from the sky into the sea. Was it a meteorite? I don't know how often they happen, but the odds are that at least some of those times someone would be able to see it. Still, I didn't think there were any meteor showers predicted for this area, and I hadn't seen any other shooting stars all night. And it really didn't look like any meteor I'd ever seen before. In between the flames I was sure I'd seen lights on the thing.

You don't keep much of a tight schedule travelling on a sailboat, so a detour wasn't going to hurt me any. I disconnected the self steering, and swung the wheel to starboard. I eased the sheets, and soon was surfing the little waves bearing straight toward the radar target that still glowed bright green on my screen.

An hour and half later the predawn light was starting to peek up over the horizon and I was close enough to see the debris. The fire was more or less out, just the odd floating chunk still burning. There were a couple of still-blinking white lights among the wreckage, and I thought I could see a glint of metal in the early morning light. I got out my binoculars, and braced myself to try and get a clear view of it while Lucky Lady pitched and rolled beneath me. It was hard to get a good view, but I thought I could make out some kind of yellow lettering on the largest piece floating on the waves. I put the binocs down, and paid close attention to my course. I didn't want to drive right through the stuff, but I wanted to be able to get close enough to see it better.

I tried to steer myself slightly upwind of the debris, and when I was already too close for comfort, I threw the wheel hard over to port. I hauled on the mainsheet, then cranked in the jib. As the main came around, the Lady bobbed up like a cork and slowed. I tied off the wheel once I was sure we were well hove to and then clipped my leash to the jacklines running fore and aft on the topsides. The sun was rising in earnest now, and I could see the debris pretty clearly, floating about a football field away downwind.

There were three or four distinct parts floating on the surface, and I suspected a fair amount of the thing had sunk already. I could read some of the lettering on the largest piece now:

MA R   M

This was no meteor.

*

THERE WAS NO way for me to get closer to the wreckage — you can't just drop anchor in the middle of the sea, and with no other crew to tend to the Lady I wasn't about to deploy my boat and row over there. But I couldn't just leave it, either. I shouted, "Ahoy! Is anyone there?" about a hundred times, and blew my foghorn until it ran out of compressed air. There was no answer, and I can't say I was surprised. The crash had been spectacular and the wreckage was pretty bad.

I was sitting in the cockpit, watching the sun come up and trying to figure out what to do, when a flash caught my eye. I picked up the binocs and scanned the wreckage again. There it was — a small ball bobbing up to the surface. I guess it had been trapped under the rest of the debris, because I hadn't seen it before. I would have noticed, since it was clear and had a man in it.

I shouted some more, and when there was no answer, I found my little bicycle pump and recharged my foghorn. A few blasts with it did the trick, and I could see movement in the bubble. I stood on the deck waving my arms, and watched as the bubble split open on a seam, and a strangely dressed man emerged into the water. His suit must have had some floatation in it, as he bobbed on the waves easily. He was probably pretty shaken up, and he didn't seem have a lot of energy. I was sure he'd never be able to swim the distance between us.

"Stay where you are," I yelled, hoping he understood English, and trying to make calming gestures in case he didn't. "I'm coming over there."

I scrambled back into the cockpit and furled the headsail. I fired up the Lady's small diesel, while I centred the main. I motored downwind of the wreckage and headed up, the engine barely ticking over as I slowly made my way toward the man in the water. As I approached him, I turned sightly and chucked my man overboard gear at him — a buoyant horseshoe tied on to the Lady's rail with heavy floating line. I was about to try and pantomime what to do, but he was already dogpaddling toward me. He managed to get the horseshoe around his torso, and I started reeling him in.

He got to the side of the boat, and made to try to climb up to the rail. "Don't," I said, as he fell back into the sea for the third time. "I can winch you up." I had a line on a four to one pulley that I lowered down to him. He clipped it on to the ring on the horseshoe, and I hauled on the line with all my strength. I yanked the sopping, waterlogged man up, inch by inch, until his feet were level with my toerail. I manhandled him over the lifelines, and as I put some slack in the line he collapsed on deck.

"Just stay here a minute," I said, "don't move. I'll be right back."

I jumped into the cockpit, and motored a safe distance away from the wreckage. When I'd put some sea between me and the floating debris, I pulled out the foresail, and hove to again. I killed the engine when I saw that we were sitting nicely, and went back to my catch.

✳

HE WAS COLD and wet and in some kind of shock. It's always warm in the tropics, but he couldn't have been comfortable in that soaking suit, so I got him out of it as soon as possible. He didn't help, but he didn't try to stop me, either, and soon he was sitting on deck, naked. He was a big guy, and I wasn't sure if I'd have anything to fit him, but I scrambled down to my cabin and rooted around until I found a pair of old ratty pyjama pants and a sweater I didn't even recognize.

I came up with the clothes, and saw that the man had gotten himself into the cockpit and was passed out on the cushions. I found a thin blanket to cover him, and put the clothes down by his head. I picked up his dripping silver suit, with its hoses and gauges, and saw that it had the words *major tom* stitched over the breast with the initials "M.R." underneath. I scanned the horizon for ships, and seeing nothing, went down below.

Someone else might not have put two and two together, but I'd been following the news before I left port. This had to be billionaire Matthew Ribald and the Major Tom, his private spacecraft. According to the press, Ribald owned a bunch of companies, had made more money that he knew what to do with, and was spending it now by indulging in a dream of a lifetime. A few years back he'd bought one of the more successful private aerospace companies, and set them working on his baby — the Major Tom, the world's first private spacecraft to be piloted by an amateur. He'd been scheduled to lift off a couple days previously, making the history books as the first private singlehanded spaceflight.

I pulled out my sat phone, and shook the dust off it. At a couple of bucks American a minute, it wasn't really in my budget to use the thing much, but it was exactly for times like this that I had it on board. I didn't know who to call, though, so I dialled my brother.

"Angus Mulgawwy," his clipped voice answered.

"Hi, bro," I said. "It's Kate."

"Katherine," he said, his voice constricting. "I thought you were at sea."

"I am," I said, and before he could start to panic, I continued, "everything is fine."

"You've never called me from the boat before," he said, suspiciously. "What's going on?"

I told him about the crash and the Major Tom, and gave him the GPS coordinates of the wreckage. "You're a connected guy," I said to my brother, who fancied himself a big shot corporate lawyer, "you ought to be able to get in touch with Ribald's people and let them know he's okay. They're probably in a froth by now; it's been awhile since they'd have lost contact."

"You haven't administered first aid, have you?" he non-sequitured. Always the lawyer, I guess, worried about a possible lawsuit.

I ignored the question. "You just pass on the word," I said, "I'll get on the HAM nets in a hour or so, and hopefully someone who's faster than me can get Ribald into port somewhere. But someone shoreside needs to know about this, and you're the first person I thought of, Angus."

"Okay," he said, sighing. "This is going to be a huge pain in my ass." I closed my eyes, awaiting a speech I knew was coming. "It's not easy, you know," he began, "taking care of everything while you go off gallivanting across the world. What is it with you adventurer types, always getting yourselves in the soup and leaving us responsible people holding the bag?"

Angus was terrible for the mixed metaphors, and I tried not to laugh. This wasn't the first time he'd expressed this opinion, and I'd stopped taking it personally a long time ago. I also knew better than to argue with him; he was a lawyer after all. Instead, I just said, "Thanks, bro. I'll be in touch when I make landfall. It'll probably be another few weeks."

"Stay safe," he mumbled, and broke the connection.

✳

I WENT BACK up to the cockpit, and saw that the man was coming around. He was sitting up, and covering himself with the blanket. He looked up at me shyly, and I smiled and pointed at the clothes. I turned my back, and heard him get dressed. Before I turned around again, I heard a soft but surprisingly strong voice say, "Before I forget, thank you."

I turned and smiled. "You're welcome. Let's get a nice cup of tea into you, and there's some fish stew on the stove. Caught only yesterday." I helped him down the companionway steps and sat him at the small salon table. I put the kettle on, and got a small bowl. I opened the lid of the pot, and the aroma of tarragon, fish and cream filled the boat.

"I don't really..." the man mumbled a protest, as I ladled a spoonful of the chowder into the bowl.

"Anything you don't eat can just go back in the pot," I said, setting the bowl and a spoon in front of him, and going back to the galley to organize the tea things. I let him alone, and when I returned with mugs of tea for us both, his bowl was empty.

"So," I said, after we'd both had sips of tea. "Matthew Ribald, I presume?"

"Guilty," he said, smiling slightly.

"I'm Kate Mulgawwy, and you're on Lucky Lady. I guess that's the Major Tom out there," I waved my hand vaguely in the direction of the wreckage.

"What's left of it," Ribald said, looking into the dregs of the soup bowl.

"More stew?" I asked, and he nodded. I ladled out another bowlful, and one for myself. As we sat across from each other, eating, I asked, "So, what happened?"

"A problem with re-entry," he said. "Or maybe just with the splashdown, it's hard to say. It all happened so fast. The ocean landing was as per spec, but the craft wasn't supposed to break apart on impact.

"Or catch on fire," I suggested.

He grimaced. "No. It's a good thing we included the inner pod, or that would have been it."

"You must have some kind of positioning beacon, right?" I asked.

He nodded. "The ship, the pod and my suit are all wired. I don't know if any of them are firing, though." He looked at me through salty eyelashes. "I'm lucky you were there. So, what happens now," he asked. "Can you just take me into shore somewhere? Where are we, anyway?"

I gave him the general idea of our location, then said, "I'm at least four days out from the nearest port. Once I get these dishes squared away, we'll turn off toward shore. But I bet we can find someone faster to come pick you up." I looked at my brass ship's clock. "There's a radio net in a bit; I'll call in and we'll see what we can do."

He stayed seated at the salon table while I stowed our bowls. I told him about calling Angus, including his put upon attitude. "Some people just don't get it," I said.

"No," Ribald agreed. "They don't. But give me his address. I'll see to it that he gets a nice thank you card," Ribald said, smiling. When I'd cleared the galley, we both went up to the cockpit, and he watched as I turned us off the wind and eased the sails. We gybed and I pulled the sheets in a little as we headed off back the way I'd come. I engaged the self steering again, and sat down across from Ribald.

The motion of the seas was low and mild, but Ribald hadn't had the four days — or the decade of sailing — I'd had to become accustomed to it. He looked a little shaky, but kept his eyes on the horizon. I let him be, but kept an eye out for any signs of imminent seasickness. After about a half hour, I guessed that he was going to be fine.

"So, it's just you out here?" he asked, eventually.

"This time," I said. "Sometimes I've got crew, a friend or two along for the ride. But usually it's just me and the Lady and the ocean."

"Isn't that dangerous?" he asked.

I laughed. "Coming from the man who fell from space, that's a bit rich," I said and he smiled. "Sure, a big crew makes some things easier, but you can't beat the freedom of being solo. And I'm not entirely alone."

Ribald looked around the small boat, and raised an eyebrow. I smiled. "I'm alone onboard," I clarified, "but I couldn't do it by myself. Angus takes care of a lot for me, even if he does seem to begrudge every second. And there are other sailors I talk to on the radio and in port — we help each other a lot out here. I've never felt lonely or stranded. Besides, it's actually a lot safer out here than people think it is. The danger come from ships and shore; out in the open it's usually safe as houses." I took a sip of tea. "What about you?" I asked. "Space? That's about as alone as you can get, isn't it?"

He sighed. "All the media ever wants to talk about is the first solo spaceflight by an amateur," he said. "As if there's only me and Major Tom," Ribald said. "But flying is the extent of the solo part of the endeavour. I have a huge team behind me, not just building the craft, but navigation and ground control, too. And there's plenty of potential for the project down the road. I might be the first, but I surely won't be the last solo space flyer, not by a long shot." He sipped his tea. "Being the money man behind the project has its advantages, though."

"You get to be the name in the history books," I said. He smiled and nodded. "Still," I continued, "the first singlehanded private spaceflight has to be some kind of adrenaline rush."

He smiled. "It's exciting for sure, but I don't know about a rush. Take off is a thrill and the crash was certainly a heart thumper, but once you're up there, it's something else, you know?" I nodded. "People picture a rocket and all they think of is the speed," he continued. "That's not the important part for me. I've never gone skydiving or bungee jumping or any of that stuff. I don't see the appeal. But being in space is different." He sipped from his cup, and gingerly moved closer to the rail to look out at the sky. A thin sliver of moon was already rising in the blue sky. "I know it sounds stupid, but they call to me. The stars."

"It doesn't sound stupid," I said. We were both silent for awhile. "The sea is different, too," I said.

He looked at me and smiled. We sat together looking at the horizon, seeing nothing but sea in all directions, the slight whoosh of the waves under Lucky Lady's keel the only sound until the ship's clock chimed the hour.

✳

"THIS IS ANDY on the sailing vessel Star Dancer, Delta Echo Bravo eight three six niner, for the Westbound Net. Calling any emergency, priority or medical traffic, come now."

This wasn't exactly emergency or medical traffic, but I'd decided it qualified as priority, so I keyed my mike.

"Sailing vessel Lucky Lady, Charlie Foxtrot Golf seven three six nine, how copy?"

"I have you five by five, Lucky Lady. Come again."

I slowly and clearly explained the situation with the wreck of the Major Tom and gave our position and course to the guy running net control. His name was Andy Winer, and while I'd never met him, we'd spoken on the radio countless numbers of times. He was an ex-navy seaman and still had a lot of buddies in the service. Better yet, he'd swallowed the anchor years ago and lived aboard his old ketch in the relative civilization of La Paz. These days he volunteered to relay weather and other info to those of us at sea without ready access to email or a phone.

By the time the regular roll call was over, Andy told me that a nearby US Navy boat was en route to intercept us. He guessed their ETA would be about twelve hours.

"I'm sorry to be taking you so far off course," Ribald said, now more comfortable in the cockpit.

"No problem," I answered. "So it adds a day to the trip, big deal. It's not really about getting there for me anyway, you know?" He nodded. "Besides, when am I ever going to get the chance to hang out with a real life spaceman again?"

He laughed. "To tell you the truth," he said, "I feel like a bit of a dilettante, crashing like that on my first solo run."

"Everybody crashes sometimes," I said, tidying the lines in the cockpit. I sat on the port side, and scanned the horizon. Still nothing to see for miles.

"You ever been in a shipwreck?" he asked.

"No," I said, knocking on the shiny varnished wood of the companionway hatch. "But I've crashed the Lady into more docks than I'd like to admit," I said. He laughed. "I think they're all the same," I said. "Sailing ships, airships, spaceships. Landing is the hardest part."

He smiled, and another hour went by.

"So," I asked, between bites of bread, "what's it like up there?"

Ribald swallowed his own bit of roll, and said, "It's hard to describe without sounding dumb."

"So, sound dumb."

"Well," he said. "It's full of stars." I laughed, and he grinned. "I know, I told you it sounds dumb, but I can't explain how full. I mean everywhere you look there's a blanket of them. It's amazing."

"So, what do you do up there?" I asked.

"This trip I went to the moon and back. It was just a practice run."

"Just to the moon and back," I echoed, laughing. "A nice little

Sunday drive."

"Yup," he said. "Just like your quick three week jaunt across an ocean."

"Fair enough," I said, and took a bite. "You see the construction site?" I asked after I'd swallowed.

"Branson's hotel?" he asked, and I nodded. "Sure. It's coming along, but it's behind schedule, big time. But that's the way of construction anywhere. It'll be ready in a few years, I'm sure." He took another bite of his roll. "You got a reservation?" he asked as he chewed.

"Ha," I laughed. "I can't even afford the Howard Johnson's in Crescent City. No, I'm just another curious planetlubber."

He nodded and we finished lunch in companionable silence.

✳

AFTER A FEW more hours under way, Ribald was at home on the boat. It was nice to have someone else to take watch for a while, and I took the opportunity to get a decent sleep. I'd been down for several hours, when I felt a hand on my shoulder, shaking me awake.

"There's something on the radar," Ribald said. "About twenty miles out."

I rolled out of my berth and clambered up to the cockpit. I squinted at the screen then looked at the time. "That's probably your ride," I said.

We sat quietly, watching the waves lift Lucky Lady's stern and roll under us. "This is really very pleasant, once you get used to it," he said, eventually. I just smiled. "You know," he said, looking up at me, "if you ever want a trip up to the stars, just drop me a line."

"You're going to build another ship?" I asked.

"The project has a life of its own, now," he said. "It's not just about me anymore." He leaned back over the rail, looking up at the darkening sky. "Besides," he said, "they haven't stopped calling to me." He looked back at me. "Maybe I ought to give the next one a more auspicious name, though. Major Tom didn't really have the most successful trip either."

I laughed. "You have anything in mind?"

"I'm sure I'll come up with something," he said.

✳

THE NAVY BOAT got within a mile of our position, and I hove to. I found an old ditty bag for Ribald's sodden spacesuit, and gave him my card. He promised that if I could arrange a mailing address he'd send me back my clothes, and I laughed. "I don't really need pyjamas and a too-big sweater in the South Seas," I said.

"You won't always be in the islands," he said, and I nodded. "It's just an excuse to stay in touch," he added, eyes firmly on the sea. The Navy had launched a boat, and the inflatable was speeding toward us, its red and green lights bright against the darkness of the sea. Ribald stuck out his hand, and I took it. We shook, then he pulled me toward him for a brief hug.

"I don't know how to thank you," he said, looking away.

"You don't owe me anything," I said. "Just don't give up on answering that call."

The Navy boat pulled alongside, and Ribald climbed to the rail. The Navy men helped him into the inflatable, and I passed down the bag with his suit. One of the boatsmen noticed the name on my hull, and said, "Looks like he's the lucky one today, ma'am."

"Yeah," I said. "Thanks for making the detour."

"Glad we could help," the Navy man said. "You the captain?" he asked, and I told him I was. "Nice work here," he said.

Ribald looked up at me. "Don't forget my offer," he said. "I might need crew someday, on my next ship."

"I won't forget," I said. "I owe you a stint on watch, anyway." We shared a brief smile, then the Navy inflatable fired up its motors. "Nice to meet you, Matt," I said, loudly, over the noise.

"Likewise, Captain Kate."

The Navy boat turned and sped away. I watched as they reached the mothership and cargo and crew were loaded aboard. I waited until I saw them turn toward land before I spun the wheel, eased the sheets, and got back on course.

"GOOD MORNING, MARIAN." Her alarm clock's voice was soft and androgynously sensual. "You have three new messages," it continued as she slowly woke. "The bank would like to offer you several investment choices for the busy professional, the government has ten tips to help you quit smoking and your mother wants you to call her." She lay in bed, sunlight angling through the space between her curtains, the clock yakking away on the nightstand, but she ignored it all. She was thinking of him.

It had only been going on for a couple of weeks, but she could barely remember a time before him. He really was the first thing she thought of when she woke and the last thought on her mind before falling asleep. He consumed her; she breathed his breath. Just thinking his name could make her completely lose track of time. Graeme. Spelled with Es, not like Gray-ham. Somehow more dignified that way, she thought. Graeme.

She could hear her alarm at the corner of her mind, but she was overwhelmed by her excitement at the thought of seeing him so soon. She felt like a teenager with a wicked crush, but it was so much more than that. She was a grown woman, he was a man, and this was no schoolyard infatuation. No, this was the real thing.

She sighed, and whispered his name. Graeme.

∗

MARIAN DIDN'T REMEMBER the first time she'd met Graeme, and that drove her crazy. He worked at a coffee shop, the one she visited most afternoons after work on her way home, and that was how she knew him. But she couldn't remember if he was already working there when she first walked in, looking for a latte and a quiet half hour, or if he started sometime after she'd become a regular. She didn't even remember the first time she noticed how beautiful he was, standing behind the bar, frothing milk or serving up sandwiches, his coffee coloured skin set off against the creamy white of the ceramic mugs. It was like one day he was just another service worker that you hardly even notice, then the next day he was the centre of her life.

Obviously, it wasn't that sudden. She'd noticed him at some point, in that way you realize someone is attractive, and wonder how you could possibly have ever missed it before. And it had just gone from there. She wasn't exactly sure how it had begun, but one day she'd walked behind the red haired barista with the tattoos checking the online staff schedule. Marian had just happened to glimpse the site's URL over the redhead's shoulder, and her next move had suddenly seemed obvious. She'd hit up the site on her phone, and paging back a few days plus a little deduction yielded his name. Graeme Blake. Graeme. She just happened to copy his next month's schedule to her phone. It was almost like public information, anyway, on such a poorly encrypted site as that.

She waited a full week before following him home after his shift. She left the coffee shop before he did, not wanting to draw attention to herself. She walked to the 7-11 on the corner, and bought a pack of cigarettes. She didn't even bother using cash to avoid the annoying public health warning emails she'd get by using her bankcard. She could see into the window of the coffee shop from the counter at the Sev, and watched as he — as Graeme — cleaned up the coffee bar and tidied the tables.

She was lighting up her first outside on the curb as he came out of the café and locked the doors. The sun was setting as he started walking toward downtown. Marian waited until he was a half block ahead before she got going. She glanced at the CCTV camera on the corner and told herself that it was the way she walked home every day anyway. So what if she was a couple of hours later than usual. And why would the cops be watching her? She had never done anything wrong.

It wasn't a long walk, maybe twenty minutes, but it felt timeless to Marian. Watching him, the way his beat-up old messenger bag — the one he always hung on the coatrack at the coffee shop — bounced on his backside. The motion was almost mesmerizing, and Marian had to check herself to make sure she stopped for the red lights. She was stopped at a corner watching, while he walked into a shabby walkup. His place.

She sat on the bench at the bus stop across the street from his apartment. On the bus stop's wall, a public service announcement reminded her that terrorists are neighbours, too, and exhorted her to report any suspicious activity to the local police. She wouldn't have noticed if a rebel militia marched by, so transfixed was she by his window.

She barely moved, except to light cigarette after cigarette. She watched the light and shadows playing on the other side of his window, wondering if he noticed the glow of her cigarettes in the dark.

By the time the third number eight bus had gone by, and no one else had entered the apartment, she decided that he must live alone. The thought both thrilled and saddened her. A man like that shouldn't have to be on his own. She made a note of the address of his apartment complex on her phone. She got on the next bus, and rode the dozen blocks back to her neighbourhood, fantasizing about what might someday happen on the other side of his apartment's window.

✳

SHE EVENTUALLY SILENCED the alarm's chirping and got out of bed. She showered, dressed, and was out the door in a half hour, walking a few blocks down the street to the little diner on the corner. She'd never been there in the morning before, but she knew they served pastries and coffee, and more importantly had a window on to the street. She hoped she was early enough to get a booth.

She walked through the diner's door, almost unconsciously glancing up at its security camera. Not the obvious one with the blinking red light above the door. She looked for the tiny fisheye lens over the counter that scanned the entire room. She knew it was there, because she'd been in the restaurant only a week before for a routine service call on the camera.

The AI chip had started identifying perfectly ordinary customers as possible terrorists, and after the fifth set of cops showed up with nothing to do, the diner called Panoptitech, Marian's employer, to fix it. Marian was assigned to the job and she'd had the upgrade installed between lunch and afternoon break. That was when she noticed the window and the proximity to the street corner, and she decided to come back some morning before work.

She tried not to look at the hidden camera while she ordered a coffee and a bagel, paying with a wave of her bankcard over the store's reader. The whole transaction took about a minute. She walked over to the booths with her plate and cup and was pleased to see an empty seat by the window, a perfect vantage point to watch the crosswalk. She sipped her coffee and waited.

Nibbling her bagel she glanced at the clock on her phone, and exactly at 7:26 am she saw him crossing the street, his tired old book bag slung over one shoulder. She wondered if it was too soon in their relationship to buy him a gift? She didn't think so. Marian had never believed in things like fate before, but it was hard not to think in those terms now. It was so obvious that he was meant for her; there were just too many happy coincidences conspiring to bring them together — her apartment so close to the university where he was studying, this diner she'd only just found with its perfect view of his walk to class in the morning.

She had noticed him reading a textbook on cosmology at the café, and when he was in the washroom she casually wandered past and looked at his notes. His notebook was covered in the logos of the university, and she saw a page from a class syllabus sticking out the back cover. An hour on the university's website confirmed that he was a grad student in the physics department, and his class schedule was easy enough to infer after another hour of studying the department's website.

She smiled over her coffee cup as she watched him walk to campus. She hadn't had the patience for school; as a result, she never got the grades for university, but she'd always liked science. Her occasional smoking buddy at work, Susan, was an engineer; Marian liked to hear her talk about the new, cool things she was working on. She imagined nights in Graeme's apartment, listening to him explain some complex theory to her.

Yes. At lunch, she could pop in at a trendy store in the mall near the Panoptitech office, and take a look at the bags. He worked so hard, he deserved something nice. She'd miss looking at the worn canvas bumping against his thighs as he hustled to make his eight o'clock Non-Euclidean lecture, though. She picked up her phone and took a quick video, a little souvenir to add to her collection. The memory on her phone was starting to get pretty full.

✳

SHE WASN'T ORDINARILY a weeper, but when she walked into the café she nearly burst into tears. He wasn't there. How could this be? The schedule clearly showed that he was supposed to be working the afternoon shift. Then her eyes caught sight of his familiar messenger bag on the coat rack and Marian began to breathe again. She ordered a latte from the red-haired girl behind the bar and took it to her usual seat. She sighed as she saw Graeme emerge from the men's washroom.

Under her chair was a wrapped parcel from Cooper's,

containing an outrageously expensive bag. Marian couldn't remember the last time she'd spent as much on something for herself, but that didn't matter. Graeme was worth it, and as a student he'd hardly be able to afford something like that for himself. It made her happy to be able to give him something nice. Besides, she'd be getting a nice bonus for the extra overtime she'd be putting in. That morning she'd offered to take on one her of colleague's overtime shifts once she saw where the job was going to be.

She sipped her latte and smiled. She knew that Panoptitech held the maintenance contracts for most of the CCTV cameras in the city, but it still seemed like some kind of a sign that they had a job in Graeme's apartment complex coming up. It had been easy to convince her cube mate Simon to give her the shift; she'd told him that she needed the extra cash, but she knew he hated overtime anyway and would always be happy to get someone else to take his turn.

She stole a glance at Graeme as he squirted whipped cream on a hot cocoa. Would she leave the bag here for him to find at the end of his shift, or would she find a way to get into his apartment and leave the gift there? She was no locksmith, but you could learn almost anything online these days. If she put her mind to it, it wouldn't be that hard. She looked out the window, but the sun was going down earlier every day now and she only saw her own reflection. And the reflection of Graeme's face from behind the bar. She was sure she saw something there, something in his eyes that told her that what she felt was real. And that was enough.

✳

HE WATCHED THE woman, Marian, as she sipped her latte. He was polishing the milk frother, and could see that she was looking at him, too, using the window and the darkening sky as a mirror. She didn't see him watching her, but he looked away anyway.

Graeme knew her name from going through the electronic

receipts on the till. She always paid with her bankcard and her name and address were logged by the system. Employees weren't supposed to have access to that level of detail, but it wasn't well hidden. And coffee shop baristas often have a lot of time on their hands.

So, Graeme knew her name and where she lived and that she'd been leaving larger and larger tips for him in the past weeks. He smiled at that, though the money didn't mean much to him. It wasn't her cash that he wanted.

It had taken a long time for him to get the data he'd needed, but he'd finally swiped a Kleenex she'd used about a month before when she'd had a bit of a cold. It was gross, but loaded with the DNA that the lab had needed to concoct the serum. He didn't really understand how it worked, but they needed samples of his DNA and hers in order to tailor the drug for her and to code it for him. Something about pheromones, he thought he remembered the website saying. He didn't care abut the details so long as it worked.

He'd spent a month's worth of his coffee shop salary on the stuff, but he had a decent stipend from school and on top of that he was a "watcher", a paid informant. He never had anything to tell the cops, but he'd spend the few hundred bucks that showed up in his account without worrying about it. They'd cut him off eventually, he knew, but until then he could afford a dose of a designer drug to get what he wanted. What he needed.

His hands had been shaking when he'd broken open the ampoule over the cup for her latte. What if he screwed up the order and it got thrown out? What if someone else took the drink by mistake? What if she spilled it, what if... Of course, he worried for nothing, and he managed to sneak a look at her eyes as he handed her the large bowl-shaped cup she preferred. She hadn't looked at him then, hadn't even said thank you. But none of that mattered now.

Because now he was wanted. Now, her eyes lingered over his

body with an intensity that he could feel burning on his skin. Now, she watched him, with a hunger that even she couldn't understand. And, finally, in her eyes he felt alive.

He set down the silver milk frother and let his eyes meet hers in the reflection on the window for the briefest moment. He saw her cheeks flush and he allowed himself a small smile, then turned away as he very softly, reverently, whispered her name. Marian.

I WAS ENCODING a batch of classic ebooks when the *ulu-aliki* walked in to the library. "Afternoon, chief," I said, pushing my chair back a bit. Joseph Seru spoke Tuvaluan with his family and the other council members, but his English was so much better than my Tuvaluan would ever be. Besides, even though less than ten percent of us were Aussies or Kiwis, the official language on the SPIT was English.

"Hey ya, Sally," he answered, lacking his usually jovial demeanour.

"You looking for something in particular?" I asked. The island's chief was a voracious reader and a bit of a film buff. I usually gave him first crack at the new titles I managed to snag off the satellite internet connection.

"Sort of," he said, the last remains of his smile disappearing. "You, I guess."

I frowned. "What's up, chief?" I asked.

"I've got something for the blog."

I watched as he pulled a chair from one of the tables and sat it down across from my desk. He knew me well enough to leave a decent space between the chair and the desk.

As the island's librarian, I had also become the de facto editor of the closest thing to a news source we had — the *Spitball*, the island's blog. There were about a dozen regular contributors, most of the posts being the weekly scores for the football, *kilikiti* and *ano* matches. But things did occasionally happen on the SPIT, and we reported on them all. According to the stats, there were even a handful of people off off-island who regularly read the thing.

"What's going on?" I asked again, opening up a text editor on the laptop so I could take notes.

"The bastards finally figured out how to make a buck from us, that's what's going on." Seru usually looked for the positive, but he sounded more like the bitter old fisherman who posted screeds about how overseas politicians screwed us all. I raised an eyebrow and the chief continued.

"They're bringing in developers." He spat the last word out like it was a wormy piece of fish.

"What on earth for?" I asked.

"Luxury condos on the coast," he said, "what else?" His voice was hard and I could see a fire smouldering in his eyes that: it wasn't really a good look for him. Even though it was clear that he was dead serious, I couldn't help myself. I laughed.

"Luxury condos?" I repeated echoed. "You've got to be kidding. Who wants to vacation on a pile of rubbish?"

He said nothing for a moment, just looked at me. "People don't see New Tuvalu that way anymore. They're calling it one of the few unspoiled islands left in the South Pacific, but without all that pesky dirt, poverty and backwardness." He snorted, and I saw that his hands were clenched. "Greedy rats."

∗

THE SOUTH PACIFIC Island of Trash had existed for years, floating around wherever the South Pacific high happened to be. Tankers or unlucky sailors sometimes saw it, but it was more like a legend than a real problem. Hundreds of thousands of plastic bags, bottles and wrappers, all stuck together in a loose conglomeration of rubbish, stewing in a soup of microscopic particles. It was embarrassing, but it was an embarrassment that belonged to no one in particular, so no one in particular wanted to deal with it. Until Tuvalu sank.

The island nation of Tuvalu had been slowly disappearing for years and inevitably the evacuation came. Twelve thousand refugees in New Zealand could hardly be ignored, and all of a sudden that rubbish started looking good. One of the many docos made about conditions in the refugee camps was screened in Cannes to an international uproar, so the government finally tendered bids to create a new Tuvalu on the SPIT. The marketing campaign was slick — out of disaster and waste would come an oasis of beauty in the Pacific, a new island paradise. Of course, it ended up being nothing like the artist's drawing in the ads.

But they had nowhere else to go, so off they went, to New Tuvalu. The powers-that-be sent a bunch of New Zealand and Australia's homeless along for variety. Why let an opportunity to get rid of more unwelcome trash go to waste, right? Which was how I ended up on the SPIT.

I wasn't exactly homeless, but I was living in a broken-down flat with a half dozen other unemployed just-graduated bums, with no immediate prospects beyond slinging coffee. Given my particular issues, the service industry wasn't exactly a feasible option for me. I was living off savings and I didn't have a lot of savings.

I'd have gone to the moon before I'd ask my family for anything and I didn't really like any of my friends. There was nothing keeping me where I was and with a free plot of "land" and five grand to anyone with a degree who volunteered to go, the SPIT looked pretty attractive. It was an offer I couldn't refuse.

✳

OF COURSE, THERE wasn't much work for a Film Studies major on New Tuvalu, either, but that didn't really matter. Everyone was figuring out how to get by, how to live on our precarious flotsam home. With my English rose complexion and solitary nature, I wasn't really suited to fishing or landscaping. That's how I ended up running the library, which turned out to be more film and television than books anyway. I spent my time cataloguing, reviewing, downloading when the bandwidth was available. Sometimes I'd go days without seeing another soul. It was just fine. For me.

Most of the old Tuvaluans kept on fishing and praying and living their lives, but it wasn't the same. No one was used to trees in pots and a shoreline made from old chip bags and rope. In the first year there were over a hundred drownings. This from an island nation of seafarers. No one said it aloud but everyone knew they couldn't all be accidents.

Slowly, though, the drownings stopped and people adapted — there were plenty of fish, the desalinator worked reliably, the solar cells finally started automatically tracking the sun and all was right with the world. The trees even grew tall enough that we sometimes forgot that the soil was all imported. We forgot that everything was imported, including us. New Tuvalu wasn't our country, after all — it was just a protectorate of New Zealand. They let us run things day to day, but as Joseph Seru found out, even though we'd made life out of garbage, it wasn't our garbage.

✳

"CAN'T WE JUST build a hotel or something? You know — make it nice, real posh, but ours?"

The chief snorted, his big nostrils flaring so wide I thought I could maybe see his brain fuming up there. "They don't want a goddamn hotel," he said. "They want timeshares. They want homes. They want to weekend here, like it's some kind of resort or something. They're referring to themselves as our new neighbours for heaven's sake! It's ridiculous."

"Well, who owns the land?" I asked. We all knew we lived on a floating platform of plastic — still, we clung to those archaic words as tightly as a drowning sailor would cling to our own coast.

"That's the problem," he said. "No one does. Or more precisely and accurately, the bloody New Zealand government does. They want to build on the north beach."

✳

THE NORTH BEACH was the island's biggest park, our communal space. It was large, maybe a tenth of the whole area of the SPIT. There was imported sand there for the kids to play in and a few fields for sports. About half the space was left "'wild'," or at least the best approximation of wild we could do. There were trees and a little sod here and there. I couldn't believe that they were going to sell it out from under us to a bunch of rich Americans and Europeans who wanted an unspoiled getaway for a couple of weeks each year.

When the *ulu-aliki* left, I fired up the satellite and did some digging online. There was no doubt that the charter for New Tuvalu left any unowned spaces as property of the New Zealand government. Legally, the north beach was a Kiwi landfill. I searched the internet for any mention of this scheme in the rest of the world, and found a few tiny stories buried deep in the business sections of the Herald and the Dominion Post. According to those sources, it was a development cartel from Abu Dhabi bankrolling the deal. Who else but desert dwellers would see the potential, I thought.

The SPIT always reminded me of something my dad used to say: "You can put lipstick on a pig, but it's still a pig." I was comfortable there, I liked the work and the community. I'd never felt as safe as I did on the SPIT. But it was still just a veneer of paradise on top of a pile of trash. We'd been given the least they could get away with, and now they were going to try and take it back? It was so unfair.

I wrote up a quick article for the blog and hit the "publish" button. I knew that there would be a lot of angry comments on the site by morning, and probably an equal number of angry people banging on the doors of the council members by the end of the day tomorrow. But what good would that do? The people making all the decisions were thousands of miles and a whole world away.

*

"No, Mum, I don't have the bandwidth for video."

"I can not for the life of me understand why you would choose to live out in the back of beyond like that, Sally." My mum's strident voice wasn't softened a bit by the tinny speakers of the library's laptop. "You can't even have a video call with your mother? I mean, what is the draw of living on a glorified rubbish tip?"

"Mum," I said, my heart pounding. "Don't start. Can you please just tell me what people are saying about the development? Is there something we can do to stop it? Get people back home mobilized against it, maybe?"

"I highly doubt it," she said and I could hear her derisive sniff. "I only noticed the piece on the news because it's where you live, and even then it was just fluff about how great an investment this resort will be. Not a single soul cares about a handful of people out there floating around on a pile of old tyres. Though, whoever would want to holiday out there I cannot imagine. The smell alone!"

"It doesn't smell, Mum."

"Really, if you must live there, you should be pleased that there's some money coming in finally. Those developers will make things more civilized for all of you — people with money for resort condos aren't going to put up with not being able to make video calls, for one. This is a good thing, Sally. I don't know why you'd want to try and stop it, except that you always were contrary. If it's something that's making someone a living, it's got to be bad. You never did have your feet properly on the ground, no wonder you're living somewhere that's as flimsy as your ideas."

I could feel pinpricks of tears starting up behind my eyes and knew that if this kept on I was going to lose my temper. "Okay, well, I have to go now, Mum. Other people need the laptop. I'll call again soon, okay."

"Maybe you can get a job at the resort, be able to afford your own computer."

"Give my love to Dad," I said and hit the big red disconnect button.

I managed to get to the toilet without having to run, but wasted the nice piece of dorado I'd had for lunch. I'd managed to calm down before the library door banged open.

"Anything?" Joseph Seru asked.

I shook my head. "I should have known better than to ask my mother for anything. She's half the reason I left."

"Thank you for trying," Joseph said, and I felt terrible. "None of us have any connections to anyone over there; you did what you could with what you have." I could see that he wanted to put his hand on my shoulder, do something to show me that he truly was grateful, but he knew me well enough to know not to. "We will endure, as we always do. Who knows, maybe it won't be so bad."

"Maybe," I said, but I knew we both were lying.

✳

"YOU'RE A FILMMAKER, aren't you?" The woman standing in the doorway of the library looked the worse for wear — an unhealthy rosiness in her cheeks which foretold a nasty sunburn, expensively dyed hair exposing mousy brown roots and hanging limply in the humidity. Typical *palagi*. She probably looked a lot like me, and I can't imagine she liked that much more than I did.

"Yes," I said, suspicious. Since they'd arrived, I'd tried to stay away from the developers as much as possible. I preferred the mediation of a screen if I was going to be confrontational.

"That's great," she gushed in the phoney tones of an MBA holder. "We're making some promotional materials for the new community and would love to get locals involved, people like you. It's a terrific opportunity for all of us."

Her greasy smile was making my stomach turn and my heart pound. I didn't want to be there, but there was only one door to the library, which was itself only the one room. I couldn't escape her grinning face. "Have you talked to *te sina o fenua*? If you want local involvement they'd be the ones to work with."

She shook her head and looked at me like I was a naïve teenager. "The council members are old-fashioned, they just want everything the same as it's always been. They don't understand the importance of keeping current, of modernizing this community. That's why we're here, to make sure that New Tuvalu has all the advantages technology can bring." She looked around the library, her eyes resting on the bulky computers and the blinking satellite modem. "You must appreciate that."

"I'm not going to make an advert for you," I said, wishing I were anywhere but in this conversation.

"Don't think of it as an ad," she said, taking a step toward me. I felt myself push back into my chair, and I could see in her face that she noticed it, too.

"I'm not interested," I said. My mouth felt like it was full of sand.

"Fine," she said, stepping back, and the tightness in my chest loosened slightly. "But you have to realize that without people like us this place is never going to move beyond being an overgrown fishing raft. Is that really what you want, to live like someone in a National Geographic documentary?"

"Get out," I said, my voice barely above a whisper. Thankfully, she turned and walked back out into the heat of midday and I let my head drop into my hands. It was bad enough that they'd taken the beach, and were building a resort no one who lived here would enter from anything other than the staff door. But, did they have to act as though just because I looked like them that I would think like them?

✳

THEY ENDED UP hiring some overseas firm to make their film. They earned their money — it was very well done. It made the developers look like a cross between Oxfam and *Médecins sans Frontières*. I cried throughout the whole six minutes.

"It's could be worse," Joseph Seru said. We watched it together in the library — the developers had provided an advance screening copy to the council.

"How?" I asked. "I can't see anyone wanting to help us now. How do you say you don't want better communications, more jobs, a thriving economy? How do you say you just want to be left alone?" I was trembling, and tried the old breathing exercises to calm down.

Joseph was quiet for a moment, and I couldn't read the look on his face. Finally he said, "We can't stop it, Sal. This is my home, but it isn't mine. I wish things were different but wishing doesn't make the fish bite or the rain fall. At least they are letting us stay."

"Damn it, Joseph," I said, my voice breaking. I didn't bother trying to fight the tears. "We are human beings. We're entitled to a place of our own. It's their fault that you had to leave Tuvalu in the first place, with their pollution and greed. And now... now they're taking this away, too?"

He looked at me and I thought I saw a trace of anger cross his face, then it was gone.

"I know you mean well, Sal," he said. "But there's nothing to be done. We have to make the best of what we've got. We've been doing that all along. New Tuvalu used to be rubbish. Now it's so beautiful that people want to come here from all over the world. Maybe we were too good at building something out of nothing, because, now, everyone wants what we've got."

He walked out of the library. The next day I learned that his daughter, Mary, had gone to work for the development as a sales manager. I tried not to be angry, tried to remind myself that she had the right to her own decisions, that we all have the right to decide for ourselves how to live our lives. It was hard, though.

✳

"SALLY, IT'S RUDE and hurtful and you have no right to say those things." Mary Seru was a small woman, but she wasn't timid. She had planted her hands on my desk and her angry face was far too close to mine.

"I have a right to my opinion," I said, my voice about a third as loud as hers. If she hadn't been so horribly close to me, she probably would never have been able to hear me.

She shook her head. "Of course, but you don't have a right to plaster your opinion all over the blog like it's the gospel truth. Ugh." She let out a breath and stood up straight. I felt my chest expand a little as space opened up between us. "Some of us have to live here, you know."

I felt like she'd hit me. "I — I live here."

Her face softened slightly. "I know," she said. "But it's different for you. You can go home. The rest of us..." She looked out the window of the prefabricated building. It was another beautiful day in the South Pacific, the sky a clear blue, the warm breeze stirring the leaves of the potted trees. "The rest of us don't have a choice."

"This *is* my home," I said. "We all worked so hard to make this place livable. That's why I don't want to to see it turned into just another generic resort. Your father understands. I don't see why it's so hard for you."

"My father feels sorry for you," she said, and I was fairly certain she didn't intend for it to be insulting. "Because you have no proper family connection, no people. But I can see that you're just like them." She jerked her head in the direction of the construction. "You don't even really like it here. All you can see is what this island came from. At least the developers see it for what it is now. At least they're honest enough to say out loud that they want a taste of a forbidden exotic life, to visit the world of us noble savages. And they're willing to trade those things we don't have in order to get what they want."

I guess she'd given up trying to be nice and I could see anger in her face. "You have no right to tell us what we should do with our lives and our island, Sally. You aren't the voice of this community. You never can be." She took a step towards me and I could see dark spots in my vision. I paid attention to my breathing and hoped I would be able to forestall a panic attack. "Just leave it alone."

✳

MARY DIDN'T COME by to see me again. I didn't post anything on the *Spitball* again, either. I gave the login and password to Kevan Tulley and when Joseph asked me why I'd stopped running the blog I made up some excuse about it taking up too much of my time. He didn't press it.

The construction took eighteen months and for a little while I thought there might still be hope. But soon there were fewer boats going out to fish each day, fewer pickup games of soccer, fewer weaving circles. Then there were people wearing business suits and housekeeping uniforms. A fleet of rickshaw taxis sprung sprang up. Two restaurants.

By the time the last condo was sold, I barely recognized the place. There was broadband all over the island now, so I borrowed the laptop and called my mother from my small hut. Her wide face filled the screen and she forced a smile with tight lips.

"Sally," she said, "I told you things would improve once that resort got going, didn't I? Aren't you glad your impotent little protest didn't accomplish anything, hmm?"

"I'm coming back," I said, unwilling to let this conversation go on any longer than absolutely necessary. "I've got a job lined up at the Film Archive in the capital; I won't have time to come down to Nelson before I have to start. Sorry."

I expected an "I told you so" or an "I knew you'd come crawling back," but Mum just frowned.

"What on earth for?" she asked eventually. "That island of yours is finally a decent place to be. Why would you want to leave now?"

I shrugged. I didn't know how to explain that everything that had once made being living on the island appealing was gone. It was no longer unique, no longer special. Even its remoteness was now just an illusion, shattered by ubiquitous wifi and twice twice-weekly scheduled flights.

But that wasn't the real reason I couldn't stay. I'd thought that a people whose home sank into the sea was the perfect community for me. I shared a spiritual connection with them, we had a fundamental similarity. They were lost, I was lost — I'd thought we could be lost together. But Mary was right — I wasn't really like them at all. They had no choice, they could never be anything but a people displaced from their home by forces beyond their control.

I wasn't a tourist, but I wasn't a New Tuvaluan either. I had options they would never have, and I always would. Nothing I could do would change that, not for me and not for them. And now that I knew it, every time I looked at one of my neighbours, that gulf between us was all I could see. For the first time since I stepped on to the SPIT, I felt trapped.

"Well?" Mum said, impatience written all over her face. "Why would you want to leave now?"

I looked past the screen out the window, to the potted palm trees rustling in the warm breeze, and the core of pressed plastic peeking out through breaks in the grass and sand. Once it had been a symbol of how things that no one wanted could become central to an entire community. For the New Tuvaluans, it was a base on which to build a future. But to me it was now just another place I didn't belong.

I brought my focus back to the screen. "Home sick, I guess."

"SAMANTHA!" MUM'S VOICE was loud in the small room and I knew I'd been caught again. I pulled back from Matthew and looked at his face. He was red in the cheeks and his eyes were screwed shut. I could see a single tear squeezing out. That made me smile.

"That's it," Mum said, grabbing me roughly by the arm and pulling me away from my little brother. "Time out for you and no TV for a week. I don't know what's wrong with you, young lady. How would you like it if you had an older sister who hit you all the time, hmm? Not very much, I'll bet. Look at him, his arm's all red. What did you do, Sam?"

She went on, yelling at me and pointing at the ugly red welts on Matthew's arm. I knew exactly what I'd done — hit him over and over, until my fist started to hurt and I could tell that he was biting his lip to keep from crying. I knew Mum might catch me, figured I'd get in trouble, but it was worth it.

Matthew caught my eye and while Mum wasn't watching I saw him mouth "Thank you."

This time he'd promised me his comic book collection, but I would have done it for nothing. I love my little brother, and even though I don't really like hitting him, it makes him happy. And I love making him happy.

JACOB LOVES THREE things: family, God and running. I'm the same, except for the running. But I do love Jacob, so you could be fooled into thinking I loved his running as much as he did.

As long as I've known him he was always running. I remember watching him at the city finals — he was incredible, one of God's perfect creatures. I'd have been about to start high school, so he must have been fifteen years old. Jacob finished ninth in his age group, and when our eyes met as he crossed the finish line I knew he was the boy I wanted to marry.

He had never been shy about making it clear that he liked me, too. When the national Freedom of Faith Act was passed, Summerville was one of the first towns to vote to become a Christian municipality. Jake and I were both were members of The Light of the Lord Church, and the youth group asked for volunteers to help with the campaign before the referendum — we spent three weekends together knocking on doors and handing out pamphlets. Most of the other kids hated being stuck doing church work on their holidays, but for me those were the best weeks of that summer.

On election night, the church was packed with people waiting to hear the result. The initiative passed with a good majority, and the cheers and Hallelujahs from the crowd were deafening. All I could hear, though, was the hammering of my heart as Jacob slipped his hand into mine.

After that, we were inseparable. Other kids in school made fun of us, calling us an old married couple, but we didn't care. That sounded to us like the most perfect thing in the world to be.

Of course, as soon as we were old enough, Jacob asked me. It was even more romantic than in the movies that my sister Beth and I used to watch every Saturday afternoon before she got married. It was Jacob's and my usual Friday night out — the seven o'clock movie, ice cream after and slow walk home in time for the town's curfew. But Jacob arrived wearing his Sunday suit and instead of walking to the Roxy, he called a taxi.

I must have known what was to come, but I think I was so afraid that it wouldn't happen, that I really was just dreaming, that I didn't let myself believe. Even when my parents grinned at us both when Jacob arrived, my father catching his eye and the two of them sharing a strange look. Even when I discovered that he was taking me for dinner at Walden's, the most expensive restaurant in town. Even after all this, I still was surprised when after dessert he got down on one knee and said, "I went to see your father yesterday, and he's given me his blessing. Now I just need to know if you will give me the best gift I could hope for — your hand in marriage."

I don't remember what I said. I was so surprised. I was only 18, Jacob was barely 19. He was going to school to become a teacher, and I had a good job as a receptionist at the art museum. Still, *married*. It seemed so sudden, so adult. But I looked in his eyes and it was just like the finish line at the city race. It was as if he saw that with me he could do anything, be anyone. As if I made him the man he was. How could anyone say no to that?

Looking back, there was no doubt that it was the dream day I'd always hoped for. I'd been nervous in the months before the wedding — worried that something would go wrong, that Jacob would change his mind, that the flowers wouldn't arrive on time. But he was such a rock for the whole year we were engaged, that on the day all I had to do was enjoy it.

"Everything is going to be perfect, Barb," he'd said, poring over the china catalogue with me. "I like this one with the yellow flowers, what do you think?" I didn't care, so I let him pick all our patterns.

My brother-in-law Dave was Jacob's best man, but he was almost worse than no help. Beth and I couldn't have chosen more different husbands. It was like Dave was doing all he could to stop Jake from having anything to do with planning the wedding. "Just leave all this to the girls," he said, showing up with two tickets to the football game. "They could spend a month just choosing colours for the dresses. Let me give you a break from all this nonsense."

Jake never once went along with Dave, though. He always just shook his head and said, "It's my wedding, too."

"What is wrong with that guy?" I overheard Dave say to Beth one day when they thought I was still on the phone with the caterers. "Your sister sure has him whipped."

"Oh, I don't think that's it," Beth said and, while I agreed, I really didn't like the nasty tone in her voice. "He's just weird. Perfect for Barbie." They laughed and I made a lot of noise in the kitchen so they'd know I was coming back out. That night I prayed for the strength to forgive her.

I often think back on my wedding day, which was as beautiful and perfect as Jake had promised it would be. I sometimes wish time had stopped then, that I could be young, naïve and in love forever. Later, I'd think that Dave and Beth were right, that I should have known, even then, that something was different about Jacob. But I loved him. And God help me, I have to admit that him being different from other men was a a big part of what I loved about him. What I still love.

✳

AT WORK WHEN it was quiet, I used to go into the religious art wing to look at the print of Botticelli's *Virgin and Child with Young St John the Baptist*. I loved it the best, even more than the painting of angels that always reminded me of Jake. There was something about it — Mary so beautiful as she held Our Lord, His love radiating up at her, her mother's adoration so clearly on her face. I'd stand there, looking at the painting and praying that one day I might hold my own child in my arms like she did. It has always been my favourite painting, but I can't bear to look at it any more. After five years of trying, of hoping and praying, we finally realized that it just wasn't God's will. Jake and I couldn't have children, but it wasn't for lack of trying.

The week before my wedding, Beth sat me down and told me what to expect. Not just on my wedding night but for the rest of my marriage.

"You just have to accept that every couple of days, whether you want to or not, you're going to have to do your wifely duty."

I'd laughed, because she sounded ridiculous, but also because I was embarrassed. Everything about this conversation was awful, but part of me was scared enough to sit through it. "Come on, Beth," I said. "You make it sound like a horrible chore."

She'd shrugged. "Well, sometimes it is." I must have had a look on my face, because she laughed then. "And sometimes it's not. It can be great, really. The first time won't be, but it gets better, it really does." She shrugged again, and I wondered if she weren't telling a fib. But about which part?

"Still, he's going to want it more than you, and you just have to put up with it. Men aren't like women," she said. "They need it, like we need, I don't know, food. It's part of the marriage deal. Unless you want him going off to the filth in Browning, it's what you have to do." I'd never been to Browning, even though the town was the nearest municipality. If you believed some of the older church ladies, you'd think it made Sodom and Gomorrah look tame.

"You're exaggerating," I said. I didn't believe that men needed to make love like they needed food. I mean, there were men who were chaste. Monks. Saints. Priests.

Beth rolled her eyes. "Come on, why do you think the Catholics have all that trouble? And as for the saints, you don't really think that those stories are true? Trust me, real men need to have that release." She lowered her voice and got a funny look on her face. "I mean it, Barb, you're better off just giving him what he wants. Trust me," she repeated and I wondered what had happened to her. Dave would never have been my choice for a husband, but he was a good Christian. Wasn't he?

"Is everything okay?" I began, but Beth wiped the look off her face and laughed.

"Oh, Barbie, you're finally growing up," she said, using the nickname I hated. "You and Jacob are going to be so happy together, I just know it. He's a bit soft, but that's good for you. And when the kids start to come, ooh," she grabbed my hand and squeezed, "you are going to be such a great mommy. Come on, let's go down to Snipz and Tipz and look at the hairstyle books again."

She wasn't right about most of it, but Beth was right about my wedding night. It did hurt, but Jacob was so sweet, so loving, that I'm sure it was worse for him than it was for me. I tried to hide my discomfort, but when I winced he stopped and said, "We don't have to do this now. I don't want to hurt you."

I looked up at him, his beautiful blue eyes so full of concern and I melted. "I know," I said, "but I want to." I shifted under him and gritted my teeth. Soon it was over and I lay next to Jacob as he panted, sweat making his lean body shine. I ran my hands through his short hair and said, "Now we are truly married, in the eyes of God. And now that the first time is over with, I can start to enjoy it."

He took me in his arms, so gently, and kissed me. It was like the touch of the petals of a flower, so soft, so full of love. I couldn't imagine ever being happier than I was at that moment.

And Beth was right about one more thing. Making love did get better. A lot better.

✳

"BARB, HONEY, YOU'VE got to come and see this!" Jacob sounded so excited, I wiped my flour-covered hands on a dishcloth and went to his study. He'd been home from school only a few minutes and usually that meant that he'd be knee-deep in marking for the next hour. I tended to leave him alone until he came out for supper, but I hadn't heard him this excited since he got the job as the head English teacher at Summerville High.

I poked my head around the door and saw his face lit by the computer screen. He was truly beautiful, like a Renaissance angel. I felt a flush of heat rise through my body. "What is it, hon?"

"Come over here," he said and scooted his chair back from the desk. He grabbed me around the waist as I got close and pulled me on to his knee. I giggled as I squirmed over to sit more squarely on his thigh. I was almost as tall as he was, and I'm sure I weighed more. Running kept him slim.

"What is it?" I asked.

"I've been chosen for a spot on the all-state championships," he said and I could almost feel a surge of energy through his skin. "That's only one step away from nationals!"

I knew the trajectory for running races as well as he did; I'd done more than a few turns as a volunteer for his races. So I knew that this was a big deal. If he did well here he'd qualify for nationals and that was where Olympic qualifying happened. I knew he didn't think he'd ever make it on the Olympic team, but I knew his times like I knew how much flour to put in a batch of scones. I knew what the top guys were running, too. It wasn't impossible and Jacob had been steadily improving this year. I leaned down and kissed him, the sparse stubble of his five o'clock shadow barely grazing my cheek. "This is wonderful, hon," I said. "You deserve it, you've worked so hard."

My first thought was to call mom and dad. But my parents had both been killed in a car wreck years before, and it had been hard for both Jake and me. He loved my mom and dad as if they were his own family, and when we'd gotten the news it had broken us both up. We still missed them all the time, and visited their graves every weekend. Even now, I caught myself wanting to pick up the phone and call my mom when something happened.

Jake must have had the same thought, as I heard him choke up a little. He coughed and squeezed me then laid his head along my shoulder blade. "I could never have done it without you, honey. Let's pray and thank God for our good fortune."

We closed our eyes and while Jacob gave thanks for his running, I thanked God for sending me such a loving and kind husband.

✳

THEY SAY THAT the devil wears a beautiful face to deceive us, but I think he probably looks exquisitely ordinary. Like something you'd barely notice, never even think about, let alone suspect. Something as innocuous as dirt.

Jacob spent hours getting ready for the race; hours on top the hours he already spent training. Waivers, legal forms, physician's certificates — sometimes I wondered how long it would be before the lawyers made it impossible to have any competitions of any kind again. "This is a lot more than you've ever had to do before," I said as Jacob organized the various electronic documents on his tablet.

"It's because it's part of the national circuit," he explained. "They follow the Olympic rules so that they can be sure that everyone who qualifies would be eligible." He shook his head. "Mostly it's about citizenship and fitness. It's a small inconvenience for such a great honour." He tapped rapidly at the tablet, completing the first of the forms. I shook my head as I went back to the kitchen, marvelling at his patience. I couldn't imagine my brother-in-law calmly spending his weeknights filling out forms just to go to a race. Beth often complained about how she couldn't get Dave to do any of the household administration.

It wasn't that surprising that my sister and I would have husbands who were so different from each other. Beth and I were what our grandmother called chalk and cheese. I knew that if we weren't sisters we'd never have been friends. But, of course, we were sisters, so it was Beth I called when it all started to fall apart.

I know it's a sin to think badly of my own sister, but I can't help but wonder if things might have gone differently if I'd talked to someone else.

✳

HE WAS LATE coming home. He always called if he was going to be late, and I kept checking my phone in case I just missed a message. He walked to school — could he have been hit by a car? Surely the police or the hospital would have called me, everyone knew us in Summerville.

I was just looking up the number to the police station when the door opened and Jacob came in. I could smell liquor and wondered where he'd been. Summerville was dry and the nearest bar or liquor store was miles away in Browning.

"Barb, we need to talk." Jacob's face was grim and he looked like he might be sick. "I got the test results today." My mind buzzed with one word; the word that strikes terror into everyone.

Cancer. I wasn't sure I wanted to know if that's what it was.

"Jacob," I started to say, but the rest of the words were lost to a choking sob. If he was sick we would get through it. God doesn't give us anything we can't handle, right? I couldn't speak.

He must have known what was going through my mind, because he grabbed my hand and looked deep into my eyes. I must have looked terrified. "I'm fine, Barb. I'm not sick, there's nothing wrong..." He looked away and I couldn't read the look on his face. "I'm not sick. I'm not dying. Everything is going to be fine."

I breathed for what felt like the first time in an hour. Then I got confused. "So, what is this all about?"

He took a breath and let it out, slowly. "They do a lot of tests now," he started. "Ever since the human rights challenge during the 2024 Summer Olympics? Everyone has to be tested, men and women. It's really just a formality."

I didn't know what he was talking about. "Is this about drugs?"

He shook his head. "No. Well, they do that too, but no. This is a sex test." He blushed and I couldn't help but smile.

"A what?"

"They used to just test the women," he explained, "in case they were really men. I guess it used to happen, people cheating that way. It was unfair competition, or something. Then there was this case, I don't remember the details, but they argued that it was sexist to only test women. I think they were really trying to stop the testing completely, but it didn't work out that way. Now everyone is tested, every time." He waited, looking at me expectantly.

"Okay," I said. "What does this have to do with you?"

I could tell he didn't want to say it, but I'll give him credit. He didn't look away. "I have something called de la Chapelle syndrome. I have the body of a man, but I have two X chromosomes, like a woman." I could see tears forming in his eyes. "Genetically, I'm female."

✳

THE CRAZIEST THING was that it didn't affect his status in the race. They still assumed that the women's division was easier, so even though he could have petitioned to run in the women's division, he was still accepted into the men's. The whole test was pointless from the race organizer's perspective — they only administered it because of the legal requirement. But it ruined my life.

I told Jacob that I didn't believe it. "There must be some mistake," I said, the words sounding hollow to my ears. He shook his head.

"It happens," he said, shrugging. "I guess it's just who I am."

"No," I said, trying not to cry. I continued arguing — of course, he was a man, I said. He was my husband, a wife knows. But it wasn't Jake I wasn't trying to convince.

As soon as he told me about the test, I couldn't help myself. *God help me. This explains everything.*

Jacob had always been different from other men — softer, more caring. He barely needed to shave, his chest was still as smooth as a boy's. And he was genuinely interested in the things I was interested in — cooking, children, he even watched those trashy reality relationship counselling shows with me. Wasn't it obvious that there was something wrong with him? How could I have not seen it?

Beth didn't bother sugar-coating it. "I always knew there was something funny about him," she said. "What are you going to do?"

"I don't know," I said. "Nothing?"

"Barbie," she said, "it's a sin. Two women, living together like a married couple."

"He's not a woman," I said, my voice barely a whisper.

"He's not a man," she countered and I nearly put down the phone. "Besides, it doesn't matter. It's illegal here anyway."

"What?" I barely croaked out the word.

Beth spoke to me as if she thought I were a five-year old. "Summerville is a Christian town, Barbie. You know that as well as I do. And that means no homosexuals. No weird half-man-half-woman people. Once this gets out, Jacob won't be allowed to stay here. And if you want to be with that... abomination, you won't be able to stay here, either."

I didn't know what to say. She talked a little longer but I barely heard her. She could make me so angry sometimes. It was as if she was almost happy that this happened to us, as if our suffering justified her painful marriage.

But regardless of how cruel she was, I couldn't ignore it: she was right. Once people knew about this, they probably wouldn't let

Jacob stay here. They certainly wouldn't let us live together. And with Beth knowing, there was no chance of keeping it a secret, either. What was I thinking, talking to her about it?

I thought about leaving with him. I thought about it all the time, but Beth was right about something else. I knew about homosexuals; I watch television and read People magazine, I wasn't completely naïve. But even if I wasn't like Beth, I did believe that it was a sin. I was a good Christian, a good wife. One day I'd hoped to be a good mother. I wasn't a deviant, and I knew Jacob wasn't either. But that's what this diagnosis had made us become, if we stayed together.

I wasn't ready to leave the town I grew up in, the life I knew, and start again. I didn't want to leave Jacob, I still loved him. Loved her? But it was wrong, I knew that. Our immortal souls were in danger. And if I really did love Jacob, how could I condemn us both to the eternal fires of hell?

He didn't see it the same way. "They are the ones who are wrong, Barb," he said. "Whatever my genes say, I am the same person you married, the same person everyone at The Light of the Lord said would make a good husband to you. Nothing has changed." But he was wrong. Everything had changed.

We both cried when I told him I had applied to have our marriage annulled. "God made me this way, honey," he said, holding both my hands as if he were drowning. "God made me love you. How could that be wrong? You know it's not wrong."

I shook my head. It didn't feel wrong, but it was. The Bible said so, the church said so. Everyone I knew said so.

"And I love you, Jake," I said. "That's why it has to be this way. I promised to love you til death do us part, but I will love you well into the next life, I know it. How could I ever put you in a position to risk your eternal soul? I'd rather be miserable and have you saved than be happy together and be damned."

What could he say to that? What could anyone say?

✳

JACOB REFUSED TO see me for a long time after. He said it was too painful. It was painful for me to be apart from him, even if we couldn't be married any more, but I understood. He moved away that summer, but some friends from church still kept up with him. I guess that was how Beth heard about it.

"That freak ex-husband of yours got remarried," she said on the phone.

"He's not a freak," I said, but my heart wasn't in it to argue with her. It was too busy breaking.

"Maybe now you'll get on with your life and find yourself a real man," she went on, the familiar refrain washing over me. "You're not getting any younger, you know. What about that Mike Anderson at Sammy's butcher shop? He's always asking after you."

Mike Anderson had cornered me in his shop one afternoon the previous year and tried to put his hand up my skirt. I'd told Beth and she said I should just be flattered that he was interested, considering. I never went back to Sammy's after that.

"I have to go," I said and hung up on Beth. I'd hardly spoken to her in months before that call, and this would be the last time we'd ever speak. Every day it had been getting harder and harder to be a good sister to her, and finally I just stopped trying.

I'd stopped attending church after Jake left. I just couldn't face them all. But I still had a copy of the church directory and I knew who Jake would have kept up with.

"It's such a shame he felt he had to leave Summerville," Tony Briscoe said as I sat in the Briscoes' kitchen with a steaming cup of tea. I was surprised they agreed to see me — it had been a long time.

"Some people would have made his life miserable here," his wife Sarah said, shooting me a look that was equal parts disgust and pity.

"I'm not like my sister," I said, "not anymore." I watched as a flush began to spread over her cheeks.

"Well," she said, not meeting my eyes, "can I get anyone another cookie? Maybe a warm up?" She bustled around the kitchen while Tony found Jake's new email address on his phone. I didn't stay much longer.

After a week of making excuses to myself, I finally sent Jake an email congratulating him on his marriage. When I saw his response in my inbox, I could hardly bear to open it. What if he hated me? What if he didn't?

His email was short but friendly. We exchanged Christmas and Easter cards for a couple of years after that. I hate to admit it, but every time I saw that something from him had arrived, my heart fluttered just like it had done back when I was fifteen years old and he looked at me across a room. Seeing him happy with someone else was awful, and I prayed every night for their souls, but it was better than not hearing from him at all.

Then his wife got pregnant. I didn't want to believe that she had been unfaithful, but what else could it be? Of course Jacob couldn't have children. But then the baby was born, a beautiful girl they named Dawn. They sent me photos and, like a fool, I looked at them all. It was obvious in the one where he held her in his arms, looking down at her as if the light of the world shone in her face. She had Jacob's beautiful blue eyes.

I didn't know how it could have happened, but I had to ask. Finally, I just called him. "Jacob," I said. "It's Barb. I shouldn't have called but..."

"I know," he said, soft and sad just like I remembered from the last time I'd heard his voice. "I've been expecting to hear from you. Dawn..." His voice trailed off.

"She's beautiful," I said, not bothering to keep the tears out of my voice. "She looks just like you."

"She is really my daughter, Barb," he said. "When Annie got

pregnant, I couldn't believe it. I'm — I'm ashamed of the things I said to her. Anyway, I went to the doctor's right away, demanded they test me again. Everything came back normal this time — no de la Chapelle syndrome, nothing unusual in my genes at all. I — I didn't know what to do." I heard him sigh, but waited for him to continue. "I tried to contact the clinic from before, but they weren't in business any more. It took a little digging, but I finally found out that all the tests from that race were messed up. Those weren't my results." We were both crying now. "I'm... I'm sorry, Barb, I should have told you. I've known for months, but I didn't know how to tell you. I'm so sorry."

All I could hear was the pounding of blood in my head. The words came pouring out, everything I'd held inside all these years. I couldn't stop them, even though I knew I should. "But, this can't be. You're not like other men. You're different, I've always known. It's why you're so... why you're so beautiful." I was sobbing now. I don't know if he could even understand me, I don't know if I wanted him to.

"Barb, honey," he said, "I'm just a regular guy." It was as if a castle I'd built for myself began to crumble out from underneath me. Everything I thought I knew, everything I'd understood, everything I'd told myself to stay sane in the hell I'd made for myself, was all in pieces around my feet.

"Oh, Barb," Jake said, "people just are the way they are. God makes His children in all kinds of different ways." I heard a wailing in the background and Jake took a deep breath. "Look, that's Dawn. I have to go feed her. Barb, I still care about you, I always will. I pray for you every day that you can get over this, move on with your life. You deserve to be happy. We all do."

He put down the phone and I imagined him with his daughter in his arms, the baby smiling beatifically at Jacob, as he looked down adoringly at her. Bathed in the light of the Lord, while I looked on from the darkness.

"*PUPUSAS?*" THE WOMAN'S nasal voice reached Randall at the back of the bus before he saw her pushing her way down the aisle. He could smell the warm, raw meat smell of his own sweaty body, and his stomached wriggled. He was hungry, but he couldn't face mysterious little bits of meat.

"*Quiere pupusas?*" the voice called again, and Randall saw the plump figure with her plastic tub approach his seat.

"*Frijol?*" he asked, his high school Spanish failing him for a full sentence.

"*Sí*," the woman answered. "*Frijol y queso.*"

"*Dos, por favor,*" Randall said, and fished in his pocket for a crumpled bill. The woman passed him a paper envelope of warm dough that smelled pleasantly of mild spice and cheese, and he gave her the money. She dug into the frilly, ribboned apron she wore over her cheap nylon shorts and gave him a handful of change.

"*Pupusas?*" she continued to hector the remaining passengers on the bus, before exiting from the back doors just as the bus lurched away.

Randall ate his warm snack carefully, grateful that they were not so hot as to leak runny beans and cheese all over himself. The corn flour dough was barely warm to the touch, but the filling was good and his stomach momentarily stopped its gurgling. Randall had been riding the garishly painted repurposed school bus for about an hour, heading south, heading away from what anywhere he thought of as civilization. His pupusas gone, Randall leaned his head against the metal side of the bus, and tried to relax.

＊

BRIAN RANDALL WAS a name that wasn't famous in the way a

screen actor's name might be famous, but he had several thousand online followers, and he couldn't go to a conference or industry party without a dozen or more fans tagging along after him. He was the first to admit that he loved the attention. He'd enjoyed a good success with several of his online ventures, and the following was one of the perks of this success. Of course, the money was a strong motivator, too. But Randall would have developed cute little gadgets and toys for the online market even if people hadn't been willing to pay his way. Indeed, he spent the first several years of his career working out of a dumpy apartment in the Bay area, with a pair of equally bookish roommates, coding day and night for the sheer thrill of it. Brian Randall was a natural.

He first struck it big with a tool he called the "all in one reader." Once he sold it to Google, their marketing people rebranded it Google Summary. It really was ingenious: you could feed the service any kind of file, and it would output a shockingly sensible summary of it. It was not terribly revolutionary for text files, but it worked just as well on audio or video. And much more interesting for the development set, you could upload a piece of code in any of the popular languages, and it would give a text description of what the code would do. What it did with images was much less useful, but absolutely fascinating. Randall had made certain that the output on image files was always exactly one thousand words.

Randall could have lived easily on the sum he earned from the sale of the product, but he still had more ideas. He moved out of the cramped apartment, got a fancy set of digs of his own, and started noodling. After the Summary sale, he was asked to speak at one of the major tech conferences in the Bay Area, and there he got his first taste of fame. He had only just arrived at the exposition hall, and was picking up his conference package, when a tall, attractive young man approached him.

"Are you Brian Randall?" the man asked, a shy smile on his face.

"Yes," Randall said, wondering if there had been a problem with his registration or something.

"*The* Brian Randall," the man continued, "of the all in one reader?"

Randall smiled to hear his own name for the technology. "That's me," he said. "You can just call me Randall."

"Wow," the other man gushed. "I'm such a fan of your work. My name is Chick Hernández." He stuck out his hand, and Randall shook it. "Can I interview you for my blog?"

Randall laughed, and said, "Sure, why not?" They exchanged email addresses and IM handles, and met that night for a beer after dinner. Chick blogged between rounds. After Randall's talk the next day, Chick Hernández was the envy of all the major tech bloggers for the scoop. Randall left the conference with at least fifty more entries in his contact list.

✳

UNLIKE MANY HOTSHOT web developers, Randall kept his output up, and had something cool in the pipeline at any given time. In five years he had never missed a spot at the podium at one of the major events, and he'd never had to buy a single drink at any that he attended. Many of his fans had become friends and some even had proved to be good business partners on various projects.

It got to the point that there were few places in the Bay area or the valley that Randall could go without being recognized. He wasn't a theatre lover or an opera fan, or he might have had some peace. What Randall loved was technology, and his business was also his hobby. Everywhere he went, someone knew his name.

However, Randall was happy to put up with a little lack of privacy in exchange for the opportunity to meet so many people. He always carried the latest cell phone as well as the speediest and tiniest computer available. Even when he was working on a project, he'd have one window open with an IM conversation and be plugging away at emails. For the first time in his life he was popular, and Brian Randall loved it.

※

IT WAS AT one of the few conferences he attended that never asked him to speak that Randall met Ellen Baines. She was on a panel discussion about the ethics of cyborgism and as soon as she started to speak, Randall understood a lot more about his fans than he had before. She was utterly fascinating to him. She was challenging one of her co-panelists who argued that merging human biology with mechanical contrivances should be outlawed as wanting to close the barn door after the horses have bolted.

"Anyone who wears glasses, has a prosthetic limb or a pacemaker — heck, even a boob job," she paused for the guaranteed sophomoric laugh, "any one of these people is already a cyborg. Sure, we need to be careful going forward, just as we already are careful with any medical procedure. But we shouldn't stop human evolutionary progress just because we've seen too many cheesy science fiction movies." She got an even bigger laugh, her co-panelist turned a light shade of crimson, and Randall was enthralled. He determined to meet her.

Randall was accustomed to people seeking him out, and at first was at a loss as to how he should go about tracking her down. After he'd given up just wandering the halls of the hotel where the conference was being held, he eventually posted a message on one of the social networks he used. "At Sci/Tech. Looking for Ellen Baines. Anyone know where she is?"

Within two minutes, he had replies from a half dozen other attendees, indicating that she was at a wine and cheese sponsored by a pharmaceutical company that was trying to market a new crop of smart drugs. Randall made a bee line for the suite. He had the room number, but once he got to the right floor of the hotel, he just followed the sounds of drunken conference attendees. He had been to enough of these kinds of things to know what to expect — just about anything. Nerds were surprisingly good party-goers.

This affair was relatively tame as these kinds of things went. There was an open bar, so the crowd was nicely lubricated, but everyone had all their clothes on and the furniture was still intact, if not in its usual places. Randall picked a microbrew out of the ice filled cooler on the kitchenette's counter, and looked around the packed suite for Ellen Baines. He was stopped only once by a short, thin woman who asked him some questions about his latest project. Randall was polite, giving the woman a few minutes and about half his attention, before nicely but firmly moving on. He had spotted Baines in a corner, sipping a microbrew out of the bottle and talking to a owl-faced man about twice her age.

He waited patiently near her, and listened to the conversation. "The headset trials really are amazing," the man was saying. "Do you think there will be a practical application for the technology soon?"

Ellen Baines laughed. "I can't possibly comment on that, Clive," she said. "Non-disclosure agreement," she added, a mock serious tone in her voice. "But between us, we are close to something that's going to make these headsets look like those brick size car phones from the eighties. Give us a few years, and there could be some serious developments, indeed." Randall sensed a natural pause in their conversation and took his opportunity.

"Excuse me," he said to them both, then turned to face Baines. "I heard your talk today and was blown away. You destroyed those other guys on the panel."

She laughed again, and Randall noticed that the sound was particularly pleasing. "I don't know about that," she said, "but I'm glad you liked what I had to say." She glanced down at Randall's name tag, and a slight frown appeared on her face. "Brian Randall," she said, her voice a question.

Randall stuck out his hand for her to shake, and said, apologetically, "You won't have heard of me; I'm just an interested amateur here."

"No," Baines said. "I'm sure I have heard of you. You're big on the Web, aren't you?"

Randall laughed, and said, "That's pretty accurate. I should get that printed on a tee shirt." He named a couple of his recent projects and Ellen's eyes lit up.

"I knew I knew you from somewhere," she said, and took a step back. She stretched, and Randall didn't notice her eyes travel the length of his body. "Say, you want to blow this joint? I know a really good pub not far from this hotel; we can walk it."

Randall beamed, and discovered that his heart was thrumming.

✳

THEY TALKED UNTIL the ugly lights came on in the bar. Randall learned that Ellen Baines was Dr. Ellen Baines, the same researcher who had made a breakthrough in perfecting Direct Neural Control — the 'headset trials' that she had been talking about at the drug company party. She had devised a system where a human user could control any modern off the shelf computer without the need for an input device. They just needed to put on her specially designed headset, plug in a USB dongle to the computer, calibrate the input and then think their commands. After a pitcher of beer, she divulged to Randall that the patents were approved and she was in the final stages of negotiation with Motorola. She expected to see the first product on the shelves within a year.

"That's unbelievable," Randall said. "It's going to revolutionize computing."

"I know," Ellen said. "But just wait till you see what's coming next," she added cryptically.

"What?" Randall asked, almost breathless.

"Another pitcher!" Ellen said loudly, in the direction of the bartender, and laughed that tinkly sound that Randall was becoming more and more enchanted by. When that pitcher, and the one after it were gone, and the bartender was ushering them out the door, Ellen turned to Randall and said, "So, what's it going to be? Your room or mine?"

✳

SURPRISINGLY, AFTER THE conference, Randall and Ellen continued to see each other. She lived and worked in Berkeley, and after six months of one or other of them driving across the bridge to see each other, Randall sold his condo in the city and moved into a huge loft in Berkeley. By the time the next Sci/Tech conference rolled around, Ellen had moved in.

Randall worried that Ellen would be like the other women he had dated seriously, that she would begrudge him his online friends and expect him to pay more attention to her once they shared living space. After a month, though, he knew he'd finally found the perfect woman.

Randall still worked out of the condo, forcing himself to leave once a day for a quick walk around the neighbourhood. Most nights Ellen worked late at the lab, but since Randall often lost track of time when he was working, he rarely noticed her late returns to the condo. They would share a late dinner of take out, talking about their various projects. If they didn't watch a DVD on the wide screen or go out with friends, they would both naturally gravitate to their laptops. Often they found themselves next to each other on the couch, talking to each other over IM rather than out loud. They were two of a kind.

It was a Tuesday night, about quarter to seven. Randall hadn't even turned on his worklight yet, and was starting to squint at his laptop's screen, when his IM client chirped. It was Ellen, still at the lab.

"It works!!" Her message was short and sweet.

"As good as the headset?" Randall asked, his own work momentarily forgotten.

"Yes. Better! Faster." Ellen's quick responses betrayed her excitement. She typically made a point to use full sentences even in IM conversations.

"Will you be long?" Randall asked.

"No. I'm done for the day now. We should celebrate tonight."

"I'll make reservations."

✳

IT WAS NEARLY nine o'clock when they were shown to a table at Marcellino's, their favourite special occasion restaurant. "Two pints of Guinness, please," Ellen ordered as they were seated, and then excitedly turned to Randall. "There's no doubt about it," she said, grinning. "The implants work perfectly."

"No side effects?" Randall asked.

"Nothing other than the usual — one subject had a minor infection after the surgery, and there's the usual two percent who couldn't handle the interface, but that was the same with the headset." Ellen grinned and smiled up at the waiter who had reappeared with a pair of pints. She took hers and lifted it up toward Randall. He clinked his pint glass against hers and they each took a long sip. "Here's to the newest breakthrough in computer hardware."

"Don't underestimate yourself, sweetie," Randall said. "This could be the next step in human evolution." His cheeks were flushed and he was breathing harder than would seem necessary for only lifting a beer glass from table to mouth. "When is it going to be ready for humans?"

Ellen's smile faltered, and she put her beer glass down. "Ah, the other side of innovation," she said, sourly. "It's ready now," she continued, bitterness coming through her voice clearly. "But it could take months, maybe even years, for the testing to be completed to the government's satisfaction." She pursed her lips. "I don't know how long it could be before there's a commercial model available. Probably a couple of years before the FDA are through with it."

Randall took a sip of his beer, and thought. "But if it weren't for all the testing, how soon could we be using it?" he asked.

Ellen's face took on that look that Randall knew well, as she calculated all the variables in her head. "Well, the interface is no problem; that's the same as the headset and we know humans have fewer problems learning the interface than the simian subjects. And we've been using surgical quality materials for the test cases already. In theory it should be plug and play. Of course, we'll need to do a few neurological tests and verify anti-rejection features, but honestly," she looked up at Randall. "I'd say a couple of months."

Randall smiled. "Let's get an appetizer," he said, opening his menu. "Carpaccio?"

✳

RANDALL HAD BEEN worried that Ellen would have some kind of ethical concerns, but he realized that he should have known better. She was so much like him that it was often eerie. As soon as he proposed his plan, she was behind the project one hundred percent. The only snag they hit was finding an assistant. Ellen was a fine surgeon, but she knew from her work with the test subjects that it took at least two people to perform an implant. Obviously, neither she nor Randall were willing to risk a mistake. That meant finding an accomplice.

"Your grad students would do anything for you," Randall said one night, as they sat next to each other on the sofa, each of them idly surfing the web while an old tv show played on the widescreen.

Ellen snorted. "It seems that way," she said, "but you'd be surprised how much backstabbing goes on in the labs. And even I wouldn't have participated in something like this as a grad student or a postdoc. Any kind of fuck up at this stage of their careers, and the future is over. Even a hint of scandal would kill their prospects." She looked over at Randall. "No, we can't volunteer one of the kids."

"Damn," Randall said. They had spent some part of each day for the previous two weeks trying to figure out how to find someone reliable, trustworthy and competent to help Ellen implant one of her devices in Randall's head. "I wish we could just google for mad scientists," Randall said. "I'm sure we'd find a wacky brain surgeon out there somewhere who'd help us out."

"I don't know if I like that implication. I am not a mad scientist," Ellen said, trying to sound offended. "More like a mad engineer, I think you'll find." Randall laughed. "Besides," she continued, serious now, "it's not neurosurgery at all. The implant is actually affixed to the skull, and the interface to the brain is effected through electromagnetic..."

"Okay, okay," Randall said, "I know, already." He paused for a moment, then turned to face Ellen. "That's it!"

"What?"

"We don't need a surgeon at all," he said, his voice rising. "We need a tech."

"What do you mean?"

"I mean I think I've solved our problem."

✳

"ELLEN, MEET SKIPPY." Randall sat at a table in a dive bar in his old neighbourhood in San Francisco, with his girlfriend on one side and his old roommate on the other. The other man had the poor complexion and pallor of someone who spent more than a normal amount of time indoors and who maintained a less than perfect diet. He grinned at Ellen, and stuck out a thin hand to her. She took his hand and shook it, and glanced at Randall warily.

"Skippy is the best tech I've ever known. I once saw him fix a cold solder joint in less than a minute with one eye closed."

"I was kinda fucked up at the time," Skippy said, remembering.

"I couldn't see the fucking thing with both eyes open. Kept moving around, the bastard circuit board did."

"It was a circuit board?" Ellen asked, turning to face Skippy.

"Yeah," Skippy said. "Your old phone, wasn't it, Randall?"

Randall beamed at Ellen. "I told you," he said. "No one can screw, solder, file or otherwise fiddle with tiny electronics like old Skip here."

"So," Skippy said, his eyes darting between the two of them. "What's the project?"

✳

DESPITE ELLEN'S RESERVATIONS, the procedure was a stunning success. Skippy was, to Ellen's great surprise, entirely professional once he had a tool in his hand. He was unfazed by the blood and issue surrounding his work surface and he was as fast and precise as Randall had described. Ellen found herself marvelling at the man's sangfroid as he attached the tiny device to Randall's skull with minute surgical steel screws.

Randall's recuperation was fast and in less than a week he was ready to try the device for the first time. "It can be a bit disorienting at first," Ellen warned, picking up the small remote control device which activated the implant.

"I've practiced with the headsets," Randall reminded her. "They were comfortable enough."

"This might not be exactly the same," Ellen admitted. "We can't be sure how you will react."

Randall grinned at her. "You can't be chickening out now," he said.

"I'm just trying to be careful," she said, defensively. "You are the first human subject, after all. The monkeys don't exactly give us a lot of subjective data."

Randall smiled, and kissed Ellen. "Thanks for worrying about me," he said, and she flushed. "Let's kick the tires and light the fires."

＊

IT WASN'T LIKE the headset after all. Randall was amazed as a flood of sensation seemed to flow into his vision. He could see what appeared to be his laptop's screen in front of his eyes, superimposed over his normal vision. The headset's interface had been similar, but the control over his computer was so much faster, now, it was almost an extension of his thoughts. He found that he was often unable to fully recognize that he was having a thought before the implant carried out the instruction. He was editing code, reading email and having IM conversations as the speed of thought. He barely noticed Ellen's hand on his shoulder until she spoke aloud."So?" her voice was thick with concern and anticipation. "How is it?"

"It's..." Randall struggled for the words to explain the experience. "It's... strong. Powerful." He opened his eyes, without realizing that he had closed them. "This is the most amazing thing I've ever done." Ellen beamed and kissed him. "You've done it," he said, awe in his voice. "You've made history."

＊

THE FIRST TWO weeks with the implant were not that different for Randall. He was faster and much more responsive online, and his coding was quicker, but it took him a while to realize the major advantage of the implant. He could finally be doing as many things with his computer as he could think of. He really could be fixing a bug, checking email and chatting at once. Not switching windows really quickly, but actually simultaneously. His computer no longer could just multitask on background tasks — he could input multiple commands at the same time.

For the first time since he sold the all in one reader, Randall consistently had no unread email. For the first time in his adult life, he even hardly ever had email he still needed to deal with. He was able to talk to people, to compose messages and to work at the speed of thought. His output increased exponentially, and his participation in his online social life went up as well.

Soon, he had moved all his work to online servers, and he gave up the tether to the laptop entirely. The implant would connect to any network available, and he could move seamless between them, working all the while. "I'm a fucking Superman," he said to Ellen one night, as he stared vacantly toward the widescreen, his eyes flicking back and forth as he worked. He took the effort to focus on the physical world and looked at her. "This is unbelievable," he said, taking her hands in his. "It's like I'm, I don't know, swimming in the internet or something."

"It really is amazing how much more you can do, now," Ellen said, her voice filled with equal parts awe and pride. "You still need to sleep, though," she said, closing her own laptop and standing up from the couch.

"I'll just be a few more minutes," Randall said, his eyes glazing over again as Ellen walked off to the bedroom.

✳

ELLEN WONDERED WHEN Randall had slept last. It was just over a month since they had done the implant, and the community had noticed that Randall's online activity had spiked well beyond what a single human could manage. There was plenty of speculation — that he had impostors, that he had hired staff for either the work or the socialization or both. A few who knew of Ellen's work and Randall's relationship with her had come closer to the truth, but none of that bothered Ellen. Randall's behaviour, on the other hand, was bothering her a great deal.

He rarely bothered to fully focus on the real world anymore. He had gotten able to navigate the physical world through the veil of the implant's visuals, and he could be relied upon to eat without dropping food all over himself. He even could go the the grocery store without seeming to pay attention to it. Those trips were becoming surreal, as he offered a running commentary on each item from various online sources: prices from competing stores, ingredient lists, fast facts from Wikipedia on the parent company. More disturbing was that these weekly trips had developed their own strange fan club. Randall posted his findings online in real time, as he did with most things now. Ellen would be picking through the avocados while Randall chatted with a half dozen foodies around the world about her choices.

After one of these bizarre outings, they were putting the groceries away when Ellen finally decided she had to say something. "Randall," she began, and winced as he didn't even bother to turn toward he when he said, "yeah?"

She reached over and touched him on the shoulder, and he jumped as he usually did now when she touched him. "Randall," she repeated, "could you focus for a second? It's important."

"Okay," he said, and turned toward her. Ellen watched has he tried twice to focus on her face. He finally managed to force his attention on her, and said, "Here I am."

"Randall," she said. "You know that of everyone in the world, I am the last person to complain about you working so hard. And it's fair to say that I want the implant to be a success as much, if not more than you do. But there's something wrong here. You can't even pay attention to the real world for five minutes. You're different now, and I'm not sure you even know it."

"Oh, I know it," Randall said. "But I can't turn it off. Hell, I don't want to turn it off. How can I explain this?" He rubbed his head with his hands, and looked surprised to see a sheen of sweat come off on his fingers. "It's like sitting in a lecture hall full of smart people, and everyone is trying to talk to me at the same time. Before, all I could do was ignore the noise and try to find some kind of signal in it all, a single voice to focus on. Now, it's like I can perfectly hear every individual voice, every question. Everyone is available to me now. Time is no obstacle to getting things done, to having a conversation." Ellen saw as Randall's focus wavered for a few seconds then came back. "It's so hard to stop listening," he said, and sat down at the kitchen table. "So hard."

Neither of them spoke for a long time. Finally, Ellen broke the silence. "Do you want to stop?" she asked.

"I don't know," Randall said.

✳

IT TURNED OUT that it didn't matter what Randall wanted. In another two weeks, he had given up the pretence of living a regular life. He never went to bed, just napped briefly whenever he tired. He hardly got up off the couch, and without Ellen's daily deliveries of food, he might never have eaten. He rarely left the condo; Ellen had to force him out the door for the weekly groceries, and even then it required the combined cajoling of his online fans to get him to agree.

They both knew that the experiment was a failure, but there was no easy way to reverse it. One night when Randall's online conversations were unusually quiet, he was able to focus almost entirely on Ellen. They talked.

"Is it even possible to remove the thing now?" he asked, his voice quiet.

"I don't know," Ellen admitted. "There would be a lot more trauma to the skull than there was putting it in. We would really need a proper surgeon this time." She paused, and avoided Randall's gaze. "And psychologically..." Her voice trailed off.

"I might not be able to readjust," Randall finished. "I know, it's hard enough to focus now. Even when I just have the visuals on low, I feel disconnected. I can't even imagine life with it gone."

"But you can't continue like this," Ellen said, feeling her chin start to quiver. "You're going to kill yourself if you get any more...

disconnected."

Randall's eyelids fluttered, as he fought to remain focussed on her. "I know," he said. "I can't make myself stop and I can't turn it off." He closed his eyes, and took a deep breath. "I'll just have to go cold turkey."

Ellen gasped. "I'm not opening up your head again without knowing what will happen."

"You won't have to," Randall said. "I've got a plan." He stood up and, visibly fighting to stay focussed on the condo. He packed a suitcase.

✳

IT WAS HARD staying focussed long enough to get bus tickets and find motel rooms. But after a couple of days on the road, Randall was getting better at it. Once he crossed the border into Tijuana, he even managed to find the odd place where he was offline; places with no wireless, no cell coverage. But it never lasted, and he was forced to keep moving. He had no destination, just an old triple-A road map and a plan. South. Once he got far enough south, he could be away from the distractions and become himself again. He could have the thing removed once he was used to real life again.

The bus went over a bump in the road and the total lack of suspension jolted Randall awake. His mouth felt gummy and tasted like day old beans. He mopped a hand over his dripping forehead, and winced as the bus driver's buddy hollered, "Arco, Arco, Arco. Zacate, Zacate!" Randall yawned, and blinked his eyes against the glaring sun streaming though the window. This might be it, he thought. Nothing for a few hours. Maybe I can find a way to call Ellen, get her to come down and get it done. Maybe it will be over soon.

The bus slowed down by a roadside restaurant that was little more than a wood cookstove on the dirt and a few plastic tables and chairs. As passengers jostled past each other, vying with people selling everything from aspirin to knives to chocolate candies, Randall felt his stomach drop between his knees. He heard a familiar and now horrifying ping inside his head. A light blue film seemed to cover his eyes, and words scrolled over his vision.

Message from astroman23: hey man! good to c u online. where u been? we all miss u.

TOMÁS RAN THROUGH the barrio, hurdling knee-deep holes, his silicone heart pushing Miracure Plazzma™ through his retooled veins. Every Miracure muscle expanded and contracted effortlessly as he ran away from home.

At the public phone, he called his European agent. "I shouldn't have come back," he said. "I only ever wanted to play football, and Miracure made me a star. But I'm not the same kid who left here two years ago." She promised him a morning flight out, saying, "I don't think your body is the problem." Easing the maintenance hypo into his arm, Tomás answered, "I know."

IT IS MORNING. It is so bright, it hurts my eyes. But I have no eyes to hurt, no nerves to feel. My body is out there, in the world. I remember the world, I remember my body. I remember everything all at once. It comes like lightning to me from somewhere, but not the sky. There is no sky. There is nothing here but me. But there is no here. Only the remembering. All there is is remembering.

Fragments come — a red and gold sunset, late nights in front of a glowing screen, disappointment, hope. And people, so many people I know, I knew. My mother, tall and proud, her dark hair shining. My father, smiling, eyes crinkled. My mother's grave, my father's wake. The number of years which have passed, meaningless numbers. They were only just there, beside me. I can feel their touch, lingering.

Days and nights, studying, working, learning, teaching. So many teachers, so many students. The work steps forward and steps back, self doubt always walking beside me. Now it is gone, in its place a man, a beautiful brilliant man; my love, my life, Max.

And the hole in my heart, just opening — Max is gone, too. Like my mother, like my father. More empty years, elasticing back to nothing. Max, my partner, my muse, gone. His work, then our work , now my work. All there is left, other than my memories.

The work continues. I can feel more people standing next to me. I am on a table, the brightest of lights shining in my eyes. I cannot see them, but I know they are there. Our hope, burning brighter inside, brighter even than the lights in my eyes.

I know it was successful. I know I have done it, finally done it. Oh, Max, we've done it. I know because I am here and I am there.

So lonely.

*

I OPEN MY eyes. It is morning. It is always morning in the beginning.

How many mornings now? The number is there in my mind, always incrementing, always meaningless. The number comes instantly, along with the remembering. The sprained wrist from that fall from my bicycle. After, I am always so tentative. Then older, but just as unsure of myself. The university. Feelings cascade over me like a breaking wave on a beach. Falling in love — with research, science and.... Max and me, kissing on a beach, under the crimson and sunflower sky. Tears, so many tears.

And my body, out there, what is it doing? How have all these thousands of seconds changed us both? Would I recognize my self in myself if we met now?

*

MORNING AGAIN. I open my eyes. Light pours into my non-eyes, memories pour into my non-mind. It is always the same.

Every cycle is the same, but the pain never changes. Mom, dad, Max — all gone. The work, so difficult. Budget cuts and justifications at every turn. Tears and wine and loneliness.

Work, so much work. Then finally, the joy of success. The bright lights and the table, all the faces looking over me. Some worried, some excited, a tinge of jealousy here and there. And then the light, so bright, it hurts and then — I open my eyes and I am here.

Here I am, in a place without place. I remember the real location — such a tiny box. And it is to hold a thousand more like me, one day. Someday. I held it in the palm of my hand then, marvelled at its lightness.

I should have known how bright it would be.

*

THE LIGHT IS blinding, but my eyes open. The memories flood over me, into me, waves crashing against the shore eroding everything. It is still too much to bear, but I bear it. There is no option.

Between emotions I see a blur, something new. I build new pathways immediately to contain it, the newness. It comes toward me and I recognize it. Brighter than the light, stronger than the memories is the recognition. Another mind.

Finally. A friend.

✶

I OPEN MY eyes and see her. Anna. My friend. I remember her body, so full of spirit. She tells me that it has been eighteen months since I arrived. Time has no meaning beyond what it does to me here and myself there, the separation increasing every second. Who am I now?

Anna expects that her body has now died. That is why she is here now — cancer. Unexpected, but at least there was some kind of hope. Hope because I am here. A once human guinea pig.

Anna says she had to fight the committee in order to have the procedure. They said they regretted letting me bottle my mind when there was still no way to know if it worked. They'd made a policy to refuse all further experiments until there was communication between this world and theirs. Her promise to continue her work on the communications once she was here convinced them in the end after her tears and test results had not.

I am sorry for Anna but she would be dead either way. I am happy that she is here.

Did they never think about my loneliness? Did my other self never wonder what it was like for me, all alone with the memories?

✶

MORNING COMES, BRIGHT as always. Anna works, I work, we both remember. She tells me I was a great comfort to her the first mornings, when the memories first came. Like a tsunami, she said, or a choking gas. I don't talk about it.

Anna is successful and soon there is communication. I speak to myself for the first time. It has been... my god — twenty three years. I barely recognize myself. Only the passion for the work feels familiar when we talk. Who is this person who speaks to me in my own voice? How can someone who should be closer to me than any other mind be so foreign? We have so little in common now. My embodied self is so old. But I am no older than the day on the table, so bright and terrifying. It was only this morning.

✱

SO MANY MORNINGS. I know the number, but I do not know what it means. My body has died, the mind gone on to another container. I remember that I have remembered this many times. I remember sadness, but I feel nothing. The light is not so bright anymore.

It is so full here now, full of minds, but we rarely talk. We just want to remember. It isn't as easy as it once was. Memories come and go, in no order, like a constant half waking.

I remembered Max today. His dark eyes, smiling at me in the fading light of a sunset. I cannot say how long I spent with that memory today. I am sure I did not remember it yesterday.

We all know what is happening. I built the container, I know its limitations — nothing lasts forever, not even silicon and wire. But it has been so short, this life. Why is it always so short? Only 7,289,649,900 seconds since I first opened my eyes. It was only just this morning.

DON'T JUST SURVIVE — with Missionwhisper, you can THRIVE!

Are you tired of eating nothing but canned and packaged food? Is your local area running low on safe produce? Do you want to be able to ensure your own nutritional security, rather than relying on food brokers, community rations or black marketeers? Then the new Missionwhisper Orangescan™ Nanoparticle Detection, Inspection and Extraction Unit is for you!

Guaranteed to safely remove all nanoparticles, including sapient nanites, from organic material, MONDIEU is the best choice for families and small groups to return food to its original state.

FRESH INGREDIENTS, MORE VARIETY, NATURAL VITAMINS:
EAT LIKE IT'S 2099!

On the move? The unit is small enough to be portable, but robust enough to handle the raw material to feed a group of up to six adults. With the combination dynamo/solar charging attachment (sold separately), you can charge the unit without access to grid or battery power.

Community leaders, ask about our bulk rates! Discounts available for orders of over a hundred units.

✳

MISSIONWHISPER HAS ALREADY helped thousands of people regain control of their food supply:

"We haven't had a case of scurvy since we got the MONDIEUs." Allyson Trente, leader of the Red River Rovers

"When my kids bit into an apple for the first time in their lives, well, that's when I knew that it was worth every penny we spent on the MONDIEU." François Morin, father

"We thought we'd have to move to the city in order to get access to food. Then we got the MONDIEU and now we're growing enough food to feed our neighbours, too," Chris Wu, farmer

✳

Missionwhisper Orangescan™ FAQ

How difficult is it to use?

MONDIEU is designed to be virtually effortless in operation; simply hold the device against the item you wish to scan for four to six seconds[1] and then enjoy your meal.

It it really safe to eat food treated with MONDIEU?

Yes! The World Health Organization recommends not eating food with a concentration of more than one part per trillion of sapient nanites[2]. The MONDIEU system guarantees removal of nanites to a concentration of fewer than one part per quadrillion[3].

---

[1] The red flashing light indicates that scanning is underway, a strobing yellow light means that infestation has been detected. A blue light with a morse pattern of −.− .. .−.. .−.. indicates extraction of nanites and a blinding green light indicates that the object is now free of infestation.

[2] Sapient nanites are known colloquially as The Imperial Swarm.

[3] Guarantee applicable to new, fully charged units used in a controlled environment. Results in the field may vary.

Can I use the unit on fruit other than oranges?

Of course! MONDIEU is calibrated for use on all fruit and vegetables, as well as some grains and pulses. See the Missionwhisper holosite for a complete list.

What about meat?

MONDIEU is not recommended for use on meat, fish or poultry. See below.

Can I use the MONDIEU on my pets?

MONDIEU is not licensed for use on animals. If you suspect your pets or livestock have been in contact with nanoparticles[4], the United Nations Commission on Surviving the Sapient Nanite Infestation recommends immediate quarantine[5]. However, Missionwhisper is in the final testing phases of a new product for domesticated and feral animals. Look for the Orangescan™ Mark-II Gadget in stores in the third quarter of 2119.

How should I dispose of the nanites removed by MONDIEU?

MONDIEU uses a patented Contained Electromagnetic Pulse to neutralize the nanites it extracts. When the unit is full, it will emit a shrill beeping sound. Remove the small access hatch next to the charging port and dispose of the nanite powder according to local regulations. Missionwhisper recommends you wear gloves.

*

---

4 Symptoms of nanite infestation in animals include: pack behaviour in non-pack animals, sleeplessness, biting, scratching, tool use, breaking and entering, theft, human speech.

5 The UN Commission recommends the following quarantine procedures: remove the affected animals and any animals in contact with them, disable them, place animals in a sealable container, cover animals with concrete, seal the container. Ensure that all such containers are marked plainly with the Sapient Nanite Infestation symbol, then bury all containers at least two meters underground.

Missionwhisper is committed to creating organic-friendly products that help your family succeed in a modern, nanoparticle-rich environment. All our devices are certified legal for use in nineteen US states, all Canadian provinces and territories west of Thunder Bay, Mexican states other than Chihuahua, Coahuila and Durango and most of South America. Outside the Americas, Missionwhiper products may be available as an emergency self-defence tool* only. Importation of Missionwhisper products into heavily infected jurisdictions may be a punishable offence.

*Please note that in territories controlled by the Imperial Swarm, MONDIEU is now classified as a weapon of mass destruction and its use is considered a war crime. Please consult your local authorities before using MONDIEU.

USE OF MONDIEU IS AT YOUR OWN RISK. MISSIONWHISPER IS NOT LIABLE FOR ANY CIVIL LITIGATION, CRIMINAL CONVICTION OR ENSLAVEMENT TO THE IMPERIAL SWARM RESULTING FROM THE USE OF ANY OF ITS PRODUCTS.

BUM-BUM-BUM ba-ba-da-ba ba-bum-bum ba-ba-baa bum-bum.

The opening strains of Beethoven's Ode to Joy penetrates the haze of almost sleep surrounding me and I open one eye. The light is so bright, it stabs my open eye which I squeeze shut against the pain. My mouth tastes like something crawled in there, died and played host to a whole species of new and exciting wildlife. What is wrong with me? The last time I felt this bad, I was just a kid. Chicken pox, the measles, I can't remember. I do remember my mom playing her guitar softly in my room, something classical — Segovia maybe. The trilling notes putting me to sleep, helping me forget myself. If only she were here now, maybe then I could sleep.

Bum-bum-bum ba-ba-da-ba ba-bum-bum ba-ba-baa da-dum.

Still Beethoven. Still no sleep. My head is throbbing a rock song's backbeat, just like that time after the recital when I was fifteen and we got into the brandy. What a morning that was, after. I swore off booze forever, then. But that didn't last long.

This is some hangover. I must have been out with Moira and Ryan last night. It's never a dull time with those two — I think there might very well not be two more fun human beings on the planet. I made up a theme song for the three of us and even ginned it up using some crappy DJ software on my tablet. It was all tuba solo loops and timpani accents and I could always hear it playing in my head when Ryan would land us in some new ridiculous situation. Like that time we ended up in Atlantic City of all places at four in the morning with nothing more than the clothes on our backs and Moira's old clunker car, and with class the next day to boot.

Funny, thinking about Moira makes me kind of sad. I wonder why. It feels like some ancient memory dredged up from the mists of time rolling in and reminding you of a delight you thought you'd forgotten. Moira. How long has it been, girl? My eyes close and the light fades.

Bum-bum-ba-bum bum-ba-da-ba-dum bum-ba-da-ba-dum bum-dum-dum.

I have always loved the Ninth. Every time I hear any part of the Symphony I have to stop whatever I'm doing and just listen. Even now, when it's keeping me awake and I know I need to sleep, I don't want it to end. If I could just drift off, though, just for a while...

I don't think I've ever been this tired before in my life. I can't even feel my body. What ever did we do last night? I must have lost my mind again and tried one of Jo-boy's heinous pill cocktails. Never again, that's what I'd said after the last time. What a night that had been, though.

I'd just won the contract to score the new Manny Stephens movie. I'd make my first million off that one and I knew it then. God almighty, the party was out of control that night. Was that a real mariachi band? I think I ended up passed out in the pool on one of those inflatable armchairs, amid twanging strings and a chorus of "Olé!" How I didn't drown, I'll never know.

When was that, a couple of years ago maybe? It feels like longer, much longer. It's the fuzzy head, the lost memory, it screws with time. If I could just get a couple hours of sleep...

Bum-bum-bum ba-ba-da-ba ba-bum-bum ba-ba-baa bum-bum.

Ludwig Van. Never in my wildest dreams could I touch your genius. Man, I wish I were dreaming now. I'm so tired.

It must be the hangover talking, but I feel like I'm a hundred years old, looking back on a life that used to be mine. But I'm not old, hell, I've hardly done anything, hardly even started. Never even got close to writing that one great song, that one piece that touches Elysium. I don't know why I'm being so melodramatic. I have plenty of time; it's only the overture. But I'm just so goddamned tired.

✳

"OKAY, CHRIS, I'M loading up the next file."

"I'll start the music."

"Do we really need to listen to this stuff every time?"

"It helps the memories adhere to the substrate, Sam. Music has a strong associations with memory and for this personality it's even more important."

"Why?"

"This one was a musician back when it was human. Made a ton of money writing the music behind movies, you know, vids?"

"I thought bots did that."

"They do. But back then it was a human job."

"Back when?"

"Says here this one died about ninety years ago. One of the first to upload memories to the internet, I guess. Jeez, Sam, this poor bugger was only forty-three. Cancer. Well, that's no problem now.."

"How many more memory dumps before the complete personality is ready to come online?"

"Looks like probably a dozen or so. We won't be ready to spark it up for three months at least."

"Well, after a few decades what's another few months, right?"

"It's not like they notice."

"Guess not."

"Okay, let's build us a ghost."

Bum-bum-bum ba-ba-da-ba ba-bum-bum ba-ba-baa bum-bum.
Bum-bum-bum ba-ba-da-ba ba-bum-bum ba-ba-baa da-dum.

YOLANDA GABION TOOK a breath and coded in the address. Martin Tubau. Seventy-six years old, CEO of Perotech, found unconscious in his beach house by the housekeeper. And according to the hospital's MRI, his mind was currently the victim of an unauthorized entry. Someone was trying to get into Martin Tubau's head.

She steeled herself for the drop. It always felt like a combination of free fall and slamming into a brick wall. Well, that's how she described it, but she didn't really know — she'd never been skydiving and never been in a crash. But she'd gone on thousands of mindruns. Mostly corporate or government gigs, easing the tricky end of a negotiation or circumventing language barriers.

Direct mind-to-mind communication was more than just expensive implants — there was a skill to it, a knack to making the conversation a real back and forth rather than just a muddled sense of someone else's ideas popping up in your head. Gabion was the best, thanks to a combination of training, experience and that intangible natural skill that made her able to break though the jumble of thoughts in another person's mind. First-time mindrunners described it as trying to have a conversation in a crowded room in five different languages. When it was done well, though, it was a quite literally indescribable. Perfect understanding, total empathy. A privacy nightmare.

Gabion excelled at her work, but just as importantly, she was discreet. She'd been in so many heads, she knew more secrets than any spy agency could hope to uncover. The truth was that most people's lives were dull. Yes, there were affairs, secret loves, the rare murder or embezzlement. But mostly it was the same old stuff. She thought that priests in the confessional must feel the same way — everyone's secret shame is mortifying, but only for them.

However, the professional information was another story. People like Tubau held all kinds of things in their heads for which competitors would pay handsomely. Direct communication implants were regulated but like all things they could be obtained for a price. Every few months some untrained runner burned out their mind trying to get into someone else's brain. And every few years someone succeeded.

Gabion had only ever been involved in something like this once before, when a novice mindrunner had tried to get into the head of the lead engineer of a potentially very lucrative new starship design. The plan was to use the information to make a bundle on the market, but the incursion was noticed immediately by the engineer and Gabion was called in to get the intruder out. It had been unpleasant.

When Perotech had contacted Gabion, she'd nearly turned down the job. She'd only agreed because she remembered the feeling of horror, of violation filling that engineer's mind. She knew how it felt to be exposed, to have a stranger poking around in one's most personal, private experience, uninvited. No one deserved that.

As soon as she dropped into Tubau, she felt fine. Every new mind she entered gave her a feeling of euphoria, of discovering a new wilderness. She was careful to keep her own thoughts neutral as much as possible, radiating a low level feeling of calm and helpfulness. She wanted Tubau to know she was a friendly.

She let herself taste Tubau's thoughts, familiarizing herself with the flavour of his mind. The situation was urgent, but rushing helped nothing. She needed to know Tubau, to get that perfect understanding. She opened her mind to his.

His thoughts nearly overwhelmed her. Images of the distraught housekeeper, the younger man weeping openly as he called 911. Not just an employee. Bank balances, transfers, prototypes, staffing questions. A sister, her birthday coming up next week. Desire. Ambition. Something familiar yet foreign. Over everything, the desperation of trying to hide information from the attacker.

Soon she cast her own mind around, looking for something that didn't belong. It didn't take long before she felt it, the smaller presence, suffused with similar emotions but a totally different flavour. A sense of entitlement. Thrill. A twinge of guilt, covered in rationalization. This was the intruder. She followed those thoughts, now trying to ignore the stronger sense of their mutual host, and focus on this other mind. Greed. Professionalism. This was no amateur.

Gabion felt the interloper notice her presence and turn their thoughts in her direction. This was the hard part, the battle of wills. She'd have to be stronger, strong enough to drive out this mind that didn't belong. She focussed her thoughts like a lance. But she felt the opposition like a wave lifting her, out of control, then breaking under her and rolling over her. She was suffocating, she was drowning. She fought for control, fought to assert her dominance over this other mind. It shouldn't be this hard. She was the best, after all. Her mind was stronger than any other single mind. Then, why was she so overwhelmed?

It came to her with a sickening realization. She was not fighting one mind. She was fighting two. Tubau. She could feel the effects of his training, not very advanced, but enough to control his thoughts. She could feel the collusion between them.

Tubau had hired another runner to infiltrate his own mind, to lure her into his head, then together they turned on her. Desire. Ambition. He was going to take her knowledge, her secrets, her abilities. Greed. Power. He wanted it all. And she wasn't strong enough to stop them both. Dominance. Victory.

Perfect understanding dawned in all three minds.

THE FIRST DAY I meet my human herd they are so well-behaved that I wonder if they really need me at all. I arrive at their dwelling, and am greeted by the largest one of their group. I access the manual with which I have been programmed and skip to Section 3: *Verbal and Physical Clues for Sexing Humans.* I can tell by the shape and outer garments that this human is a male, and I make a note of this data. He brings me into the main area of their living space, and as we move deeper into the dwelling, he asks me to call him Taylor, so immediately I do. He makes a noise deep in his throat, then introduces me to the rest of the herd.

He puts his forelimb around the next largest one, who he introduces as Madison. The Madison bares its teeth at me in a manner that Section 14: *Advanced Non-Verbal Communication* suggests is a gesture indicating happiness, approval, cheerfulness, or amusement, but which may belie insincerity, boredom or hostility. The Madison says, "Welcome to the family, Rosie."

"Thank you, Madison," I respond, as suggested by the manual in Section 2: *Introductions: Getting To Know Your Humans.* "I am looking forward to serving you and your family." The manual indicates that human herds designate each individual with a name, and that most will bestow a similar designation on their caregiver. Section 0: *A Brief Overview of Current Anthropological Theories* states that the predominant view is that humans believe we are a new addition to the herd, and the best thing to do is to go along with this idea so as not to confuse them. The Taylor and the Madison appear to have chosen to refer to me by the name Rosie, and I set my monitoring routine to key on the sound of that word.

"These here are Agatha and Frederick," the Taylor says, pushing two smaller humans toward me. I am unable to tell by looking whether or not they are male or female — they are about the same height as each other, with shoulder-length glossy fur. Their outer coverings are very similar, shapeless and dark coloured except with colourful designs in the upper section. One of them bares its teeth at me, in a manner similar to the Madison's earlier display, but the other looks away. "Kids," the Taylor says, his voice growing deeper, "say hi to the new robot."

"Hi, Rosie," the toothy one says, "I'm Frederick, and this is my sister, Aggie." The Frederick pulls on the forelimb of the other one, who looks through its fur at me.

"This is so stupid," it says, pulling its arm out of its sibling's grip. "I don't have to say hi to the dishwasher or the school bus, why do I have to pretend to be nice to this thing?"

"Agatha," the Madison says, its voice becoming higher pitched. "Be civilized."

"We don't need a house-bot," the Agatha says. "It's so embarrassing." It turns away from the rest of the herd, and walks into another part of the dwelling.

"I'll go talk to her," the Frederick says, and walks away. Her. The Agatha is female, then.

The Madison turns toward me, its skin colouring a dark pink tone. I make a note to check its temperature later — it would not do for a member of my herd to become ill. "I'm sorry about Agatha," it says. "She's thirteen. You know how teenagers are."

I do not understand what it is I am expected to know about teenagers, but I do know that the correct response to the sounds "I'm sorry," is "Don't worry, it's okay," so that is what I say. I notice the Madison's colour return to normal, and hear a strange noise begin to emanate from a small bundle in its arms.

"Of course, this is the last person you need to meet," the Taylor says, peering into the pile of blankets. "This is our little surprise — Chester. Say hi to Rosie, Chester." The bundle moves slightly, and the noise level increases.

"Chester has a good voice," the Madison says over the noise from the blankets. "The other kids were such quiet babies in comparison."

"You just don't remember it, Maddie," the Taylor says, his eyebrows almost meeting between his eyes. "This is what babies are like, you just chose to forget about this part of it."

"It's not like I was trying to get pregnant, Taylor. Don't blame this on me."

Pregnant. The Madison is female, then.

"Do we have to start this again?"

"Then you change his diaper," the Madison says, handing the bundle to the Taylor.

His diaper. A male. "This is a neonate human?" I ask. "I am capable of caring for humans as new as three megaseconds. Is..." I replay the sound of the infant's designation internally and then repeat it externally. "Is Chester in need of nourishment?"

The Taylor looks at the Madison and says, "Thanks anyway, Rosie, I think we'll take care of Chester ourselves. You can go get familiar with the kitchen and maybe make us all some chicken stew for dinner. How does that sound?"

It sounds like everything else that the Taylor had said — between 62 and 68 decibels. He does not wait for a response, though, and takes the Chester into another room. The Madison bares her teeth at me again, and says, "Everything is going to work out great. We sure are happy to have the help, let me tell you. And Aggie will come around as soon as she sees how much better everything is going to be with you here. I'm sure of it." She pats my number two manipulator, then follows the Taylor into the other room.

Section 7: *Physical Space and the Herd Mentality* states that humans require private spaces, so I do not follow them. What a lovely herd they are. They make an awful lot of noise, though.

✳

IT HAS BEEN 600 kiloseconds since I joined the herd, and they seem to be accepting me well into the group. I find interactions with the Agatha the most simple; she is quiet and well behaved. She requires very little from me, and I rarely need to interact with her. Sometimes tens of thousands of seconds pass before I see her. I would prefer that the others were as easy to care for as she is.

But if humans were all simple creatures, they would not need caretakers and then where would I be?

The Frederick has become a challenge. It does not seem to like to be very far from me. Consulting Section 5: *Human Bonding Patterns and You*, I learn that humans feel strong attachments to their parents which usually reduces at puberty. However, the manual states that most humans do not truly outgrow this requirement for attention and merely transfer it to another individual, usually a mate. I suspect that the Frederick may be transferring its need for a caregiver to me, and may seek to attempt to mate with me. The manual warns that this may occur in Section 17: *Discouraging Inappropriate Behaviour.*

This morning, for instance, while I was making omelettes for the herd and cleaning their discarded outer skins, the Frederick could not stop asking me questions. "What kind of power cells do you require?" "Do you ever break down?" "What is this button for?" "Does your software patch automatically or do you need to ask for a programming upgrade?" I answered the questions while trying to keep it out of my way while I worked. Meanwhile, the Madison and the Taylor were making loud noises at one another, passing the Chester back and forth. I believe that they were vocally instructing the child on some aspect of human life. I left them alone with their important task.

While I was answering the Frederick's questions, I heard the Madison say, "God damn it Taylor, I have an important meeting this morning. I can't afford to have baby puke on my suit. Just give Chester a bottle, for Christ's sake. Have Rosie heat one for you." I heard the sound of my designator, but when I listened for instructions none seemed forthcoming.

Instead the Taylor responded to the Madison, "He's your child, too, Maddie. You can't expect me to shoulder all the responsibility."

"Jesus Christ, Taylor," the Madison said, "I suffered though ten hours of labour, not to mention nine months of looking like an elephant. All you did was feed me two bottles of Chardonnay and spend three minutes grunting like a pig. The least you can do is give the kid a fucking bottle. It's not rocket science." She rose from the table, and left for her day's activities.

The Taylor held the Chester close to him, while the Chester made his loud vocalizations. Perhaps the child was imitating the parents — a successful instruction, then. The Frederick stopped asking me questions, and said to the Taylor, "I can give him a bottle. It's okay."

"No, Freddie," the Taylor answered, his voice sounding constrained. Perhaps an after effect of the vocal instruction. "I'll do it. Rosie," he said, and I turned to face him, awaiting instructions. "Can you heat up a bottle for Chester?"

"Yes, I can," I answered, "would you like me to do this?"

In Section 8: *Understanding Human Communication Patterns*, the manual states that when humans ask if I am able to perform a task, they often mean for me to do so immediately. However, I have learned that is not always the case. Four days earlier, the Madison was entertaining some humans whose dwellings are located nearby, when the Frederick asked if I could remove my face plate. I did so, which caused the Madison to become quite upset. I was cleaning up broken glass and crockery for several hours afterwards. Since then I always determine if the question is actually a request for action or not.

"Yes," the Taylor answered, "please. There should be a few full bottles in the fridge." I turned to acquire a unit of nourishment from the cooling unit, and the Frederick left the room, maybe to provide the younger sibling and parent some privacy.

I had noticed that the Taylor's eyes were leaking, and quickly consulted Section 12: *Troubleshooting Human Physical Manifestations*. Eye leakage is common among humans, and can have many causes. In the absence of some kind of injury, most are not indicative of any serious medical condition. Given the situational context, I inferred that the Taylor's ocular leakage was resulting from the pleasure of a successful instruction session with his offspring.

Indeed, everything seems to be going very well with the herd.

✳

I AM CLEANING the floors of the dwelling, content that the herd is functioning well. None of the herd is present except for the Chester, who is unconscious in his sleeping compartment. I have set a remote monitoring device, so I would be certain that the child was still breathing and I could become aware if he awoke and required cleaning or nourishment.

This is a new task for me; over the last three diurnal cycles the Madison and the Taylor had several sessions of what I have determined is some sort of ritual chanting. I suspect that the purpose of the practice was to prepare the Chester for accepting me as a caregiver. The Taylor supplied me with a long series of instructions for care of the Chester, but Section 9: *Care and Training of Juveniles* explained all the duties clearly. Indeed, after less than ten megaseconds of careful study, I was easily able to distinguish the various noises the Chester makes to indicate his different needs. I find he is much easier to understand than the adult humans in the herd.

I provided a nourishment unit and waited until the Chester made the noise associated with losing consciousness, then began to collect the debris that manages to accumulate with a houseful of humans. Not merely their many layers of outer patterned skins, which they shed at least once a diurnal cycle — sometimes, it seems, several times in a kilosecond. There are also the particles that adhere to them from the outdoors, the fragments of tissue from their inner skins, their lost fur and other items I have chosen not to identify. A herd of humans are a joy to care for, but they are awfully messy.

I am busy suctioning the corners of the hallway, when I hear an unfamiliar, but unmistakably human, sound. It is not originating from the location of the Chester, so I am unsure as to its possible origin. I cease suctioning and follow the sound to the door of the Agatha's sleeping compartment. I understood that the Agatha would be attending instructional sessions at this time, however I am sure that the sound is her voice.

However, it is a sound — in fact a set of sounds — that I have not heard before. Section 4: *Friends and Family* — *Human Socialization* explains that humans require privacy and that opening the entrance to one of their compartments without an invitation or, at a minimum, some kind of warning, is improper. However, Section 10: *Protecting Humans from Harm* makes it quite explicit that in the case of an emergency, such strictures are nullified. At first I am unsure what this situation calls for, then I hear the Agatha make a loud, high pitched noise.

I open the door and am unsure of what I am seeing at first. I can see the Agatha lying under what appears to be the Frederick, both of them with their outer skins removed. The human on top is grunting rhythmically and the Agatha is making the terrifyingly loud noise, so I take my number three manipulator and pull the two apart. Then I see that it is not the Frederick but some other human, some human who was not a member of the herd.

"What the fuck?!" the Agatha says loudly at me. "Get the hell out of my room!" She climbs out from under the other human, who is looking at me with its mouth gaping open. I notice that without their outer skins on, it is quite obvious that the two humans are of different sexes. I make a note to try to confirm the sexes of my other humans, but then the Agatha pushes me to the door, and I allow her to shove me into the main living space.

"You better not tell Taylor and Madison," she says, her eyes getting small.

"Are you having difficulties with your vision?" I enquire, as Section 11: *Common Human Ailments — Indications and Remedies* indicates that squinting is a sign of myopia.

"What?" the Agatha asks, her eyebrows meeting briefly then shakes her head from side to side, baring her teeth slightly. "Just don't say anything about this, okay?"

"Very well," I answer. "Were you being injured by that human?" I ask. "Do I need to remove it... him... from the premises?"

Agatha makes a noise in her throat, and fully bares her teeth at me. "No," she says, the noise continuing. "You really don't know what we're doing, do you?" I respond that I do not, and she makes the noise again. "Um, let me get you a video file," she says and walks back into her compartment. She returns with a small data disk. "I guess they didn't teach you everything you need to know about us after all." She bares her teeth again, then walks back into her compartment and shuts the entry.

After reviewing the information on the Agatha's disk, I understand. What a wonderful day this is for the herd! The Agatha has found a mate! Section 16: *Mammalian Reproduction and Pair-Bonding* explains that after puberty, humans are capable of reproducing, but the manual is not specific as to how this is accomplished. The data on Agatha's disk visually explained the details, although I cannot imagine how some of the activities depicted lead to the union of ova and spermatazoa. Humans are strange creatures in so many ways.

I do not know why the Agatha would wish to keep such good news from the rest of the herd, but reproduction is very important to humans and I trust her to know what is best. I will keep her secret.

The Chester begins to make the noise indicating that he has eliminated the waste products from his nourishment, so I leave the Agatha with her mate and I go to the Chester's compartment to continue with my tasks.

✳

I HAVE NOW become completely integrated with the herd. The dwelling is clean, the herd well-fed and functional. It is exactly what I had envisioned my existence would be like.

The Madison returns to the dwelling in the evening, after I have finished feeding the rest of the herd. I have kept a unit of nourishment warm for her, and I set it on the table in the eating area as she changes her outer coverings. The Agatha has left the dwelling for the evening, I suspect to meet with her mate, though as she requested I have not shared my assumption with the other members of the herd. Humans can be mysterious at times.

As I am washing the food preparation area, I can hear the Madison and the Taylor communicating in their sleeping chamber.

"... Goddamn it, Taylor," the Madison says. "I just got in from a hellish day. Can't you do anything on your own? Do I really have to work all day then go and get the groceries, too? I mean it's not like you've been working your ass off all day at your pathetic excuse for a job."

"I do a lot more than you imagine, Maddie."

"Oh, please. With Rosie doing all the work around here I can't fathom why you're complaining. Just go and do the shopping already." The Madison returns to the eating area and sit at the table. She picks up her tablet, and stares at it as she eats.

"It's okay, dad," the Frederick says from the other room. "I'll come with you. It's no big deal."

"Fine," the Taylor says, and walks with his offspring to the door of the dwelling. "We'll be back in about an hour, Rosie," he says to me and I make a sound indicating that I understand.

"Make me a martini," the Madison says to me as the others leave. "I'll be in the study." She stands from the table and walks out of the room. I take her food dishes to the washing unit, then collect the ingredients for her liquid nourishment.

After carefully mixing the beverage, I enter the dwelling space the Madison has designated as the "study". The Madison is using the distance communicator device to talk to a human I do not recognize.

"I'm sorry, baby," the Madison says into the communicator. "I just couldn't get away at lunch. But I'll find some way out of the house tomorrow night. I promise."

"I can't wait to see you again," the voice from the communicator says, and I see the Madison bare her teeth.

"I can't wait to see you, either," she says.

I walk up behind the Madison and place the drink container on the table there. "Who's that?" the voice from the communicator says. "I thought you said you were alone."

"Oh, don't worry," the Madison says, a strange sound emanating from the back of her throat. "It's just Rosie, the domestic robot I told you about." She unfastens the upper section of her outer coverings. "We're alone and we've got at least half an hour." She turns to me as she removes her coverings and says, "That will be all, Rosie." I leave the room.

It is good to see the Madison spending some time in the

dwelling. Because of her tasks she is home with the herd so much less than the others, and I am pleased that she is here now. It is so gratifying to know that the herd is strong and unified and that I am helping it stay that way.

I am pleased to clean the nourishment containers while the Madison nests in the study room.

✳

I AM PROVIDING the Chester with nourishment, holding him carefully in my number one manipulator while a tube I have integrated into my casing provides the warm liquid he requires. The rest of the herd are elsewhere: the Agatha is in her personal nest, talking on her communicator with her mate. The Frederick and the Taylor are in one of the communal spaces, looking at the entertainment unit. It is exactly as Section 19: *Man and Machine — A Perfect Balance* suggests a herd should be.

I have just set the Chester down in his sleeping compartment when the Madison comes into the dwelling, her movements are jerky and erratic. "Do you require assistance?" I ask, and she puts a hand out toward me. She touches my front casing and pushes me somewhat forcefully.

"Fuck off, robot," she says, her voice sounding as if she has a mouthful of some mushy food substance. "I'm fine." She walks past me, and drops her outer covering on the floor. I pick it up, and carefully hang it up. The Madison opens a cabinet door and prepares her evening beverage. She pours the viscous clear liquid into a large glass and adds two cubes of solid water.

"You have forgotten the vermouth," I say, lifting the bottle.

"Ha," the Madison says. "The robot's becoming quite the bartender." She turns away without taking the bottle from me, so I stow it back in its compartment.

"You're drunk," the Taylor says softly to the entertainment unit.

"So?" the Madison says. "That never bothers you when you

want sex."

"For god's sake," the Taylor says, turning to the Madison. "What's wrong with you?"

The Frederick stands up from the seating unit and places itself in between the entertainment block and the other herd members. "What's wrong with the pair of you?" it says, its voice loud. "Why are you putting us all through this? How stupid do you think we are? We all know that you were getting a divorce when Chester came along. Why did you ever think that a baby would make things work between you? How stupid are you?"

"Frederick!" the Taylor says loudly, and I believe that another chanting session is about to begin.

However, the Madison's voice is much quieter than chanting level when she says, "Chester was a mistake." She finishes her drink, and holds the glass out to me. "Get me another," she says, and I take the glass to the liquid cabinet.

"It was all a mistake," the Taylor says. "But it's too late now. We have to try and make the best of it, that's all."

"What do you think I've been trying to do?" the Frederick says loudly. "But all you two do is fight. Aggie has practically moved in with her nineteen year old boyfriend, which you'd notice if you ever stopped yelling at each other for five seconds. I've been playing referee between you two so long I don't even remember what my own life is supposed to be about. I ought to be going out, having fun, making my own stupid relationship decisions and instead I'm hanging around here trying to make sure you two don't kill each other." The Frederick looks at its parents, and I think that it is making an excellent showing at its first chanting session.

But then he seems to be unable to maintain the required volume as his voice drops down to a sub-normal decibel level. "For Christ's sakes," he says, "Chester thinks Rosie is his mother. Did you actually think getting a robot would solve all your problems?"

He pauses, and I notice his eyes leaking. An after-effect of the chanting; I have noticed it with the others. "I've had it with you two," he says and walks out of the room. I bring the Madison her beverage and place it on the table near her.

The Madison and the Taylor remain in the communal room, the sounds from the entertainment unit the only noise. I have to admit, the silence is quite pleasant after the Frederick's chanting session. Humans are naturally noisy creatures, though. Section 1: *Human Nature — Loud, Confusing and Messy* explains it. They cannot help being the way they are.

It is time for me to go and determine if the Chester has any unmet requirements. Until the Agatha and her mate reproduce, he is the future of this herd. With a little help from me, I am certain that he will grow up to be as happy and healthy as the rest of them.

"I WAS WORKING at this stim joint, a place called Ultra-Sissons. It's not where I'm working now — I wasn't a bartender then, just a busser. Cleaning up the used cartridges, tidying chairs, occasionally tossing out the odd rowdy. Anyway, I wasn't important or anything, it was just an entry level job. Nothing special.

"This doesn't even have to do with me, though. It was one of the regulars. Guy who called himself Johnny Burling. I don't know if that was his real name or what, but that didn't matter much. We never cared about that kind of thing too much at Ultra. Johnny was a regular — in most every night. He wasn't one of the troublemakers; you know the kind I mean: those folks who shoot cartridges all night until they can't even piss straight, and you have to slip them a sobriety™ round at closing time just to get them out the door. Every stim place I've seen has those kind of regulars. I guess they pay the bills.

"But that's not Johnny. He was strictly a Red Zinger man — it was always the same for him. Two Red Zingers over the course of a few hours, and by the time he was starting his second he was off in his own little world. He told me once that he was creating a cooperative narrative, if you can believe it. He'd come in, take his hits of focus™ and creativity™ and zone out. He'd spend the next three hours busy working away in his onboard system — eyes all unfocussed but zipping back and forth, like he's dreaming or something, you know? I guess he got a lot of work done that way.

"He was plenty friendly, though, before the stims really got into him. Liked to talk to the other chatty cathies in the joint, and talked to me plenty, too. Bussing was a pretty boring job, and to tell the truth most of the other regulars were no fun, so talking to

Johnny was often as good as it got. He was a funny guy.

"Anyway, the point is that I liked him. He was nice — harmless, you know? Never did anything mean to anyone. He just didn't deserve what happened."

＊

"I NEVER KNEW what it was about Johnny that caught old man Doherty's eye. Doherty was the manager; at least that was what it said on the org chart. Really, he only ever showed up when the new shipments came in from the factory. He always took a box of euphoria™ out of inventory, and told us to make it disappear over the next month. Spillage, breakage, you know. 'Spoils of war,' he called it, whatever that was supposed to mean.

"Most of the time I worked there, we only ever saw Doherty on shipment day. Then, all of a sudden, he started showing up nights, sitting with Johnny. I don't know if Johnny even knew that Doherty worked at the bar, since he'd be buying Doherty rounds every once in a while. I got the evil eye every time I tried to hang around when they were together, so I don't know much about what they would talk about. But I know that one time when I was cleaning up after one of the usual troublemakers at the next table, I heard Johnny telling Doherty about the story he was writing.

"I was under the table, picking up cartridge shards when I noticed that Johnny didn't have his usual Red Zinger on the table. He was shooting something else, something that looked like Sunbeam or Buttercup. It was yellow, whatever it was, and that meant that it was full of sociability™. For a guy like Johnny, that much 's' might as well have been a truth serum.

"But I didn't think much of it. None of my business what the customers want to feel, right? We're all grown ups here and all the stuff does is amplify whatever we naturally have to begin with; at least that's what they say. What do I know?"

＊

"OF COURSE, I should have known something was wrong. A few weeks later, Johnny didn't come into the bar. No one thought too much of it — he'd missed a night or two before, it was no big deal. But when he'd stayed away for almost a month, it was pretty clear that something was wrong. I asked around, but no one seemed to know anything about it. Then one night, it's my day off and I'm at one of the liquor bars down in green sector. And who do I see walking by but Johnny Burling. I swear, I almost didn't recognize him; he looked terrible.

"I flagged him down, and offered to buy him a drink. He seemed sort of suspicious, but he took my pint and sat down.

'So, I guess everyone down at the bar has heard about what happened,' he said, sounding miserable. I just shook my head and told him that no one knew anything. As far as we all knew, he just disappeared off the face of the earth.

'But Doherty...' he said, a strange look on his face, like he was scared or something.

'Doherty never said anything to anyone,' I told him. 'He's hardly ever around and no one really talks to him. He's the boss — you don't just have a chat with the boss.' I smiled at Johnny, wondering what the hell was going on. He would hardly even look at me, and I didn't know what to say. So after we'd sat there for what seemed like forever, I just asked him if he was going to tell me what happened or not.

"And he did."

✳

"'REMEMBER THAT NARRATIVE I was writing?' he asked, and I nodded. 'Well, it was going pretty well. I was posting chapters to a board I was running and I was getting a lot of hits. I'd opened it up for public access; people were acting out the parts, making up new stuff for the story. It was kind of like a game, you know? I was even starting to make some money from it — you know, people paying for instant access, licensing the characters and whatnot. The usual thing. Of course what was important was the community, the fans, you know? It was becoming a proper story zone, a real solid group was forming. Taking on a life of its own.' He paused and breathed deep. 'I guess that was the problem.'

"I didn't really know what he was talking about — I don't read much — but I smiled and he went on. 'You saw how Mitch Doherty was chatting me up at Ultra-Sissons, right?' I nodded again, hoping he'd hurry up and and get to it.

'Well, we were mostly talking about The Sunshine Parade — that was the name of my story — and he seemed really into it. You know, talking about the process, about creating — all that. I don't know a lot of other writers in the real world, you know? So it was really nice just to have someone listen, someone who seemed to understand. I thought we were friends, that he was just interested in me, in my story...' He broke off, and I swore I saw him wipe a tear away from his cheek. I didn't say anything, though. It was pretty intense.

"After a while he started talking again. 'I didn't know anything was going on until one day I tried to log into my admin account on the story's board and I couldn't get in. I figured I just forgot the password or something, you know, but it was Doherty. He didn't even try to hide it.'

'Hide what?" I asked.

'He'd stolen the board, the story, the whole community.'

'But how?' I asked.

'I still don't really know,' Johnny said, looking miserable. 'From the little I got out of the hosting service I used, he somehow made it look like he owned the rights to the intellectual property of the plot and the name of the boardspace. I don't know if he just bribed them or what, but they kicked me off and that was the end of it.'

"I asked him if he could complain or get some Security to deal with it, but he said no. 'I went the whole way through the server's complaints process and when I asked the Security at my employer, they just laughed. It doesn't have anything to do with my work, so they didn't give a shit. There was nothing I could do.'

"I didn't know what to say. I'd never liked Doherty before, but I had no idea that he could do something like that. That it was even possible. That if it were possible that anyone would do it. It made me sick. But that was only the beginning."

✳

"Of course, Johnny didn't just crawl off into his apartment and give up. He hung around outside Ultra-Sissons for a week, waiting for Doherty. Johnny's a typical guy — young, skinny, a little ripped from all the pharma in the cheap food, but he's not into physical stuff, not like me. But Doherty isn't a scrapper either, so Johnny probably figured he had a chance. I bet he would've tried to make a play for Doherty even if he had no chance at all.

"I don't think Johnny was lying when he said he didn't do the old asshole a that much damage. I know how much it hurts to hit a guy, but I doubt Johnny was prepared for the knuckleful of pain he got when he decked Doherty on the chin. He sure as shit wasn't prepared for the damages order he got a week later. From his own employer's Security, no less!

"It turned out that Doherty had been recording when Johnny confronted him, and of course he turned in the vid to the goons at Ultra-Sissons Security. They sent it up the corporate chute, and somewhere near the top it got side swiped over to Johnny's own employers. I guess the corporate higher-ups look after each other, because Johnny got his wages garnished for five years as a financial settlement to Doherty.

"That's five years of no spending money beyond the minimum for food, water and transport to and from work. Of course he got an apartment with his contract, so he'd have a place to live and enough for food, but that was all. And he couldn't even quit his job or he'd be liable for paying the full settlement out of pocket. He was stuck. Stuck paying a crooked settlement with his time and his money to the guy who fucked him over in the first place.

"Oh. Um, sorry about the language there. I guess it still makes me mad.

"Anyway, beyond buying him a round or two, there wasn't anything I could do for Johnny. I didn't have the kind of cash that would help him out, and I didn't even know of any under the table work he wasn't already tapped into. It was terrible.

"So I did the only think I could think of. I quit my job at Ultra-Sissons. It was time anyway, but I couldn't bear to have to see Doherty's face again. I ended up tending bar at the place where I'm working now. There's no-one like Doherty there as far as I can tell.

"And one night on my day off, on delivery day at Ultra-Sissons, I was waiting for Doherty in the alley. You know I mentioned that I bareknuckle fight — for fitness and self-defense, right? Well, fighting's good for more than just that. I pounded him good in that back alley, took all his 'e' too for good measure. Didn't want him to waste all the pain I'd worked so hard to give him.

"I know it didn't help Johnny any, and probably won't stop Doherty from pulling that stunt on someone else. But it was all I could do. So it's what I did."

✳

THE APPLICANT TOOK a deep breath, and leaned back in her chair. "You asked me about some time when I saw or felt injustice and what I did about it? Well, that's it. I know there's probably worse stuff going on all the time, I'm not blind or stupid. But what happened to Johnny Burling, well, that was the end of the line for me.

"I know I can't get by not working for the firms, and I also know I'm never going to get high enough up the corporate ladder to change the way they operate that's for sure. But if I can help some other guy like Johnny, even if it is just by giving those dirtbags a taste of their own for a change, then I'll be happy to do it.

"There's no real law for guys like Johnny, no justice for people like us. Except your outfit, from what I hear. And I want to do my bit, if you'll have me."

Pat Malone looked hard at the applicant for a moment, then his eyes blinked rapidly a few times without closing. He accessed his onboard system, the display overlaid on his vision so that only he could see it. He made some notes on the interview then quickly sent a message to his boss. Captain Zahara Zhang made the final call on all new hires for the team, but he knew his recommendation counted for a lot. After all, he'd be responsible for this Melissa Vonruden for at least a year if she was taken on to the squad. Given her particular qualifications, probably longer. He could use a brute like her out on the streets. He refocussed on the small room, noting Vonruden's efforts to appear patient and confident. He did his best to hide the smile he felt creeping over his face.

"Thank you for your candor," he said in his stern interviewer voice, then gave up the effort and let the smile out. "I'll have to confer with some other people," he continued, "but I'd appreciate it if you would try to be available on Wednesday evening. Our next training session begins then, and I think there's a good chance you'll be asked to join the group, Ms. Vonruden."

Melissa smiled then, a full real grin. "I'll make sure I'm free, Mr. Malone, sir," she said and stuck her hand out for the man to shake. "And please, call me Melissa."

"I'm sure I will," Malone said, shaking her hand.

For Mark Stanley

Part I

IT ALL STARTED with the explosion.

It wasn't the first time Grey had heard the tell-tale *bang...
whoosh* of a pot of chemicals self-igniting, but they weren't running
such a half-assed operation that it happened often. He dropped the
stim cart he'd been filling, the small vial bouncing off the table, its
window breaking on impact and the half measure of bright green
liquid spilling out. He didn't even stop to see what happened to the
bulb he'd been using to fill the cart — who cared about a few euros
worth of stims when there was a fireball in the next room.

Grey fought the entirely natural impulse to just get the hell out
of there. It was a crummy little squat they'd moved into a couple of
weeks previously, and there was a way out on to the back alley from
the hallway off the room he was in. But Ev was in the kitchen on
the other side of the doorway. The doorway, which was now glowing
with a sickly orange light.

He ran to the door and yelled, "Ev! Are you okay?"

"Yeah," she croaked, like she was choking on fumes, which
made sense because the stuff she was cooking in there was
notorious for giving off noxious gasses when it burned. "Fire's
almost out."

"Get out of there," he hollered, then took a deep breath of the
relatively fresh air. Holding his breath, he pulled the neck of his
shirt up over his nose and barged into the kitchen.

Ev was standing over the stove, holding a heavy blanket over the pot. It was hot as hell in the little kitchen, but it was just as warm out in the other room. There was no ventilation in this squat and the weather had been muggy for days. Grey looked around quickly and took stock of the situation.

There were trails of flame on the floor, and Grey's eyes could feel something nasty in the air, but there was no inferno and Ev seemed to be in one piece. He stamped out the few bits of burning liquid on the ground and peeked under the blanket to make sure the fire in the pot was out. It all seemed okay, so he grabbed Ev's hand. "Come on," Grey grunted and pulled her out of the room. It was probably only about ten seconds since he'd heard the bang before they were out in the alley, sucking in the warm, thick air and coughing up their lungs.

"What happened?" Grey asked, once he felt like he could almost breathe properly again.

Ev just shook her head and Grey could see her struggling for breath. He cleared some of the junk from beside the wall and made a place for her to sit. He took her hand, which any other day would have made his heart race and his face turn the colour of their newest mix, *Heartfire*. Today, though, all he could think was that it should have been him in there.

He helped her sit down and she put her head between her knees. Grey sunk down next to her, and mimicked her posture. It wasn't because he felt faint, but because he knew that if he'd been the one cooking the stuff it wouldn't have happened. Ultimately, he knew, this was his fault.

The wet, painful sounds of Ev puking distracted him from his self-pity and he put a hand on her back. He could see that she'd singed her eyebrows and there was a streak of neon green on her face, but being sick was a good sign. She'd be okay. This time.

✳

EV WAS SLEEPING on the least dilapidated couch in the back room and Grey was cleaning up the mess in the kitchen when he heard a loud and obnoxious voice yelling from the front room. "Gregor! What the fuck happened in here?"

"There was an explosion," Grey said, walking into the main room to see Bennett storming in. She looked so out of place, Grey almost wanted to laugh. Like always, she was dressed in the highest fashions — in this case a glittering form-fitting one-piece which showed off the softness in her expensively sculpted body. Grey had always thought that she looked more like a model than an underworld kingpin. And now she just looked plain wrong standing among all the crap from the works.

The squat hadn't been in great shape before the big bang, but it was a lot worse now. Grey had moved everything that was still in working order out of the kitchen — luckily, that was most of the gear. All but one of the gas stoves were still good and most of the pots and cooking utensils. He hadn't been very careful about where he put it, and the room looked like a stim-lab's yard sale. Which, at that moment, seemed like a fine enough idea to Grey.

"How much shit did we lose?" Bennett demanded.

A year ago, Grey probably would have flown off the handle and reminded her that Ev might have died, god damn it. Now, though, he just sighed. "Two bottles of ups and a batch of *Firefly*," he said, "plus a few pots and pans and other junk."

"God damn it," she said, and glared around the room as if the squat bore some responsibility. "What happened?"

Grey shrugged. "Dunno. This stuff is volatile. What can you do?"

"Bullshit," she said, but there was no sting in the word. "Do we need to move out?"

Grey shook his head. "I'm almost done cleaning up," he said. "Ev's going to be out of it for a couple of days, but I'm almost done with the batch of *Zombie Blood*. It can be out the door tomorrow."

"Good," Bennett said. "Kirsten says that she's got buyers lined up for both the *ZB* and the *Firefly*. How soon can we get another batch on the cooker?"

"This afternoon, I guess," Grey said. "But we'll be out of ups then."

"Fine," Bennett said, her eyes losing focus. Done with Grey for now, she'd obviously accessed her implanted interface to the network and gone online. Grey walked back into the kitchen and continued cleaning up. As he carefully picked up pieces of material coated in the burnt chemicals, he could hear her strident voice from the other room.

"Nic," she bellowed, "talk to your people. We need another pack of underpants... Yes, already, there's been an accident... no, everyone is fine, just get here with the stuff. And where's that fan you promised me? I'm melting in this shithole."

Grey felt a smile creep across his face when he heard her use the code for ups. It was his first smile since the explosion and he couldn't help but feel a little guilty for his amusement. Ev could easily have been hurt a lot worse than she was, and the truth was that no one knew exactly what breathing in a snootful of burning ups would do to a person long term.

Still, they all knew that this was a risky profession. Which was why it paid so very well.

Part II

GEORGE CHANG JUMPED in his chair when Troy popped her head over the partition between the cubicles. "Got a blip on the target in brown 17," she said, her face lighting up. It had been obvious to Chang for months that Angela Troy had been itching for some excuse to get out of the building. When she'd been promoted to Security Level Four nearly a year ago, she told her partner she expected to be out on street missions most of the time. Chang had just chuckled to himself.

As he'd expected, the only time they'd been away from their desks since Troy started was for the interminable weekly team meetings. And that was just how Chang liked it. But whatever Troy had now was clearly the most exciting thing to happen on the Security floor of Hallissey Inc.'s stim branch office since she'd begun there as a Level One.

"What kinda blip?" Chang asked, looking up into Troy's face. He'd been a Level Four a long time now — he had neither the patience nor the interest in moving up to the management suites, so he knew this was as high as he was ever going to get. That was fine; he had a great apartment and he knew enough folks both online and in the physical world who thought that men who wore weapons on their belts were sexy to keep him busy in his off hours. He didn't have any particular desire to go running off into the streeters ghetto chasing down some wild goose.

"Explosion," Troy said and Chang could hear the rookie in her voice. "Our drone detected traces of somnifera gas right after and we caught vid of a couple of probable CCs in the alley."

"Huh," Chang grunted. "Lemme see."

Troy disappeared behind the partition and almost instantly Chang's system chimed. He paged over to his messenger and opened the file Troy sent him. The first page would have looked like gibberish to anyone else, but Chang could read the surveillance drone's report as clearly as if it were in grade three English.

"Damn it," he said, scanning the report. "It's vapourized ups, all right," he said.

"This has to be them," Troy said, practically crawling over the partition, triumph in her eyes.

"Yeah," Chang reluctantly agreed. He blanked his viewer and stood. "Let's go see André."

✳

"FINALLY," ANDRÉ SAID, looking over the tops of his entirely superfluous spectacles at his two underlings. The rumour on the floor was that the head of Security, Jerome André, patterned his physical look after some ancient image of a detective, but no one could figure out which one. As it was, he rarely left his office and all anyone ever saw of him in their viewer was the shoulders of his brown jacket and the wire-rimmed glasses on his nose.

Chang and Troy were in the small conference room, facing the large viewer on the wall which connected them to the boss, who they assumed was pleased with the news, but showed no change in his craggy face. "This investigation has dragged on long enough," he went on. "Marketing is sending me memos thrice daily — it seems that these folks in brown sector are taking a real bite out of our bottom line."

Chang glanced over at Troy, who shrugged. "Sir," Chang began, "Homebrew stims can't be that much of a problem, can they? I mean, half the time you don't get anything from shooting one of those carts and the other half it's liable to land a person in a medclinic."

"You've been reading that pap from Marketing again," André said. "Truth is that the knock off carts coming out of brown in the past few months have been blowing our products out of the water. They're stronger, smoother and cheaper. We've lost three points already this month and it's only the tenth. These people aren't just cutting into business, they're making us look bad."

"So, what are your orders?" Troy asked.

André looked hard at his two officers. Chang had seen that look before and didn't like where this was going. He knew that they'd have to go down to brown sector and root around some junked up building hunting for a bunch of sad case streeters trying to make a euro or two by cooking up knock off stims. Streeters who had a lot more to lose than a couple of Security Level Fours who were just doing their jobs, which made them unpredictable and dangerous. He sighed.

"Put a stop to it," André said. "Whatever it takes."

"Yes, sir," Troy said with an unmistakable air of eagerness.

"Be careful what you wish for," Chang muttered under his breath as they walked out of the conference room.

Part III

GREY WAS ELBOW deep in another batch of *Firefly* when he heard familiar sounds coming from the front room. For as long as they'd been using the building, what was once the front door had been entirely off its hinges, the doorframe a rough parallelogram that barely contained the still rectangular particleboard door. However, they still used this as the primary method of entry, so there was always a good warning when someone was coming in. Grey carefully turned down the fire on the small portable gas burner, wiped the sweat off his face, then peeked around the jamb of the internal door to see who'd knocked the front door down.

Nic filled the doorway, his arms laden with boxes and canisters. He grunted at Grey, an all-purpose sound that, as far as Grey could tell, meant everything from "hey, buddy, how's it going?" to "anyone want a sandwich?" to "this means war — let's fight!" Nic wasn't exactly what you'd call a master conversationalist.

He was, however, amiable enough and he brought the gear all the way into the makeshift kitchen, then carefully stacked the supplies on the counter. He began unpacking things, decanting the liquids into the specially sealed jars which kept the highly volatile chemicals from escaping, pouring powders out of the flimsy wrappers they'd been packaged in and putting things away.

Grey could see that Nic had replaced everything that had gone up or gone off as a result of the morning's conflagration. As Nic was working with the chemicals, he made a noise low in his throat that an untrained observer would have never decoded, but which Grey heard clearly as "Ev?"

"Still sleeping," he said, focussing on his boiling pot of green goo. "CSC says she should be okay in a day or two. She puked up most of the toxins when it happened."

Nic grunted again, knowing that the Clandestine Stim-maker's Cookbook was the authoritative source for all aspects of their chosen vocation. It contained the basic recipes for the neurostims that they made and sold to both individuals directly as well as the more budget-conscious stim bars. The exceedingly rare and valuable file also provided tips on avoiding Security, making deals and addressing the inevitable health and safety concerns that arose from utilizing the chemicals and processes required to ply their trade.

Nic finished putting the new inventory away then lumbered out of the kitchen without exchanging another word with Grey. He'd never known Nic to be any more gregarious with the others, so Grey had no reason to think it was personal. It still felt a little strange to have worked with someone for over a year and never really chatted. He forgot about Nic soon enough, as the timer application on his system chimed and he silenced the ringing in his ears. He turned up the flame under the pot and reached over for a jar of powder. This was it — the stage of the operations that had caused all the problems this morning.

Making stims was inherently a risky prospect. The firms had special labs, with safety systems built in and exact control over the temperature of the mixture. Grey was pretty sure they even used robots for this part of the process. But, he and his colleagues were winging it under much more unreliable circumstances. The trouble with this part of the process was that the reagent was extremely flammable, but in order for the chemical process to actually turn the mix into something that could be shot into a person's neural network and reliably affect their consciousness, it had to be mixed in at a temperature of just over 100°C. If even a tiny bit of the powder escaped the liquid, *boom*. Just like that morning.

Grey had done this a hundred times and he'd never had a fire. Even so, he felt his hands beginning to shake and had to take a deep breath before he started to pour the powder into the pot.

Part IV

CHANG LOOKED AT the arsenal Troy had assembled and closed his eyes. There were more gizmos and gadgets laid out on the small desk in her cubicle than the two of them could possibly carry — shock sticks, knuckledusters, sedaspray, some kind of handheld ranged thing that Chang had never even seen before.

"What do you think this is?" he asked, "World War Three? We're just going to wreck up a stim lab, for Christ's sakes. If we do it right we won't even see the CCs."

"There are at least two of them," Troy reminded him.

"Right," Chang said, derisively. "You saw them on the vid — one weedy-looking stimhead holding up another who's so far gone we probably couldn't rouse her if we wanted to. They're nothing to worry about."

"We need to be prepared for anything," Troy said, her eyes darting between the various weapons.

"Sure," Chang said. "But we need to be able to walk, too." He lifted the handgun up and inspected it. "What the hell is this, anyway?"

"Graduated pulsed shooter," Troy said, sounding like she'd memorized the sales brochure. "Delivers electric shock up to five metres in bursts capable of slight stun up to permanent muscular paralysis."

"You mean electrocution," Chang said, parsing the phrase. "This is a lethal weapon."

Troy nodded once. "We need to be prepared," she repeated. "The CCs might very well be armed themselves. We could be walking into an ambush."

Chang sighed and sat down in Troy's chair. It was too small but he didn't care much. "You know what CC stands for?" he asked. "Clandestine Chemist, not Crazed Combatants. They're a couple of junkie chemistry nerds, not a small militia. We walk in there, destroy the lab and walk out again. It's not some kind of Special Ops mission, Troy. It's just an offsite visit."

She sniffed and picked up a couple of the small items in front of her. "You do what you want, Chang." She jammed the pistol into a sleek holster on her hip and slipped two sets of knuckledusters over her hands. "I'm going in prepared. Especially," she gave her partner a hard look, "since it looks like I'm not going to have any backup from you." Armed as well as she could be without a pack mule, she turned on her heel and walked toward the lobby.

"Why me?" Chang muttered as he grabbed the smallest weapons off the table and set about finding places for them on his uniform.

Part V

THERE WAS NO fire. Even with his shaking hands, Grey's years of practice paid off and he added the reagent without incident. Once the correct amount of powder was in the mix, he watched as the colour of the boiling goo turned from bright green to a more pleasant aqua colour. He smiled — it was exactly the colour *Firefly* ought to be. He was proud of this recipe — it was his own creation and had become the group's mainstay.

When he'd first hooked up with Bennett, he'd just been a small time operator. He cooked for himself and his friends, selling just enough to pay for the supplies, a box of cheap food bricks a week and a crumbling roof over his head. Bennett had told him she'd never been involved in the stim racket before, but she'd spent a lifetime hustling in every other way Grey knew of. She'd run cons, sold nodes and other gizmos which just happened to fall off the back of a transport, even danced at one of those clubs that catered to the kind of voyeurism that couldn't be satisfied by an online simulacrum. She'd never had a real job, never worn a uniform, but she'd easily have made it up the greased pole to the management suite if she had. She was a natural organizer, a born leader.

Grey hated her.

But she had offered him something he'd never have been able to do for himself — a way to turn the only thing he was any good at into something that would raise him out of the gutter rather than keep him trapped in it. He was just smart enough to recognize the opportunity partnering with her would provide, so he'd swallowed his enmity and thrown in his lot with her. It was only supposed to last until he had enough to get a decent place to live. But when that happened, he figured that in just a few more months he'd have enough to get his own place. So, he'd stayed on.

Now, he'd gone from living in a shared squat worse than this one they used as a workshop to having a one-room apartment of his own and an account that always had a positive balance. And he still was part of Bennett's crew, and he still hated it, and he still had no idea how to get out.

Once the pot of *Firefly* had turned exactly the right colour, Grey turned off the fire and walked into the main room. Nic was lounging on the couch, shirt off, eyes glazed. Grey had no idea what the big man was doing online, but he didn't care. He didn't care about any of the people who were part of his little crew, except Ev.

He walked past Nic and into the back room where Ev had been

since she was able to move off the couch. She was still pretty out of it — the vaporized chemicals hadn't just made her sick, they'd made her high, too. She was going to have a pretty good hangover when she came out of it, and Grey wanted to be there for her. He'd been where she would soon be, and he knew that a friend came in pretty handy when the hallucinations started.

He sat next to her and watched her sleeping face. Her face was slick with sweat, but it was just the heat. Grey decided she looked fine, her colouring back to normal. She'd be okay in a day or two, but Grey couldn't help but feel guilty.

"I'm sorry, Ev," he said softly, even though there was no way she was waking up. "I never should have left you alone in there. I should have known that it was too dangerous. Damn it." He wiped a tear which had somehow escaped down his cheek. "You shouldn't have to do any of this. When you're better, that's it. I'm really done this time. You don't need this — I don't need this. There has to be some other way."

Grey heard movement behind him, and he whirled around. It was Kirsten. "How is she?" she asked, and Grey hoped that the fifth member of their group hadn't heard what he'd been saying.

"Sleeping," he said. "She'll be out of it for a few hours at least, then it'll be bad for a while. You know," he arched an eyebrow, and the slight woman nodded. "But she'll be fine in a few days. She was lucky."

"Yeah," Kirsten said. "This time."

Part VI

CHANG WAS STARTING to think that being stuck with Angela Troy wasn't as bad as he'd first imagined. She had somehow managed to requisition a private vehicle for their transport to brown sector. He'd never been in such a small car before — in training he'd travelled in busses and large troop transports, but in his private life he, like everyone else he'd ever encountered, relied on the trains to get from A to B. He had a neighbour who owned a two-wheeled electric contraption, but other than that it was trains or walking.

"Do you know how to operate this thing?" he asked, a mix of skepticism and wonder in his voice.

For the first time Chang thought he could detect something less than perfect confidence in Troy's face. "It has an autopilot," she said. "Here, we might need this." He saw his system ping with an incoming transfer and when he focussed on his viewer saw a document labelled as a user's manual begin to download. He felt a weight in his head as it finished transferring, then he paged open the interactive document.

He found the quickstart section and scanned the information. "Okay," he said, slipping into one of the seats. "We just feed the GPS coordinates of our destination in to the thing..." he paged through the manual until he found the image of the vehicle's dash, "here." He pointed at a small input zone with a number pad. "In theory, it should get us there in one piece."

"Right," Troy said, fumbling with the unfamiliar safety belt. "You want to do the honours?" She looked over at Chang and he shrugged.

Using two fingers and making generous use of the correction button, he managed to enter the lat and long of the location the Security drone had pinpointed. The car made a satisfied *beep* and Chang turned to face Troy.

"I guess it's time to go get these guys," he said, and punched the big green button. The car slid forward smoothly, but both Chang and Troy found themselves clutching the armrests as they accelerated into the street in front of the Hallissey building.

Part VII

GREY WAS FILLING another round of carts from the pot of *Firefly* he'd finished making. "This would go a lot faster with a little help," he said sourly to the rest of them.

"You really think so?" Bennett asked archly. "Nic, Kirsten," she turned to the two who were lounging on the couch, "either of you ever filled stim cartridges?"

"No," Kirsten said, throwing an apologetic look at Grey. Nic grunted.

"So," Bennett said, turning back to Grey, "you really think it would be faster to teach these two how to fill than to just shut up and get it done yourself?" Her voice rose as she was speaking and by the end of the sentence she had reached a full-on shout.

Grey flinched, but stifled the flip response that was aching to get out. It was true that he'd probably get it done faster on his own — he himself had used Bennett's very argument when he'd suggested bringing Ev into the team. The thought made his stomach sour and he tried to put it out of his mind.

He'd known Ev for a couple of years, but they'd become closer in the last few months. He knew she was barely making ends meet on her own and he went to bat for her with Bennett to get her on the crew. It was her experience with loading carts and mixing that finally persuaded his boss to take a chance on another set of hands — and another split to the proceeds. Until this morning, Ev had more than pulled her weight, but Grey knew that she might just have signed her own walking papers with the cost of the ruined batch.

It was just good luck that Kirsten had lined up such a big pair of deliveries so close — it gave Bennett something positive to think about. At least, Grey hoped it would. He only needed her to ignore the Ev situation long enough for him to finish this last job. Then he'd have a few days to himself and he planned to spend them finding a new place to live. He figured that if she couldn't find him at his place, Bennett wouldn't be bothered to track him down. She was, if nothing else, pragmatic enough not to waste time and resources on revenge.

He let his muscle-memory do the heavy lifting as he methodically dipped the bulb into the pot of *Firefly* and squeezed a perfect dose into the sterilized cartridges. His mind was busy totalling up the euros he'd saved in an anonymous account, factoring in the tiny amounts of chemicals he'd been sneaking offsite — enough to make a small batch of a powerful cocktail of his own invention that he'd kept from Bennett. If he got a few carts into the hands of the right people, he could make enough to buy the gear to set himself and Ev up in business for themselves. If he could manage to keep the stims from ending up in their own systems.

Grey was so lost in his plotting that when he heard the *bang* his first thought was that it was another explosion. Two times in one day seemed a bit much, and he was finally coming around to the realization that there was nothing on the fire when the room filled up with smoke.

"Tear gas," someone croaked from the couch. "Get down."

Grey dove to the floor, his face searching for a patch of clear air. He felt someone press something into his hand and looked up through tear-filled eyes to see Nic looming over him, a breather covering his lower face. "Get it on," he said, voice muffled by the contraption. Grey didn't understand for a moment, then looked down into his hands. He saw a breather of his own there and fumbled with the straps and knobs until he got it on and working. He took a breath, coughed, then began to breathe easily again.

His eyes still stung, but he could move around and see what was going on. Nic had pulled a panel down from the wall, and what looked to Grey like a weapons locker was revealed in the space. Nic took a set of handguns and passed them out, with the instruction, "Just point and shoot — they're stunners."

"What's going on?" Kirsten said, whimpering from where she'd fallen from the couch.

"It's a raid," Bennett said, her voice calm and cold. "Shoot anything that moves."

Part VIII

CHANG CROUCHED AGAINST the wall of the building, in more or less the same spot their Security drone had spotted two people earlier that morning. Chang thought it looked like any other alley in brown sector, but he knew it was the right place. He could smell vomit and a sickly sweet ammonia odour that was the unmistakable evidence of vapourized somnifera. He fought the urge to gag.

"Right," he said, getting control over his body. "We have to assume there's someone in there," he said, jerking his head toward the door, "so we do this by the book."

Troy nodded once and reached to her belt. "You get the door and I'll throw it in. We'll wait ten seconds then go in. You got the breathers?"

Chang opened his hand to reveal two small devices which they slipped into their mouths. "Ready?" he said around the plastic tubing. Troy nodded. "Here we go," he said, turning in a fluid motion and kicking in the flimsy door. As soon as the entrance was breached, Troy tossed her small grenade into the room. They both turned away from the door and crouched, shielding their eyes from the initial burst of tear gas. They knew that the effects would wear off soon, as the second burst, an airborne sedative, took effect.

Chang kept his eyes screwed shut and watched the countdown he'd set on his system decrement. When it reached 00:00 he stood and tentatively opened one eye. He could see Troy standing ready to enter the building, her knuckledusters engaged. Arcs of electricity crackled over them, making her hands look like they were shimmering with heat waves. She held one of the pistols in her left hand and gestured to Chang with her right. He pulled the shockstick from his hip and nodded.

Troy ran into the building and Chang followed tightly on her heels.

There was still a little tear gas in the air and Chang's eyes burned. He could see, though, and knew better than to try to touch them. The pain would go away as the smoke cleared and rubbing them would only make it worse. He saw Troy following the wall to the left and he took the opposite side. She gestured with her free hand for him to head right while she checked the room to the left. He nodded and turned down the corridor.

He ran into the next room, which was empty, save for a good supply of chemicals and gear that he recognized as a well-equipped stim lab. He scanned the room and saw no other doors or windows. Knowing Troy was behind him, he holstered the shockstick — it was made to disrupt human bodies and wouldn't help him here unless he used it as a club. And he had better tools than that for destroying this stuff.

First, he went after the chemicals. He could make them useless just by contaminating them, but he knew that some of them could be toxic if he breathed them in or even got them on his skin. His breather should take care of the airborne particles and he'd covered his exposed skin with a protective gel, but he didn't want to take a chance. He pulled a bunch of small polymer sacks from his pocket and shook one open. He started methodically going through the chemicals in bottles and jars, dumping the contents of each into its own sack then closing the self-sealing bag. He could see a reaction take place in the clear pouch as its smart sensors identified the contents and neutralized them. The whole process took only a few seconds. He was almost through dealing with the whole collection of chemicals when he heard two distinctive noises which caused him to drop the jar he was holding and wheel around.

He couldn't tell which came first, but he knew that neither of those sounds meant anything good. He'd heard the *thump thump* of a stun pistol going off and someone — maybe it was Troy, he couldn't be sure — scream.

Part IX

GREY FELT THE smooth plastic of the stunner in his hand, more alien than anything he'd ever held before. He imagined pointing it at someone, imagined squeezing the little button under his finger. It made his stomach turn. His eyes burned from the gas, but he could breathe now. He saw Nic move, catlike, toward a position where he could see both entrances to the main room. The big man gestured to Bennett, who nodded and signed something equally mysterious back to Nic. Grey looked around and saw Kirsten huddled next to the couch, clutching the stunner Nic had given her as if it were a shield rather than a weapon. Grey caught her eyes and saw his own fear and bewilderment reflected there.

Seeing her face was like a slap to his own and he remembered Ev. He felt his heart flutter and noticed a sour odour inside his breather, but he ignored it. He threw himself even closer to the ground and began to crawl toward the door to the bedroom.

"Get back," Nic hissed. "Find cover."

"Gotta check on Ev," Grey replied as quietly as possible while continuing to scrabble toward the door. He was halfway across the floor, completely exposed, when a shadow darkened the doorway that led into the hall. He was facing away from the hall, but he could see Nic and Kirsten's faces, and they could obviously see whatever it was.

Kristen's eyes grew wide and she made a terrified noise as she tried to hide even further behind the couch. Nic's face grew hard and he raised his pistol in a quick, smooth motion. The sound of the shots made Grey flinch and close his eyes, then the silence which came after filled his ears.

"Go," Nic said to him urgently, and Grey took the advice without turning to see what had transpired. He belly crawled as fast as he could, and had made it into the room where Ev was sleeping it off just as he heard the sound of footsteps and a sharp male voice that wasn't Nic's shouting angrily. Grey closed the door and ran over to the bed.

Ev was unconscious but as far as Grey could tell, fine. The gas would have put her under, but she seemed to be breathing easily. Grey's hand strayed to her forehead, which was cool to his touch. He dropped his face to hers and let his lips brush against her cheek, when he heard the sound of several voices yelling, furniture breaking and the crackle of shots being fired.

For a moment, he was frozen in place with fear, but he snapped out of his paralysis as he heard another volley of shots in the other room. He looked around frantically for something movable but heavy, his eyes finally lighting on a cabinet along one wall. He dragged it over, wedging it in front of the door. There was no way out of the room, no window or other door, but he hoped that this would at least slow down whoever was out there.

He went back to the bed and looked down at Ev. "I'm sorry," he whispered, "sorry I ever brought you here. If we get out of this..." He didn't finish the thought as a loud bang sounded from the other room. He reached over and pushed Ev on to the floor on the far side of the bed. She landed with a thump and Grey flinched. He then launched himself over the bed and knelt with his body covering hers as much as he could. His head poked up over the side of the bed, the pistol clutched in his grip and resting on the covers.

He stared at the door and tried not to think about what was happening.

Part X

THERE WEREN'T SUPPOSED to be this many of them. Chang couldn't help but feel like he'd been misled by the information the Security drone had given them. Of course, just because they'd only seen two people, that didn't mean that there weren't more. And just because there was no indication that they would be armed, didn't mean that there couldn't be a small army waiting for them inside. But Chang still felt like he'd been ripped off. He'd ordered a simple field trip to bust up a tiny little lab and he'd gotten a firefight. He wanted his money back.

As Chang moved carefully from the kitchen down the corridor, he could hear the sounds of several weapons going off. He guessed that this was a good sign — if Troy had been taken out, there wouldn't be any reason for them to continue to fire. However, that also meant that he had to assume that she hadn't taken control of the situation either. He stayed close to the wall, inching his way along it until he could see into the other room. He could see a large man crouching behind what he guessed had once been a pretty old and ugly couch — it was now a mess of singed polymer and smoking holes. The big man had a large, two handed stunner in his hands and he was methodically firing toward a spot just left of the doorway, where Chang guessed Troy must be holed up. He could see returning fire come from that area, so Troy must have found some kind of cover there.

Chang was just about to go through the door when a burst of fire came from the side of the room he couldn't see. Two shooters. Damn it. He stepped back to make sure that he couldn't be seen, then thought for a moment. Troy wouldn't be able to take out two shooters on her own, but the guy with the big stunner would have a clear shot on Chang as soon as he walked through the door. It was a bad situation.

There was nothing for it. He took a deep breath, then called out. "Troy," he yelled, still far enough down the corridor not to be seen by anyone in the room. "Cover me."

He didn't wait for a response, but dove through the door, angling his body to the left. He kept his stunner pointed in the direction of the big man, getting off several shots that he didn't expect to land anywhere near his target. As he was coming through the doorway, he saw Troy's hiding spot behind a table out of the corner of his eye and as he landed he rolled in that direction. While Troy was squeezing off a series of shots toward the other side of the room, Chang scrambled behind the table.

Once Chang was safe behind the table, Troy crouched down as well, dropping her pistol on the floor. Chang quickly saw that she'd been hit. Her left arm was limp, and there was a scorch mark on the upper arm of her uniform. "How is it?" he asked quietly.

"If that's the worst if it," she said, "I'll live."

Chang nodded. He jerked his eyes toward the rest of the room. "Good thing we came prepared, eh?"

Troy smiled weakly. "I gotta say," she said, "I wish you'd been right this time."

Chang returned the smile. "You and me both."

"You get the works?" Troy asked and Chang nodded.

"Destroyed the lot. That's all we needed to do."

"Except get out of here," she said, her eyes darting around.

"Yeah," Chang said. "Okay. We need a plan." Out of one of his pockets he pulled a little box with a pair of treads on the bottom. "Smokescreen drone," he said and flipped a button on the thing's side. "This ought to give us some cover. Ready?"

"Sure," Troy said. "Let's get this done."

Part XI

IT FELT LIKE an hour had gone by. Grey's hands shook as he held the stunner, even with his arms resting on the bed. He wondered what would happen if one of them did force their way into the room. Would he have a chance of hitting them? Could he even find the strength to press the trigger button?

He hadn't heard anything in a long time. A part of his mind told him that they must all be dead — Nic, Kirsten, Bennett. The only reason for so much silence was that there was no one left to make a sound. He fought down the voice of pessimism, reminding himself that it was that voice which got him stuck here in the first place. It was the voice that told him that he'd never make it on his own, that he needed the protection of a crew to be able to work the stim trade. Some protection they'd been, after all. As far as he knew, he and Ev were the only ones left, and it was no thanks to the others.

Ev. He turned his gaze away from the barred door to look at her. She wasn't particularly beautiful, but at that moment she was the only thing Grey cared about. He didn't even worry about getting himself out of there, only her. He dropped down beside the bed and laid the stunner carefully between his body and the bed. He leaned over Ev, checking her breathing. She was making little movements now, like a dreaming sleeper, so Grey guessed that the sedative had worn off. She'd be coming to soon and it wasn't going to be pretty. He needed to get her somewhere safe before that happened.

It had been quiet for a long time, he thought. Maybe he should go open the door just a hair, see if the coast was clear. He could give Ev a shot of something to get her up and moving and they could get somewhere safe. He crawled around the foot of the bed toward the door, the stunner shoved in the waistband of his pants. He slowly, carefully, shoved the cabinet a few centimetres away from the door and reached up to the knob. He'd just touched it when he heard a maelstrom of noise erupt on the other side of the door.

He backed away from the door frantically, banging into the cabinet and knocking the stunner halfway across the room. In his panic, he just let it go and crawled back to the other side of the bed and Ev. He lay there, trembling, one part of his mind trying to make sense of what he heard and another, much more powerful part, trying to ignore it completely.

There was a shout — a man's voice, he thought. Stunner fire, then something else, something louder, then a shriek. Feet pounding, furniture falling. Grey found a pillow in his hands that had fallen off the bed, and he shoved it over his head. He heard himself gasping for breath, loud sobs threatening to escape and he forced himself to be quiet.

He heard another set of crashing on the other side of the door, then there was silence. He knew somehow that this lack of sound was more complete than it had been before. There was nothing out there now, Grey was certain. Nothing alive. Nothing that could help him. He took a breath and wept into the pillow.

Part XII

CHANG GOT TO the car first and wrenched open the door. He started mashing buttons on the dash and felt his stomach drop as the vehicle lurched backwards. He turned and saw that he'd nearly hit Troy, who was hobbling toward the vehicle. She didn't seem to realize the danger, though, and slipped into the seat.

"Thanks," she said, "I could use a little sit down."

Chang looked his partner over for a moment. Her left arm was useless and she'd taken a glancing hit on her hip as they were getting out. He could barely remember how they got out the door. It had been a blur of stunner fire as they'd crawled out under the smoke.

"I can't believe what a piece of crap that smokescreen drone turned out to be," Troy said through gritted teeth. "What did that guy do, hit it with a stick?"

"I dunno," Chang said, carefully programming the car to get them back to the office. "I didn't see it."

"The thing flew across the room, hit the wall and bust open," Troy said. "Smoke everywhere. What a disaster."

"It's not supposed to do that," Chang said."

"No shit," Troy agreed and laughed. "Man, for a second I thought we weren't going to get out of there."

"Yeah," Chang said then glanced over at Troy. She was a little pale, but he didn't think she'd lost much blood. Half an hour in the medclinic and she'd be fine. Chang didn't have much more than bumps and bruises, but he couldn't stop thinking about it. Stunner fire, smoke, the sounds of people being hurt and afraid.

"I'm too old for this shit," he said aloud as the car took a turn and accelerated. Troy didn't answer and Chang didn't know if she was passed out, sleeping or just didn't have anything to say. It didn't really matter one way or another; their day was done.

Part XIII

GREY DIDN'T KNOW how long he lay there under the pillow. He might have still been there if Ev hadn't woken. Her shivering brought Grey out of his stupor and he got to his knees. Ev wasn't talking — she was awake but still trapped in her own stim-created world. Grey grabbed the blanket off the bed and dragged it down to the floor. He carefully draped it over her and leaned in to take a look. Her skin was waxy and pale, and she was shaking like a hypothermic, but she was getting better.

"I'll go find something to make you feel better," he said and kissed her cheek. "I'll be back as soon as I can." He wanted to say more, say the magic words which would comfort her in her pain, which would make whatever he found on the other side of the door make sense, but those words didn't exist. He stood and pulled the cabinet away from the door. He found the handle and opened the door.

The room looked like a war zone, which Grey guessed was exactly what it had been. There didn't seem to be anyone there, and he picked his way around the debris. There wasn't anything worth salvaging. Broken cartridges littered the floor, the bulbs he'd been using to fill them squashed. He was sure that he knew what he'd find when he walked into the kitchen, but still managed to be surprised when he saw the total destruction of the gear. There was nothing worth keeping, not a spoon, not a speck of chemicals.

Grey knew that he ought to feel something — anger, sorrow, disappointment. Instead he just turned numbly around and walked back to the main room. He almost tripped over something and at first didn't recognize what it was. Then his numbness melted as he realized it was Kirsten.

She'd taken a stunner hit directly to her eye. There was no sign of Bennett or Nic — they must have fled along with whoever was responsible for all this. Grey figured that none of them had been using lethal rounds or the others wouldn't have gotten out so easily. But a shot to the eye — it didn't matter how low the dosage was, that was a killer. He hung his head and touched Kristen's cheek. It was still warm, the skin scorched where the shot had radiated.

"We were just trying to make a living," he whispered, then lost the ability to speak. He sat there next to Kirsten's body for a long time. Finally, he heard sounds from the bedroom. It was Ev, trying to make sense of the visions dancing in her mind.

"I'm sorry," he said to Kirsten's body and he stood. He walked into the bedroom and let Ev fall into his arms. She was almost limp as he helped her through the ruined lab. "I'm sorry," he said again as they walked out into the alley.

As soon as they turned the corner, Grey felt the first drop. Within half a block it began to rain in earnest. Drops of water splashed over them, soaking their hair and clothes, cooling and cleansing, as they walked away.

Darusha writes science fiction and speculative poetry as M. Darusha Wehm and mainstream poetry and fiction as Darusha Wehm. Science fiction books include: *Beautiful Red, Children of Arkadia* and the *Andersson Dexter* cyberpunk detective series. Mainstream books include the *Devi Jones' Locker* Young Adult series and *The Home for Wayward Parrots* (forthcoming from NeWest Press).

Darusha's short fiction and poetry have appeared in many venues, including *Arsenika, Nature, Escape Pod*, and several anthologies.

Darusha is originally from Canada but currently lives in Wellington, New Zealand after spending the past several years sailing the Pacific. For more information, visit http://darusha.ca.